QUEST FOR A QUEEN
The Jackda

QUEST FOR A QUEEN
The Jackdaw

Frances Mary Hendry
illustrated by Linda Herd

CANONGATE KELPIES

First published in Great Britain in 1993
by Canongate Press Ltd, 14 Frederick Street,
Edinburgh EH2 2HB

British Library Cataloguing-in-Publication Data
A catalogue record for this book is available on request from
the British Library.

ISBN 0 86241 437 7

The publishers acknowledge subsidy of
the Scottish Arts Council towards
the publication of this volume.

Typset by The Electronic Book Factory Ltd, Fife, Scotland
Printed and bound by Norhaven A/S Rotation, Viborg,
Denmark

CANONGATE PRESS
14 FREDERICK STREET, EDINBURGH

To Mum

Contents

Author's Note

In this story I have, as usual, fitted imaginary characters into the actual events of the time. Frank, Susanna and Jack, and their families, are invented. Lark and Kate are characters from 'The Lark' and 'The Falcon', earlier books in the 'Quest for a Queen' trilogy. Walsingham, Babington, Phelippes, Gifford, Savage, Ballard and the other named people were real, and are as accurate in personality and action as I can make them.

There is no doubt that the Babington Plot was whipped up by Walsingham to dispose of Mary. I have tried, through Frank's story, to explain the course of the conspiracy, which is here slightly simplified. Frank takes the place of three of Walsingham's men; Maude, Scudamore, and especially a Treasury official named Poley. Everything which he does in the conspiracy was done by one of these three (except warning Babington, who in fact saw the warrant himself and fled to warn the rest).

The theft of Mary's letter is my invention. In spite of the additions which he and Phelippes had forged to Mary's letter, though, Walsingham met Babington four times and tried to get him to turn Queen's Evidence against Mary, which seems to me to show some doubt about the quality of evidence which he had on hand.

Since Ruth didn't exist, Gifford didn't elope with her. He did, however, go to France when I said, and stay away for several months while Mary's trial was going on, though Walsingham was very displeased with him. He was no fool; Poley was arrested and kept in prison for some months, Walsingham's agent or not.

Once again I should like to thank Dr Rosalind K. Marshall, of the Scottish National Portrait Gallery, for checking my historical accuracy.

In this trilogy I have tried to give some insight into

the events and motives of the life of Mary, Queen of Scots, by the device of inventing unimportant people around her whose lives were somehow linked with hers. I hope you enjoy reading it as much as I've enjoyed writing it.

The Prologue

Straw rustled. Jack rolled out of his bed behind the counter, not quite fast enough. He yelped as a boot caught his hip. 'Starvelin' pup! Lollin' about like ve Earl o' Leicester, eh? Up an' earn yer keep!' Tom. Good. Billy'd have been far worse.

Jess lay silent, frail and tiny, thumb in her mouth, smiling placatingly. After a moment Tom's thick mouth twitched in an almost shamefaced smile in answer. Tom wasn't bad, if Sal and Billy weren't about. He lifted her by her ragged shift, limp as a rag doll in his huge hand, and slung her at Jack. ''Ere, take 'er out wiv yer,' he grunted. 'Whined all day yestidday, she did. Mam near killed 'er. Get 'er out ve way, eh?'

Nodding thanks, Jack ducked by him, hiding his sudden hope. Joe wasn't back; he'd been taken to work outside last night. Was this their chance . . ? Acting casual, he had squelched half across the yard when a harsh, hearty voice behind him stopped him dead. 'Jacky! Jacky Daw! Where d'ye think yer off ter?'

Ivory Sal, white-haired under her unstarched cap, whip-lash tough, the ruthless mistress of the best — or worst —

tavern in all the Vintry, was watching him, fists on hips. Against her stained blue gown, the thick ivory bangles and bead necklaces that gave her her nickname gleamed whiter than the teeth in her wide smile. 'Ye knows better'n that. Give 'er 'ere. Now, ye whoreson knave!' Jack's gut wrenched, but he had to turn back, past Tom's glower, to ride Sal's slap and cower, half deaf in one ear.

Sal held Jess at arm's length, studying her. Jess whimpered in fear, and was cuffed casually to silence. The tall woman chuckled jovially. ''Ow old is she? Three? Don't look it. Scarce a year, she looks. Could 'elp in findin' 'er a trade.'

Jack's scalp crawled in apprehension. 'Trade? Wot d'ye mean, Sal?'

He'd forgotten Tom, behind him. A fist thumped his sore ear, and a hand skidded off the hair he never let grow long enough to grab. Tom was bellowing ferociously, to impress his mother and draw attention from his slip in nearly letting the children all out together. 'Questions? Cheeky 'ound! Gerrout! An' don't come back empty-'anded t'day, see!'

'Now, now, Tommy!' Sal lifted a soothing hand. ''E's a good lad, our little Jackdaw, when 'e keeps 'is mind on 'oppin' round the town an' bringin' nice things 'ome 'ere to 'is Aunty Sal. Bright round silver things, eh? 'E's got 'is cheesy-'ead brother an' sister ter pay fer, eh? An' 'e don't forget it. There ain't nobody else'd keep 'em, but I'm soft-'earted, innit right, Jacky boy?'

It was an old routine. Jack nodded vigorously. 'Nobody as good's wot you is, Sal. Thankful, me an' Joe an' Jess. Right thankful, all on us.'

It was a lie, and they all knew it. One at least of the three was always kept hostage inside. Jack had run once, with Jess, but had to come back to stop Billy beating Joe to death. Sal had just chuckled, and doubled his shot to two shillings every day instead of one. Billy had enjoyed himself punishing them later, of course. It was worst when he hurt Jess. Some day, Jack thought . . .

Joe didn't blame him. Joe maybe hadn't even noticed he'd been gone. Beatings were normal for him; he neither understood nor remembered them. He laboured cheerfully, immensely strong and willing, doing exactly as he was told, having to be told exactly what to do, tunelessly humming, in any spare hour led out to earn Sal good silver hauling and hefting wine barrels on the Three Cranes Wharf on the Thames just fifty yards from the rear of the inn. He was about sixteen, but inside his mind he wasn't as old as Jess. Jack, at twelve, was the head of the family.

Worried about the baby now, he looked anxiously up at Sal, who just smiled. 'Off wi' ye!' She carelessly tucked Jess under her arm. 'But be sure an' bring in double today, to make up fer yestidday. I fair 'ates 'avin' Billy belt ye, even fer yer own good. 'Urts me more'n you.' Jack nodded, grinning, gritting his teeth, and turned to go; last night's bruises still ached. He paid them little heed; he was used to it.

Joe was lurching up the lane with his wide, disjointed stride, humming, laden with a saggy bundle. Stolen or smuggled? Don't be nosy. Keep well out of reach of Billy, slouching behind. 'Mornin', Joe! Billy!' Joe grunted happily in answer as he did to everyone, even Billy. Billy snarled.

Jack trotted up a crumbling wall as if it was a stair, to the accordeon-pleated roofs that were his usual road across London, his bare feet steady on damp tiles, thatch and slates slippery with moss as on any cobbles. The tangled medieval lanes were too narrow for the busy city, but who'd give up valuable bulding space for others' convenience? So the jumbled houses built up and out, leaning over to rub gables with their neighbours. For a daring, agile lad, this was as quick a route as wriggling between porters and packhorses, pigs and pedlars and passers-by in the tight-packed streets.

Food first. Jack pulled a double handful of old thatch, stuffed it into Fat Harry's chimney and slid down ready. When the smoke billowed in the bakehouse, he slipped in among the coughing customers, two pies under his shirt, and away. Whistling, garlicky and chin-dripping with suet, he clambered up to his private hideout in a lost attic of the medieval Plumbers' Hall nearby, to hide one pie for Jess and Joe tonight.

Now, to work. Cheapside Market was a good general hunting ground in the morning, popular and crowded. Then back up here to put on his good clothes, that he kept hidden safe from Sal, and try for a rich mark after noon. Maybe over the river in Southwark at the bearbaiting, or a playhouse crowd. If he didn't get his money during the day, he'd have to go out at night, and Jess was scared in the dark alone. And he had to steal at least four shillings today.

'So you want to be a spy, Master Verney.'

Frank frowned, puzzled. 'No, Sir F-Francis, a lawyer like you —'

The thin, dark-avised man facing him across the cluttered desk snorted. 'True, young man, it sounds a fairer calling than spying.'

Frank rubbed his long chin as he did whenever he felt uncertain, which was fairly often. 'Sir Edward's letter, sir, begs me a trial as a secretary. And surely a secretary keeps secrets, not b-betrays them.'

'Cheep, cheep, Chicken Licken!' Sir Francis's lips twisted unpleasantly in a sneer. 'You're wasting my time, you ignorant, innocent boy, which is the queen's time. Off home to your mother, ere the sky falls on your head.' He waved a dismissive hand and lifted a paper from a pile before him.

Frank was about to step back, abashed, shy and unsure; but the mention of his mother brought a spurt of anger which stiffened his spine. He took a deep breath and stood his ground with unusual determination. 'Sir, I write a clear secretary's hand, I can calculate in Roman and Arabian f-figures, I am f-fairly f-fluent in f-f-five languages.' God amend this stammer! The bent head before him didn't move, except to scan the paper. 'Sir F-F-Francis, you have no call to show me this lack of courtesy.'

That got him attention. He almost jumped back at the sudden glare of black eyes, as Sir Francis thumped down his paper and erupted to his feet. 'Lack of — Jackanapes! Cockscomb! Coystrill! How dare you speak so to me?'

'Sir, I speak you only as I f-f-find you.' For all his bold words, the pitch of his voice shot up. His knees were suddenly unsteady, and he clenched his teeth to stop the quiver spreading to his jaw.

Sir Francis saw the fright, and his mood changed again. He eased himself back onto his down cushion, smoothing the marten-fur facings of his warm velvet robe. 'Your pardon, Master Verney. I do indeed treat you with less than courtesy. Blame my ill-health, or the pressure of work, or simply the fact that you are the fifth young man in three days who has appeared before me with a letter of introduction. All with excellent handwriting, a very Babel of languages, and as much idea of my true business as a flea on a mastiff's rump has of bearbaiting.' He snorted in disgust. 'However, you at least have not fled snivelling at an unkind word.'

He motioned to a stool beside the tall window. 'Bring that over, sit down, and in two minutes tell me about yourself, and why you are here.'

Two minutes? Fighting confusion, Frank slowly drew up the stool, using the time to prepare his words before he spoke, as his tutors had taught him. 'I'm seventeen, sir. My f-father was Sir Henry V-Verney of V-Verneys House in F-Fulham. He died f-fighting the Irish rebels last year.' Why were there so many words that began with 'f'? 'My elder b-brother is presently in Ghent, f-fighting the Spanish. My second brother sailed with Drake on his

15

great v-voyage round the world, but was lost with the "M-Marigold" in the western ocean. I have good Latin and Greek, Spanish, F-F-French and German, some Hebrew and Italian. I entered King's College, Cambridge, when I was thirteen —' Sir Francis nodded; his old college; he approved — 'to read rhetoric and logic, cosmography, m-mathematics, law and geometry. In October past I was to join Sir Edward Spalding, my b-brother-in-law, a lawyer in the M-Middle Temple. But a f-friend fell ill. I v-visited him. It was the p-plague. I carried it home with me.'

The remembered horror thickened his throat, and he had to cough before he could go on. 'My m-mother — my mother is still unwell.' He'd not say more. 'But my sister and her b-baby both died. Sir Edward cannot bear my p-presence now. It's natural. But of Christian f-forbearance he wrote me a letter of introduction to you, though my f-family urge me to stay at home yet a while.' The time must be well past; he stopped and waited rather defiantly for dismissal.

Sir Francis studied him. True, the youth had the air of recent illness. He was thin, not slim. His pale skin stretched taut over high cheekbones, his dark hair was dull, and his deep-set brown eyes blue-shadowed, but something tough showed in his leanness, and he used his long limbs neatly. H'm. A good Protestant background. Test him. 'A convalescent, seeking a sinecure here to pass the time until you are fit to go whistling off to some higher master.'

'No, on my oath, sir!' Verney's protest was immediate and indignant. 'I'd work as hard as any man in your service! Besides, sir, where could I f-find a better position? You are of Her Majesty's P-Privy Council.'

'Indeed I am. But, young sir, my office extends beyond St James's, beyond even this land, all over Europe! Stay at home, indeed!' He sniffed scornfully. 'What would you deem your duties to be?'

'I scarcely know, sir. When I p-prove my worth, then travelling as your deputy. But at f-first I expect little more than scrivening. Copying letters, maybe p-preparing digests for you of reports f-from ambassadors and correspondents abroad, and, well, keeping you inf-formed —'

'Hah! There you have it, Master Verney! Keeping me informed! That, sir, is the essence of my task. Information! Treason, hidden plots against Her Majesty — it is the discovery of such evil, seeking it, prising news of it out of unwary or unwilling minds, that is my true office. I am indeed one of Her Gracious Majesty Queen Elizabeth's Secretaries of State.' He snorted. 'Huh! A better title would be her rat-catcher.'

He rose, stretched stiffly, and crossed to lean against the window, gazing sardonically down at Frank. 'It is easy, young man, to serve Her Majesty openly at court, or in the thrill of battle. My battles are fought away from the public eye, in secret, cunning ways. A hidden fight, dirty and dangerous, with dagger, subterfuge and cipher rather than banners and trumpets! And I win no honour nor glory, no wealth, nor titles, nor anything most men prize. After twenty years in the queen's service, I am still merely Sir Francis Walsingham, a poor knight. But my work is none the less vital. The good of this realm. The queen's continued safety. The knowledge that my duty to God and my country is well done. These are my ample reward.' A grim pride rang in Sir Francis's voice.

'And p-power, sir.'

Verney quailed for a second as the older man glared at him. But then Walsingham nodded briefly. The boy was right. 'And power. But not enough!'

He turned, to tap on the small panes of the window. 'Come here, young man. Look across to London. From this very spot I can see the roofs of eight men who I know support the Enterprise, as the Papists call it, to kill the queen and set her cousin, that malignant serpent Mary of Scotland, on the throne. Even now the King of Spain plans a fleet of invasion. Recusants and hidden Papists swarm around us, ready pardoned in advance by the Romish Antichrist for murdering Her Gracious Majesty!'

Frank nodded; he knew a few Catholics himself, quietly paying their fines rather than go to church, but he'd not thought them so dangerous. Sir Francis was pointing. 'See there, that red roof, and that chimney among the trees! I hear their whispers, I know their satanic plots. When I have proof, solid proof, they will every one meet the headsman on Tower Hill.' He paused. 'But unless and until I have that proof of malicious action, Her Majesty is so generous and merciful that she will not act against them. So, sir; what must I do? What do I need?'

Verney found it hard to meet the keen black eyes. He was a full three inches taller, but felt dwarfed by Walsingham's intensity. 'A s-spy, sir.'

'Hah!' Sir Francis returned to his desk. 'Nearly! But not quite!' He eased himself gently down again. 'What I need at this moment, Master Verney, is a thief. Not a secretary; a thief. I've lost two in the last week — one stabbed in a brawl, and my best man hanged but yesterday.' He shook his head in annoyance. 'Idiot! He should have taken three minutes to find the papers I wanted. But no, he had to fall down a stair and wake the household. Sheer incompetence!'

'Didn't he say you'd sent him?' Frank was fascinated.

'His brother is in jail for poaching. I hold further evidence against him. I promised to use it, have him executed too if my man spoke my name.'

'Could you not have told the magistrate you employed him? In p-private? So that he might dismiss the case?'

'Interfere with the course of justice?' Walsingham sounded appalled at the idea. 'Besides, I must never be implicated. To admit to using such methods would bring Her Majesty's Government into disrepute.'

'I see, sir. For the queen's sake you must break the queen's laws, in secret.' Verney bit his lip to hide a smile at the hypocrisy, unaware how clearly his thoughts showed to the experienced eyes studying him.

A born spy, Sir Francis thought; readily grasped the distinction between 'legal' and 'right'. Some courage, determination, intelligence. Not too nice a sense of honour, unlike most of the young fools nowadays. Something could very possibly be made of him.

'So now you must replace them. Well, London's swarming with thieves.'

'But not what I seek! See you, Master Verney, I need a paragon of virtuous vice! Someone who can force a window, pick a lock or a pocket, read well enough to find a particular paper for copying and then replace it without stealing so much as a lead token, that his presence may be quite unsuspected. And silent, even — Aah!' He suddenly curled forward into himself, grimacing and gasping.

Frank leapt forward in quick concern. 'Sir! You're ill? I'll call —'

'Call no-one! It's nothing! Nothing!' the older man insisted, grey and sweating. He fumbled for a handkerchief to wipe his face, forcing himself to speak. 'Ignore this, Master Verney. A touch of the stone. It passes.'

'The stone?' No wonder Walsingham's temper was uncertain, Frank thought. A stone in the bladder was agonising. 'I know of an excellent surgeon, sir, who cuts most speedily.'

'And how many survive it? One in three? Maybe half?' Walsingham sighed with sudden relief as the piercing stab vanished, leaving only a sick ache and the constant dread of its return. Thank the Lord; it could last for hours. 'No. I dare not.' It wasn't cowardice, Frank could tell. Why not, then? 'Even if I lived, I'd be off duty for days. I'm needed. Her Majesty's life is in constant danger, while that Scotch she-devil lives. I can't risk leaving her unprotected from the Papists.' He was in deadly earnest.

Tight-faced, his olive skin still shiny from the pain, he wiped a touch of white spittle from the corner of his mouth, and sat up, breathing deeply. 'Now, young sir. You might — might! — be worth training.' He raised a hand as a smile spread over Verney's face. 'But I shall set you a small test.' The smile faded. 'Find me my thief.'

What? Frank, in turn, took a long breath. 'Yes, sir. Er — how, sir?'

'That's your affair. Ask your friends. Bribe a jailer. Send out a crier with a bell, for all I care. But don't bring my name into it, for I should deny you, and you would never work for me. Just find me a good, silent, reliable thief.' Sir Francis raised a hand solemnly. 'The day you bring me what I seek, that same day I'll enter you on my rolls.' The hand swung down to point accusingly. 'But don't bother to return without him. Now go, young man. I have work to do.' The pain was hovering. Hand trembling slightly, he lifted a paper and held it before his face as Verney bowed himself out.

Mr Secretary Walsingham laid down the letter. From a pocket he took a prayer book, which fell open at a familiar page. 'Yea, though I walk through the valley of the shadow of death, I will fear no evil, for Thou art with me.' After a few moments his lips moved again. 'Lord of Hosts, I beg Thee, not for mine own sake, but for the safety of my queen, and my country, and Thine own true, pure, Protestant Faith, grant me this victory only in Thy name, to bring about the utter destruction of Thy most subtle enemy, Mary, the Queen of Scots, before I die. Amen.'

As he left, Frank paused in the high entrance hall. He'd find Walsingham his thief. It shouldn't be too hard, surely? Despite the off-putting description, the idea of a secret, private war of intelligence and trickery, all over Europe, somehow drew him. Yes, he wanted to be a spy.

'Tell me now,' he said confidentially to one of the guards lounging in their bright red, gold and black uniforms, 'where will I f-find the worst rogues in London?'

'Right 'ere in Westminster!' The man spat, grinning,

and considered more carefully. 'For Walsing'am, eh?' Taken aback, Frank agreed. 'Try one o' the Liberties, sir, where the law don't run. Gully 'Ole in Southwark, for bully boys, or wi' the doxies at Paris Gardens 'cross the river there. Or for cutpurses there's the bull an' bear rings, or a theatre.'

Frank nodded thoughtfully. Ruffians and murderers he didn't want. But cutpurses, now ... He didn't like baitings, nor fancy the vulgar pleasures of the Paris Gardens. But he'd lost a pouch once at the play. He'd take a boat down to London Bridge, see what was on at the Rose in Southwark or the Theatre or the Curteyn up north in Shoreditch, and keep his eyes open.

Determinedly Susanna kept her head down and ate her scrambled eggs.

Her mother and sister were at war as usual above her head, billowing puce brocatelle and elegant cream damask poised raging on opposite sides of the table. 'Only four thousand pounds! God's teeth! Father was a Master Goldsmith, not a pauper! With a decent dowry, I could wed an earl! God's wrath, I need it to counter your reputation!'

'I'd like to see the man dared whisper a word against my reputation!'

'Aye, mother, I'll swear you would! Or any other man!'

Susanna moved her plate away from the long nails clawing the table carpet. How did Ruth manage to seem so sweet and dainty in public?

Kate's dark face flushed even darker with the fury that her elder daughter so easily roused in her. 'I've no lack o' men friends —'

'And what kind of friends, then?'

'Gentlemen! Noblemen! An' they bide my friends, too! No like some young ladies we could mention, that can't keep a gallant for a month! That's one thing I've aye managed!'

Ruth's delicate fair skin was scarlet with a matching anger. 'Aye, we've noticed! God's belly, the world knows what you were, mother!'

'The best entertainer in London, that's what I was!'

'Aye — in the Paris Gardens!'

'I never performed in the Paris Gardens in my life! I sang at the Court, even! I kept the finest house in London! An' I still do!'

'You mean your friends just come for the wine an' pastries?'

'Well, it's no for your sweet conversation, ye scrape-tongued harpy!'

Screeching, Ruth hurled a silver cup to clatter off the panelling. The white cat by the fire leapt up in alarm, and washed off his embarrassment disdainfully. Susanna moved a bowl of syllabub just before whipped cream tipped all over the table. God, let her be as self-contained as the cat!

Kate's deeper, stronger voice drowned her daughter's light tones. 'Up to your room! One word more from you, madam, an' you'll bide there a week!'

'At least I can get through the door!' Ruth poked jeeringly at her mother's rigidly boned corseting.

The tight-piled heads of curls, black and flaxen, were nearly touching, their owners' noses not an inch apart as they shrieked across the table. Kate's face glowed with fury. Her hands snatched, slapped, tugged. 'Bitch!'

'Yeow! Let go my hair, you fat cow!'

Susanna had finished her eggs. Syllabub? No, it wasn't worth it. God, she must get out before she was sick! In disgust, the cat stalked out with her. Two maids giggling behind the door flushed guiltily. Susanna sighed, resigned. Why bother scolding? 'Annie, go and get on with the candles. Be sure to heat the wax properly, I want no holes nor bubbles this time.' Annie scurried off towards the still-room. 'Peg —'

As Susanna turned to the younger woman, Ruth

stormed out of the dining-room and pattered up the wide stair, pushing rudely between them without a glance, her face tight with temper. Susanna flushed slightly herself at the careful blank of Peg's face. 'Are our cloaks dry from yesterday? Bring them here.' Even the chilly damp of March was better than this house just now.

As the maid left, Susanna's mother came out into the hall. She was panting slightly, smoothing her gorgeous gown, looking for a focus for the rags of her temper. 'Susanna? Why is your hair in such a state, mistress?'

Not because you pulled it, anyway. 'I'm just going to tidy it, mother.'

Kate sighed deeply. 'Aye, well.' She shook her head. 'How does that besom aye put me in a state so easy? As if I wasn't used to tempers! It wasn't plates your father threw, it was tables. God, what a man!' She sighed again, in pleasant memory this time. 'What a man! An' Ruth's his double. You — you're more like me, the way I used to be anyway.' She smiled at last, stooping to kiss Susanna gently. They were both their father's daughters in looks, fair of hair and light of complexion, though Ruth had his blue eyes while Susanna's were as black as her mother's, and Susanna's mouth was more delicate than Ruth's wide, full lips. Maybe it was as well, she thought. Black skin like Kate's was fine and showy for an entertainer, but it had its drawbacks. Not elegantly tall like her mother and sister, this younger one, but short and sturdy like her father. 'You're the sensible, reliable one o' the family. More placid. Nothin' upsets you.'

If she only knew! Hiding her resentment as usual, Susanna curtseyed, smiling quietly. Agreeing was easier than arguing.

Peg appeared with the cloaks, and Kate raised a carefully-plucked eyebrow. 'You're goin' out? In this damp an' chill?'

'I've done my Latin and Greek for Master Green tomorrow, mother, and dinner is well forward. There's

23

a cog in at the Lion Quay with fresh spices. I need mace and peppercorns.' And to get out for a while . . . for ever and ever amen . . .

'Aye, well.' Kate's voice had mellowed, to chime deep and soft as she recovered her normal good humour. 'Keep Peg by you. The dockside thieves would take your hair off to sell, never mind cut your purse.' Susanna nodded and smiled as her mother, lips thinning, mounted the stair.

Kate's and Ruth's voices echoed down the stairwell. God, not again! Susanna seized her cloak from Peg and hurried out past the porter at the street door.

A plump little man on the threshold dodged her more nimbly than might be expected from his figure, and laughed. 'Woolgathering, my dear?'

She curtseyed politely, apologising. The peascod belly of Sir Roger's striped doublet was overstuffed, his ruff triple-piled lace, his cloak too gaudy with gold braid and ribbons, his plump, slightly bandy legs unbeautifully displayed in tight knitted netherstocks and high puffed trunks. Mutton dressed as ridiculous lamb in clashing pink and green. Poor Sir Roger! But of all her mother's friends, she liked him best.

He bowed over her hand. 'Mistress Susanna! No, indeed! Mistress Sunshine!' She smiled at the absurd idea and the exaggerated flourishes of his tall hat. The hair he carefully glossed down across his bald patch lifted to flap in the wind. She suddenly felt cheerier. He cocked his head to one side. 'What's wrong, my dear? I called to beg the pleasure of your mother's company at the play. Lord Pembroke's Men are performing "The Taming of a Shrew" over the river at the Theatre. Their new man has rewritten it, and I hear it's much improved.'

She sniffed tartly. 'Huh! It sounds most suitable, sir.'

He cocked an ear at a crash from upstairs. 'Aye, your mother has a temper, indeed. Your poor sister, so sweet and charming!' Little he knew, Susanna thought. 'No wonder you're upset.' He patted her shoulder consolingly.

Why was she always so dowdy? On a sudden kindly impulse he offered, 'Shall I escort you instead? You've not been to the play before? Your mother is a thought over-strict with you, my dear. I'll buy hot chestnuts. For all of us.' Moonfaced Peg grinned wide, delighted at the promise of an unexpected treat.

Susanna nearly refused, as she knew she should, but another outburst of squawking from the house changed her mind. When it was just Sir Roger, Kate wouldn't fret, however she scolded about proper behaviour later. Ruth might sneer. Let her. Susanna beamed up at her elderly escort, an excitement she'd not known for months starting to bubble in her stomach.

For once, Sir Roger thought, flushed and happy, the child was quite pretty. He'd brought a ruby brooch for Kate, but he'd save it for next time. 'Come along, then, my dear. Let's go and add some sunshine to the play!' he chuckled, bowing with an enormous sweep of his plumed hat and offering his arm. She rested her hand on it, wrist elegantly lifted like a perfect court lady, and Peg fell in behind them. All three laughing, they headed towards the landing-stage for a boat across the river.

The porter closed the door, grinning. It was good to see Mistress Susan getting a bit of fun at last.

The Play

'Sweet baked costards, four for a penny! Hot pies! Roast chestnuts!' The Theatre playhouse was filling up. In the light, cold drizzle, the sellers of hot foods were doing well. Jack bought nothing. He'd had little luck in Cheapside. The one purse he'd lifted held only a groat, two pennies and a three-farthing piece. He must do well here, or he'd have to go out tonight.

He sniffed in annoyance. He had competition. Martha Jessop, who 'fainted' and robbed those who stooped to help her. And old Maggie Fee, with her false arm ending in a leather-covered stump to arouse sympathy and draw attention from her own hand in ambush below her cloak, with sharp knife and horn thumb-guard ready to snip her neighbours' purse-strings.

The groundlings were the usual; a few truant apprentices and schoolboys, and a gang of bravoes, laughing loudly, hard-faced and alert. Little silver, much danger. A couple of young gentlemen were sitting on the stage itself to be noticed; coin in plenty, but out of his reach.

The tuppenny benches round the stage usually paid best: skiving housewives and maids, and yokels in for the market, all too entranced to notice skilled fingers easing pence from their pockets. A thin crowd today, though, and their cloaks wrapped tight against the drizzle. Maybe he'd wasted his money.

He seldom tried the covered balconies. He was noticeably shabby nowadays, growing out of his best clothes that he'd saved when his mother died. But needs must when the devil drives. Or Sal.

They were filling up well enough, on the sheltered side. Two courting couples; possible. A merchant giving his sons a treat; h'm . . . Children were risky, though, always turning round. An oldish man, showily overdressed, impressing a lass young enough to be his grand-daughter. A pretty girl, and fur in the hood. Could she be his real grand-daughter? No. If so, that type wouldn't be seen dead with her. If there wasn't a present for her in the man's purse, Jack thought, he'd eat his breeches. Any servants? A maid, already eyeing the men below. Right. There was his mark.

As the stage lanterns were lit against the dullness of the March afternoon Jack slipped unobtrusively through the gallery door. At the top of the stairs he walked right by a thin young man, paying him no heed. But the young man paid attention to him.

Frank's gaze had been caught by the oddity of this small lad, alone, not pressing close to the stage but hanging back, studying everyone so intensely . . . With a sudden thrill, Frank realised that here probably was a thief. Only a boy, but maybe the lad could lead him to a man?

He had enough sense not to stare directly, but leaned aside against one of the pillars, glancing sideways along the gallery. The lad stood in the darkest corner, like a pageboy watching the play over his master's shoulder. A servant came up the stairs with a message, and the lad ducked down neatly under the bench. When the man left, the boy was suddenly there again, almost invisible by the back wall.

The play was hilarious. When bold Caterina was tricked into marriage to Petruccio, their fights all over the stage had the gentlefolk as well as the groundlings cheering. Just round the corner, an excited girl in a green cloak kept everyone round her chuckling, at her gurgling, infectious laugh as much as at the play. Once, as she threw back her head to laugh without restraint, Frank saw her catch sight of the little boy in the corner, and she shared her laughter with him. After a shy second he grinned back. Frank warmed to her happiness. She howled with glee again, and he glanced at the stage to see what was so funny. When he looked round, the lad had vanished.

A fine spy he was! He'd better not have lost him!

Frank leaned back and squinted along under the bench. Nothing between him and the corner. He stood up, stretched as if stiff, and moved gently behind the laughing people. At the angle he bent and checked again, and caught a glimpse of a heel halfway along the row. He didn't want the lad arrested. H'm. He returned quietly to his seat beside the only exit.

'Look out, he's behind you!' Susanna was yelling with the crowd. For once outside herself, relaxed and free of tension, she shouted and cheered, laughed and booed at the dreadful things that happened to poor Caterina. 'Is she really a boy, Sir Roger? She's so pretty! Oh, well thrown!'

'Good, aren't they? Their new man's made a big difference. The clown, Kempe, he's always been excellent, but the main parts are vastly funnier.'

Susanna beamed. Sir Roger was treating her charmingly, just like an adult. He'd called down for a dish of roasted chestnuts, and peeled them for her with a folding silver penknife. The play was marvellous. She understood now why her mother liked going to the theatre, and from the way the men below were whistling at Peg, she could see why it wasn't a respectable thing for an unaccompanied young lady to do. She elbowed Peg, to make her behave.

Peg was in ecstasy. A funny play, and a grand seat, and hot chestnuts to nibble, and lots of men, and no guilty conscience! She pouted sexily, sticking out her ample chest, elaborately ignoring her admirers. Her attention was fixed over the rail, though not greatly on the stage; she didn't sense the small figure squirming silently, smoothly below her bench.

Sir Roger was enjoying himself more than he'd expected. Young Susanna — so fresh and unspoiled! A positive pleasure to see her blush at a compliment. Her mother was entertaining and gorgeous, of course, but not sweet and innocent — well, she wouldn't be, would she? He patted the purse at his belt. Kate wouldn't have been as pleased with that ruby brooch as this child was with some twopenny nuts! He might invite Susanna out again. Yes, definitely. He leaned forward on the balustrade, smiling, to enjoy Susanna's enjoyment of the actors throwing pans and puns at each other.

He didn't notice as a hand slid up behind him . . .

Jack felt gently up under the man's stiff, gaudy cloak. He couldn't see his hands, but he wasn't looking that way anyway. His attention was focussed on the back of the man's head, and along the balcony, ready to dive down, literally for his life, if anyone turned.

A bulge in the doublet — a small, tight pocket. Thistledown fingers eased out the contents. A watch, rare and expensive. Run with it? Anyone turning? No, go on. A pouch. His fingertips drifted swiftly up the fine suede, feather-light and sure as if they had eyes of their own. Jack was a proper pickpocket, not a low cut-purse. The purse didn't twitch against Sir Roger's thigh as the knot delicately eased open. Brooch, penknife, coins; one by one they slid out to be stowed inside Jack's shirt. What a haul! A fortune, even at the rates Ikey paid! And neat. The mark might be home before he realised that he'd been robbed.

Jack flowed back down and along below the bench.

On stage plates crashed, and the maid kicked back as she laughed. Her heel thumped him right on a bruise. He didn't even think of squealing. She didn't notice, and after a second he moved again, back to the corner; nobody looking, roll out, stand up, back to the shadows. Wait a moment; the young man by the door was going out. Off to the jakes, probably. No-one paying any heed. He drifted over to the stairs, to be off to Ikey's to sell the loot, the money hidden in his nest, and Jess and Joe safe for weeks.

In the darkness of the stairwell, a hand reached out of the shadows and gripped his arm tightly. 'A word with you!' a voice hissed.

Jack was already twisting, kicking desperately. His worn doublet tore. Nearly free — but an arm clamped right round his middle. He was still held! Then he realised that his attacker, though grunting with pain from a couple of good kicks, wasn't shouting for help. In surprise, Jack hesitated.

Frank managed to gasp, 'Talk to you! Just talk! F-for a groat!'

He didn't really expect it to work, but it did. The eel-like figure he was gripping so hard stilled, and wary grey eyes stared up at him from a broad, gnome-like face under a matted tousle of hair. 'Wotcher want, then? Lemme go, ye poxy bastard! Yer 'urtin' me wrist!'

With some dfficulty, Frank straightened up, still gripping firmly. He'd got his thief! Now what to do with him?

Sir Roger wondered what the time was. Halfway through the play; about two hours after noon, probably. Susanna would be impressed and interested in his fine watch — the pocket was empty! His pouch — light and thin — he tugged it open. Above Frank and Jack there was a furious shout. 'My purse! God's body, my pocket's been picked! I've been robbed!'

It was a common cry. The actors paused, grimacing

resignedly. Everyone checked his own purse, looked round for a fleeing thief. The groundlings laughed, and the door at the foot of the stairs was flung open and then slammed by one of the players' men running up.

As Frank's grip slackened in dismay, Jack took his chance and tugged free. No way out past the man coming up, and the closed door outside. Back up to the gallery, onto the balustrade. He'd get away over the roof!

Frank followed him. Jack was ready to kick him, but Frank hissed, 'Golden Cock, after the play!' He clutched conspicuously at Jack, but lunged past him and fell against the rail, as if he'd stumbled. The men running and reaching couldn't get at Jack past him.

Habit and self-preservation carried Jack on, swinging up onto the thatched roof. The skinny lad must mean he did just want to talk! He'd look in at the Golden Cock — but he had things to do first. To shouts and cheers from below he clambered up to the ridge and pranced along it, excited and triumphant, waving and gesturing rudely to the crowd, dodging the cobbles the groundlings hurled up at him, till at last with a mocking raspberry he ran down the outer slope, leapt to a nearby roof and away.

Sir Roger was scarlet with fury, dancing in rage, his plump cheeks jiggling like the long feathers in his hat, spluttering up into Frank's face. 'My watch! My silver watch from Germany! You let him get away! Blockhead! Nincompoop!'

Frank, who had been crushed against the rail by a dozen yelling would-be thief-takers, coughed and rubbed his ribs. For a second he quailed. Yes, he had helped the lad, but he mustn't let them suspect it! He forced himself to protest. 'Sir, I did my b-best. I turned the th-thief on the stair, when I heard your cry, and tried to catch him as he climbed. You've no call to upb-braid me f-for his escape. Unless you th-think I was his accomplice?' Drat this stammer! So undignified!

However, his complaint was too much, as he'd hoped.

The pompous little man puffed and huffed, and finally brought himself to retract. 'Heat of the moment, sir! Naturally, no gentleman would aid a thief. Hasty words, sir. Sudden shock — loss — valuable — you understand!'

It wasn't exactly an apology, but Frank felt he'd better not press the point. He bowed gravely, trying to hide his relief and glee and unexpected guilt. As he rose, the laughing girl in green danced forward to take the man's sleeve, smiling, holding something out to him. 'Sir Roger,' she cried, 'you should be thanking the young man, not scolding him! Look!' It was Sir Roger's watch. He pounced on it with little coos of delight, paying no heed as Susanna explained, 'It was on the stair. The thief must have dropped it when you caught him, sir.'

Frank frowned, considering. 'Aye, m-mistress, The lad's doublet tore. I seem to recall a th-thud, now that I th-think back.'

Sir Roger was busy winding his watch, shaking it, showing it off, making it chime to see that it was unharmed. Frank bowed slightly. 'F-Francis V-Verney, mistress, at your service.' She blushed charmingly. She was small and rather plump. He preferred tall, elegant girls, but when she smiled she was quite pretty. Her long, smooth hair was very attractive.

He was very nice, she thought approvingly. Too thin, but quite handsome. A friendly smile. And that stammer was sweet! 'Susanna Bolsiter, Master Verney.' Good, her voice wasn't squeaking as it often did when she was excited! They moved along the gallery away from the crowd.

'B-Bolsiter? I know the name.' Her heart sank. Everybody knew Kate. But his tone was interested, not disapproving. 'You live over the river in Southwark, don't you? My sister-in-law Jane has spoken of your m-mother. B-black, isn't she? And a rather — er — large p-personality, I'm told.'

Susanna chuckled again, rather breathlessly, with relief.

'Indeed she is, Master Verney. Very large. In all ways!' They laughed together. 'She says, sir, that when God made her, he was so pleased that he made plenty!'

Smiling, he studied her fair skin with interest. 'You don't — er — aren't —' He stopped in some embarrassment.

Used to it, she grinned. 'No, sir, I'm told I favour my father. And my mother's father was white.' He liked the way her nose crinkled when she smiled.

Sir Roger bobbed happily through the dispersing crowd, full of thanks now to the helpful youth. 'I care naught for all the rest, sir, if I have only my watch safe restored to me! Your most obliged servant, sir!'

Susanna set a hand on each of their arms. 'The actors are cursing us already. Pray come and sit with us, Master Verney, till the play is over, and then we may talk. You don't mind, Sir Roger? Oh — you don't know each other? Master Francis Verney, Sir Roger Frame, a friend of my mother's. Where do you live, Master Verney?' She drew Frank towards their seat.

Sir Roger looked after the two heads so close together, the dark and the fair, so fully absorbed in each other, forgetting him so easily. 'A friend of my mother's.' A fluttery pink ribbon on his shoulder caught his eye. What a ridiculous style, for a man of over forty — no, be honest! Over fifty. And he was getting chilblains in these tight shoes. Damn that boy!

He didn't specify, even in his own mind, which one he meant.

Two hours later Susanna's mother was gazing at her in some surprise. 'A new lace collar, wi' a high rebato to hold it up? Aye, of course, my dear. But why?' She watched Susanna try to cool her blushes with her hands. Thoughtfully, Kate dislodged her cat from the cushion beside her. 'Come sit down, my dear, an' tell me about him.'

'You're so sure it's a man?' Susanna laughed ruefully. 'But then, you always know about men, mother!'

Kate raised an eyebrow, smiling. 'Who better, my dear? Is it the lad brought you home from the play? It's no the proper thing, lass, for an honest girl to go out wi' the one gallant an' back wi' another, an' him a stranger. It could harm her — her reputation!'

They chuckled together, remembering the scene at the table, and Susanna blushed even deeper. 'Sir Roger felt unwell, mother. He said he'd known Frank — Master Verney's father, and asked him to escort me home.'

Kate eyed her quiet younger child's newly glowing face and considered. Roger unwell? No, most likely the old stag had been driven out by a younger challenger, who maybe didn't even know what he'd done. Poor soul. She'd be extra pleasant to him next time he called. 'Why didn't your lad come in?'

'He was already late for another appointment. But he asked if he might call at noon tomorrow to make himself known to you.'

'Very proper. What's his name? Varley, you said? What's he like?'

'No, Verney. Francis Verney. And he's — well, he's tall. And thin.' She stopped, and shrugged rather helplessly. 'He has a stammer.' It was all she wanted to say, just yet. Her head was full of fancies . . .

Kate, who was never fanciful, sighed in affectionate exasperation. She might as well ask her cat.

Susanna sighed too. She knew she couldn't match Ruth. Her face wouldn't sour milk, but she had no art to draw a man's eyes as her sister had, and her mother too. Until this afternoon, it hadn't mattered. She'd happily occupied herself and sheltered from the furious storms of the house in her studies and her housewifery, simply accepting that when the time was right, her mother would find her a good husband. But now . . . 'Mother, will you show me how to curl my hair in the court manner like yours?'

Kate pursed her lips doubtfully. 'I doubt it'll no suit you, my dear. Your face is round already. With curls, it'll look even broader.'

'But I must look stylish! Please!'

A gentleman, then. Well, that was something she'd learned. 'We'll do what we can to make you presentable!' Kate joked.

'Where's the fire?' an urchin jeered as Frank raced up the hill to the Golden Cock and dived panting through the door. The big room was nearly empty. Either the lad hadn't come, which was most likely, after all, or he'd been chased out again. Frank dropped onto one of the high-backed settles to recover his breath. If only he'd come straight here, instead of running to and fro across the river after girls! But no. He'd been foolish to expect — to hope — that the little thief would trust him. Oh, well. Try again tomorrow.

He lifted a hand to summon a pot-boy, and jumped as a small figure at his elbow flinched wildly. 'What — oh, it's you!' He grinned. 'I didn't th-think you'd come.' He looked more closely. 'It is you, isn't it?'

''Oo else? New togs, see? Elegant, eh?' Jack was proud but unhappy, bright in blood-orange velvet with black Spanish-work embroidery, some young lord's cast-offs, rich and showy if rather badly cleaned down the front. Frank restrained his comments. 'Out the flea-market. Right name fer it an' all. Me old fleas wasn't no bother. These new uns is fair murderin' me.' He scratched irritably. 'Ye said sixpence.'

Frank grinned. 'You can't need it, surely? If you can b-buy new clothes? With money f-from a certain elderly gentleman's p-purse?'

Jack's eye was cold. It had been a great haul, even without the watch; not just a dozen silver shillings and small stuff, but a gold royal worth thirty shillings, two twenty-shilling sovereigns, and four ten-shilling angels; a brooch that even Ikey would give him fifteen shillings for, and a little silver knife. Seven shillings had bought the new clothes. The rest was well hidden against bad days in the future. But this bony lad wasn't to know that. 'Wot's it t'you? Sixpence, or I'm off. Should pay for the togs, too, seein's 'ow it were you tore the old uns. An' lost me me watch.'

'Lost you whose w-watch? Oh, all right, all right!' Frank soothed him, dropping his hand to his belt. 'Here — what?' His purse was empty.

A little pile of coins was suddenly lying on the table between them. 'This wotcher lookin' for?' Jack was smirking in triumph.

'How did you do that? You w-weren't within arm's length of me!' Frank's voice rose in astonishment.

The tapster appeared at his side. 'All right, young master? 'Ere, you, gallows-bait, clear out!' He raised a hand to swipe at Jack.

'No, he's w-with me. B-bring us a j-jug of sherry sack, and glasses.'

When the drink came, Jack sniffed it suspiciously. Syrupy sweet, not like proper ale. He'd heard of it, but Sal didn't keep it. He tossed it off. Couldn't be all that strong, not if young Bony drank it. Not that much in a glass, anyway. First time he'd ever drunk from one. Frank, sipping, refilled Jack's glass, and a third time, with surprised respect. It took a good head to pour in the sack like that!

Jack studied the young man before him, aware that he was being studied in return. He leaned forward confidentially. 'Look 'ere, sir. No sense wastin' time. Ye wants a thief. That's plain. Well, then. Wot for?'

Walsingham's name couldn't be mentioned, but Frank's guardian angel made him tell some, at least, of the truth. 'There are men p-plotting against Queen Elizabeth. I need help to f-f-find out what's p-planned.' It was plain and tactless, without lure of gold and patriotic glory or threat of gallows. His teacher of rhetoric at Cambridge would have been disgusted by its baldness. But to his surprise and joy he saw Jack nodding.

'Burghley, eh? Or Walsin'am? Or Leicester? No, not 'im, puffed-up popinjay. Too busy plottin' 'imself, 'gainst Burghley. An' ol' Burghley, 'e don't trust young men. Right, Walsin'am, then.' Secrets? Huh! Frank grinned as Jack scratched again. 'Gor! 'Ungry, I suppose. Well. Wotcher want did?'

Frank blinked. 'You m-mean you'll do it yourself? I th-thought you could take me to a m-man . . .' His voice faded at Jack's insulted stare.

'I'm the best thief in Lunnon. Me name's Jack, Jack Downie, an' I'm called Jackdaw, 'cos I nips over the roofs like I can fly, an' I can steal anythin'. Never tried me 'and at the crown jools, only 'cos I couldn't fence 'em. Ain't nobody better'n me. Not nobody, noplace. Iffen I ain't good enough . . .' Jack was huffed. He poured himself yet another glass, to cool himself down. Sticky, but not bad when you got used to it.

Frank was on the point of apologising, but pulled himself together. Apologise? For insulting this filthy little scruff, in his gaudy cast-offs? 'I w-want somebody who can do more than cut p-purses and run about roofs.'

'Ain't no common cut-purse!' Jack protested, insulted again.

Frank sniffed again. 'Can you read?' His scornful air collapsed as Jack nodded defiantly. 'Truly?'

'Aye. Me dad were a priest's son, from ol' King 'Enery's time when they closed the mon'stries. 'E teached me. Can read as well's anybody.' Well, almost . . . And young Bony wasn't to know.

Frank wasn't going to simply accept it, though. He pulled the outside wrapper of his letter of introduction from his pouch. 'P-prove it, then.'

Jack took a deep breath, and concentrated. That drink was making his eyes wobble. 'Mr Secy Walsin'am, Privy Count. No, Privy Counc. Walsin'am. I thought as you was

wiv 'im.' He frowned. 'Knows wot a privy is, but 'ow d'ye
conk it, an' wot's a murr secky?'

'M-Master Secretary. And privy's not a jakes. He's a
Privy Councillor, one of the queen's advisers.' Frank
folded the paper away. 'That's fine.'

Jack preened, till he realised he was grinning foolishly.
It took some trouble to stop. This sweet sack . . . He'd
need to watch himself.

What else had Walsingham said? 'Can you p-pick
a lock?'

Jack opened his mouth to say yes, and shut it again.
Wouldn't put it past Bony to have a lock in his pocket
too. 'Well, not all on 'em. But Will Feather's a wizard
wiv 'em, an' now I can pay 'im ter teach me. This day
week I'll know all 'e knows.'

The most important thing last. 'Can you keep a secret?
Never tell —'

Jack snorted. 'Wotcher take me for? Been keepin' me
sneck shut since I were born. Else I'd've 'ad me throat
cut years back. Ain't no blabber-mouth.' He stuck his
chin forward aggressively. 'Wot more d'ye want?'

Taken aback, Frank shrugged rather helplessly. 'Nothing, I suppose. I'd thought a m-man — but if you can do it
— w-well, why not?' He grinned. Imagine Walsingham's
face when he saw Jack! 'You'll do.'

Jack looked less pleased than Frank had expected. 'Aye?
I'll do? An' wot'll you do, then? Fer me?'

Frank grinned again. 'Silver. P-plenty of it.' Well, he
hoped so. He suddenly realised he didn't know what the
going rate for thieves was.

He was surprised again when the lad in front of him,
grimy and skinny, so small that his chin barely appeared
over the tabletop, studied him as deeply as Walsingham
had. At last the boy seemed to come to a decision, and
shook his head slowly but firmly. 'That's not wot I wants.
Can get silver fer meself. But there's summat as I needs
'elp wiv. Sir, ye're seekin' a thief. Wot I'm lookin' fer —'

He paused and drew a deep breath. 'Gor, this sack's stronger'n I thunk!' Don't say yet . . . Not till Bony was in his debt. 'Tell ye some day. But you promise me as ye'll 'elp me w'en I wants it, an' I'll nick the corsets off the poxy Pope fer ye.'

What could it be? Probably a word to the Sheriff, if he was ever caught. Walsingham wouldn't approve. Too bad. 'Right, J-Jack. I swear I'll do wh-whatever I can for you, and here's my hand on it!'

Jack took the offered hand at first tentatively, and then with a clutch like a vice. He'd done it! At least, if he could trust young Bony, and he judged he could. 'Wot's yer name, anyway?' he asked, grinning. 'Ye ain't said. Could be Sir Philip Sidney, fer all I knows!'

'No, no, I'm no-one so f-f-fine — damn this s-stammer!'

Jack started to giggle, his eyes almost vanishing as his cheeks puffed. Frank couldn't help joining him, and they snorted and choked in company, while the other customers of the alehouse paused in their talk and dicing to grin in amusement at them. Jack sobered first — more or less. 'Gor, that sack fair creeps up on ye!'

The two lads gazed at each other across the table, smiling, hands still linked till Frank glanced out of the door and sat up with a jerk. 'I m-must go, it's getting dark. I'm F-Francis V-Verney, at your service.' He'd said that to three people today. 'If I need you, I'll leave word here, b-before noon, wh-where and when we can m-meet.'

'Aye. I'll check every day. But just say when. Meet under Nonsuch 'Ouse, on the Bridge. Better not near where I lives, 'case o' tales gettin' back ter Sal.'

'S-Sal?'

'Ivory Sal. Bitch as I lives wiv.'

Frank was taken aback at the suddenness of the venom in the lad's face, but judged it better not to inquire. 'I'll see you soon, then. Don't get caught in the m-meantime!'

In three seconds Jack was gone. Frank grinned to himself. He'd found Walsingham his thief. He felt marvellous!

Ruth

Mr Secretary Walsingham came hurrying towards his office with a companion, his lawyer's gown of chestnut velvet flapping round his knobbly knees, bright-eyed and cheerful. Frank, among the group waiting in the corridor to see the great man, caught a mutter. ' . . .This time, God willing. A poor imitation of a man, Gifford.' Scarcely pausing, Walsingham took a letter from one man, nodded to another, and saw Frank. His head reared up, his black eyes and tone were frosty. 'Master Verney. Did I not bid you return only if you found me what I sought?'

Frank bowed, smiling. 'But I have, Sir F-Francis.'

The change in Walsingham's face was most gratifying. 'Already? Indeed? Splendid! Come in, come in!' His companion followed them, smaller and skinnier than Sir Francis, his woolly scarf, fingerless gloves, and the bulb on the end of his pockmarked nose all matching red in contrast to his yellow hair and teeth. 'Sit, sit down! I've just received good news, Master Verney.' Walsingham rubbed his hands together with a rustly sound, fairly radiating satisfaction. 'But first your own news. You can wait, Phelippes? Good. Well, Master Verney? I scarce expected you to succeed so speedily.'

Flattered and about to speak, Frank suddenly had a thought. What had Jack said yesterday — he kept his sneck shut, or he'd get his throat cut? 'Your p-pardon, sir,' he said with an apologetic bow towards the third man. 'My tale, Sir F-Francis, should perhaps be told in p-private.'

'Ha! Discretion too!' Walsingham beamed. 'You may trust Phelippes here as myself, Master Verney. He is my shadow, my right hand.' The little man sucked his teeth, glowing with pleasure. 'I have no secrets from him.'

Phelippes sucked his buck teeth, an oddly juicy sound. 'You lie, you lie, sir! Your own right hand doesn't know what your right hand's doing!'

Frank blinked, but the two men simply chuckled. 'Come, Master Verney! Report!' Sir Francis sat back expansively. He nodded at the tale, smoothing the fur facings of his gown thoughtfully. 'So. Not bad, young man.'

'The lad is acceptable, then? Do you wish to see him f-first, sir?'

'I? How should I interview every rag-tag and bobtail who runs errands for me? Besides, I must not be involved. You found him. You deal with him. He's your responsibility.' Frank gulped. But, yes. Only a child or an idiot wasn't responsible for his actions. 'H'm. I wonder what he wants. It was important to him? Good.' Frank looked puzzled. 'You must secure a hold on him. Not just silver. Something to en- er — ensure silence.' Frank wondered what word he'd meant to use instead of 'ensure'. 'Enforce'?

Phelippes bobbed approval. 'The promise will serve for the moment, Sir Francis. Master Verney can decide whether to keep it when the time comes.'

At Frank's shocked face, Walsingham tut-tutted. 'Now, now, Phelippes! Master Verney is a man of honour.'

'And afterwards the lad'll be bound by gratitude?

Unlikely, sir. Thanks butter no pipers.' Phelippes' voice was sly. 'He'll soon forget.'

'Surely not, sir!' Frank protested, feeling suddenly naive.

The older men exchanged cynical glances. Phelippes sucked his teeth. 'Life's long, memory's cheap, young sir.'

'Nonsense, Phelippes. I trust Master Verney's judgement of the lad. Absolutely.' A twist in Walsingham's smile set Frank's hair lifting again, just as Sir Francis snapped his fingers. 'I've just the thing to try him out. On Thursday or Friday.' So soon? Frank found it hard to breathe.

Phelippes coughed gently. 'The Jesuits, sir?' He pursed his lips.

Walsingham nodded. 'You think he can't do it?'

'Untried, quite untried, sir! Both of them!' Phelippe's head bobbed apologetically.

At the disparagement, Frank's chin set firm. Walsingham leaned back in satisfaction. 'They must start somewhere. And this, while it must be done speedily if at all, is not of vital importance.' Phelippes bobbed and smiled. Frank felt reassured. 'Now, sir. What do you know of the Jesuits?'

'P-priests, sir, sent by the P-Pope to encourage the P-Papists among us to rebel against the queen.'

'And that is not all, young man! The Jesuits tell ailing fools that their sickness is the Lord's punishment for what they call the devil-worship of Protestantism. The blasphemers have female servants whom they pretend to exorcise before the eyes of their dupes, in Lord Vaux' house at Hackney, with screams and stenches and magical chants. A most convincing scene, I'm told. The false villains have tricked several weaklings into falling again before the Romish Antichrist.'

Frank frowned. 'Sir, I f-fail to see how Jack can help.'

'The priests report to Rome at the end of each month, via the French or Spanish Embassies. Now, my lord has many visitors. My agent knows who has come, but not which are innocent and which are poisoned by the venom of these basilisks, until he subtracts this letter for copying. Regrettably, he has been sent on an errand to Yorkshire. I thus need someone to slip in before Saturday, to borrow the letter for an hour.'

'Have you a spy in everyone's house?' Frank was impressed.

Walsingham beamed at him. 'Everyone of importance.'

'Sir, could you not send men to waylay the m-messenger?'

'Bullies?' Walsingham pursed his lips in disapproval. 'Plain brute force is sometimes unavoidable, but it's clumsy, and may rebound on you.'

Phelippes sucked his teeth. 'It creates a stir. Noise, witnesses, attention. Not what we want at all. Silence, young sir! Secrecy, young sir! No sense in jumping in with both feet where angels fear to tread.'

'I warned you.' Walsingham's voice was dry. 'No glory and trumpets.' He suddenly leapt to his feet, his clasped hands raised to Heaven. 'But today I feel full of the Glory of the Lord! For that she-scorpion in Chartley Hall is at last slipping into my grasp!'

Phelippes coughed apologetically. 'Sir . . .' As Walsingham turned in surprise, he gestured warningly towards Frank.

Walsingham calmed himself. 'Aye, Phelippes, you're quite right. Anticipation makes me indiscreet. Take Master Verney and show him what his thief is to seek. Come straight back. I'll crack a bottle of brandy with you to celebrate!' Phelippes bobbed, clearly surprised. However, his master hesitated. 'On second thoughts, no. We should not tempt the Lord.'

'No, sir,' Phelippes agreed. 'Don't count your chickens before they come home to roost. Come along, Master Verney.'

Frank bowed. 'Thank you, Sir F-Francis.'

Sir Francis's eyebrows rose. 'Wait a year, young man, and then thank me.' His voice was suddenly sour.

Phelippes' short legs twinkled rapidly down the corridors and jerked to a halt by a tall door, Frank rather breathless behind him. 'Master Ph-Phelippes, Chartley. Isn't that where the Scottish queen —'

'Stop!' Accusingly, Phelippes waved a huge key under Frank's nose. 'We never, never, never discuss Sir Francis's plans unnecessarily. Walls have long ears, Master Verney. As we know, who better! One careless word could spoil a whole applecart of schemes. Secrecy, Master Verney! Silence, Master Verney! Ask no questions and you'll be told no tall tales. Now. In here.'

A brazier tucked under a wide table kept the small room as hot as Sir Francis's office was cold. Shelves to the ceiling all round were stacked with boxes, bags, sheaves of paper, trays of coloured wax and chalks, books, inkwells, writing slates, a pot holding knives and a dozen quills. Phelippes smiled thinly, tossing his gloves and woollen hat onto the sill of the high window, combing his thin hair with impatient fingers. 'Not much, eh, Master Verney? For these are the most important tools of my profession.' He tapped his forehead meaningfully, and spread his large-knuckled fingers. 'My usual work is with ciphers, hidden writing, and such-like. But to our task. You realise the confidence Sir Francis is reposing in you, so early? Still, a good beginning when the devil drives . . .'

Hiding his smirk at the pride growing on Frank's face, Phelippes hunted out a sheet of paper and spread it on the table. 'Here, sir. This is a plan of Lord Vaux's house. The doors, you see? Windows, stairs . . . The letters are kept in a cupboard here, in my lord's bedroom. There is a hidden drawer inside the moulded top panel. Now, who will copy the letter? Ah, you'll go yourself? Excellent. It's the eager bird gathers most moss! But if the lad should be caught, you do not know him. And if you are . . .'

'I know, sir!' Frank smiled, his breathing already fast

and shallow with excitement. 'Sir F-Francis's name must never be mentioned.'

Phelippes nodded and bobbed. 'Good, sir! Excellent! But with care, you'll slip in and out as unsuspected as a needle!'

An elderly man knocked as he entered, holding papers. 'Sir —' He hesitated, noticing Frank. 'You told me to bring these straight to you.'

Phelippes tutted in annoyance. 'Knock and wait, Diggory! Always, Diggory! I've told you before! However . . . Yes, this will do. As you go, send in a taper, and a messenger in plain clothes. To go across the river.'

Frank cleared his throat, rather hesitantly. 'Master Phelippes, I have an appointment in Southwark at noon. I could take your message, maybe?'

The man waited while Phelippes considered, grinned and nodded, sucking at his teeth. 'Good, young sir! You're not known — yes, excellent! On you go, Diggory! Remember the taper, Diggory!' Phelippes carefully examined the papers. One was a letter, crumpled and stained, the other a fresh copy. He nodded, satisfied. 'Good! Now, watch carefully, Master Verney!'

When a boy brought in a burning taper, he lit a small lamp, and rummaged in a box of wax lumps. 'Too dark — too orange — ah, this one.' He set it to melt in a spoon over the flame. Then he folded the old letter exactly in its original creases. The wax seal which had held down the folded parchment, unbroken, perfect, extended beyond the upper flap in an irregular semicircle matching a scrape of wax on the lower fold. 'Now, sir! You see the seal has been cut free, without harm to parchment or imprint. Delicate work, sir, I say in all modesty. Now I must replace it, as if untouched. Heat it too much and the sharp impression will blur. Too little, it will not adhere. Misplace it by a gossamer's depth, and the join will show. Not easy, eh? Watch, then! Learn! And don't distract me! Don't move! Don't breathe, not so much as a hair!'

Working quickly and deftly, he heated a lump of polished brass in the flame of the little lamp, and laid it on the scrape of wax while next heating a broad, thick spatula. His eyes and hands were suddenly steady as he judged his moment. At last, incredibly smooth and fast, he knocked the warm brass aside, took the spoonful of liquid wax in one hand; with the other he lifted the cut half of the seal with the hot, heavy blade. He poured three drops of wax where the hot brass had lain and spread it with the back of the spoon exactly over the mark of the seal. In the instant before the upper part of the seal softened and blurred on its spatula, before the hot wax below cooled, he laid down blade and spoon and eased the upper flap down so that the projecting seal landed precisely on the thin layer of melted wax. He pressed it very gently, examining it minutely.

Frank was holding his breath. 'Will it do, sir?' he whispered.

'Sh!' Phelippes heated a tiny blade, removed an infinitesimal shaving from a bulge on one edge and polished the scar. At last he nodded, sucking in satisfaction. 'Perfect, Master Verney, the Lord be praised. Even I might not know I'd done it if I'd not done it.' He eased his shoulders, blew out the lamp and started to put away his tools.

In admiration, Frank picked up the letter to examine it. The seal was the Lion Rampant of Scotland. 'Er- how did it get the b-beer-stain?'

Phelippes tutted, twitching it from his hands. 'Least known, soonest mended!' He wrapped the letter in an anonymous piece of parchment, and wrote a large, spiky 'G' on it. 'The Tabard Inn. In Long Southwark. You'll find a fair-haired young gentleman there. Gilbert Gifford.' He sucked juicily. 'You'll not mistake him. The prettiest lass ever in breeches. He's expecting the letter. But no-one must see you give it to him, or imagine any connection whatever between you. You understand, Master Verney?'

Frank tucked the letter safe in his pouch. It shouldn't be too hard . . .

In fact, it was remarkably easy. The Tabard taproom held only one man, young and fair, with fine features, long-lashed dark grey eyes and full lips. Pretty was the exact word. He was on one of the high-backed benches by the fire, staring into the flames, cuddling his tankard.

Frank called for a jack of hot, mulled wine, and when it came, left it lying while he went to the jakes. Naturally, when he returned his drink was cold. He carried it over to the fire. This must look natural. His heart beating high and fast, he nodded politely to the pretty man, and laid his leather mug of wine and the letter together on the bench beside the man's knee while he thrust a poker into the flames. He knelt, ignoring Gifford, warming his hands. The cold was excuse enough for their trembling.

Gifford saw the 'G' on the envelope, and jumped as if he'd been tickled. He must know the writing, but seemed very nervous. Walsingham had said, 'Gifford — a poor excuse for a man.' This must indeed be him.

Frank bent to lift the poker and knock the ash off it. As he turned to pick up his jack again, Gifford moved his leg. The padding of his wide Venetian breeches quietly covered the flat packet. Not incompetent, then. Frank thrust the hot metal sizzling into his wine, nodded casually and moved to a bench by the window. Behind him, the pretty man rose abruptly and left the inn. When Frank glanced back towards the bench, there was no parchment there. He'd done it! His first act as a spy! It was easy!

Lord, it was almost noon! He'd have to run!

Southwark was an old settlement on the south bank of the Thames; London's wild side. Its main street, Long Southwark itself, ran south from London Bridge past St Thomas's Hospital and the Tabard Inn to Portsmouth. The Bankside beer-houses spread east, past the Gully Hole of ill repute, away along the bank to Deptford and Greenwich. To the west, the road to Lambeth threaded the more polite area of St Mary Overy and Winchester House opposite Susanna's home, and strung a long line of taverns and bawdy-houses past the Clink Prison, the bear and bull rings and the new Rose Theatre, right along to the Paris Gardens, pandemonium at night. The Puritan authorities of London were at constant loggerheads with the Southwark sheriff, who welcomed the trade and money that the baitings and plays, executions and cockfights, drink and doxies brought to the area, and cared little for the lawlessness and riots, risk of disease, and just plain sin.

It wasn't a normal place for a wealthy widow to live, but as Kate Bolsiter said herself, she might be a Lady, but she was no lady. She enjoyed the noise, the raffish crowds roistering past her door. She had married a younger son, of high ambition and great talent, and with her own talents, wealth and Court connections, had helped him build himself up to be a Master Goldsmith. They had lived in rigid respectability, roof-rattling fights and lively happiness for fourteen years. When with real sorrow she had buried him, she sold off the business and the tall house in Lombard Street, and retired in a certain relief with her two young daughters and her almost legendary jewelcases to a fine new mansion on the south bank, where her parties didn't get her into trouble with the Puritans. On foot over London Bridge, or by boat, friends could reach her house from any part of London in half an hour.

Being late did Frank a good turn. He had to knock at once, rather than hovering uncertainly outside, working up his courage, as he usually did when visiting, and so soon after the hot wine and his success, he arrived in good spirits. Cheerfully he followed a steward up a wide stair of carved oak, scarcely noticing a host of apparently oblivious servants, each busy on some innocent task which just happened to be within eyeshot of Mistress Susan's young man . . . The verdict was generally favourable.

He was ushered into an elegant parlour, expensive,

warm and comfortable, its golden oak ceiling and walls carved, gilded, gaily painted with flowers. Italian mirrors reflected and increased the light from two enormous windows hung with bright curtains. Two ladies seated on padded stools by the wide hearth were studying him smilingly. One laid down a citterne; she was black-skinned, older, enormous; the mother, Kate. Both were dressed in the fashion of the court. He didn't know either of them.

He gulped, and bowed. When in doubt, bow; it gives you time to think. It didn't help — he rose upright just as flummoxed as when he went down. 'Your —' he had to clear his throat — 'Your s-servant, l-ladies.' He felt as if he were choking. His ruff was far too tight.

The younger one, he saw now, was the girl of yesterday. But instead of the simple green dress, she was covered in fal-lals, jewels, ruff, wired collar, barrel skirt of russet satin, gold brocade under-gown. And her hair, instead of flowing smooth like honey, was frizzed. Yeugh!

Susanna saw his distaste. All her joyous anticipation, all the pleasure she'd had in being so very modest about her friend, in driving Peg to curl and pile and pin her hair, in sampling her mother's scents, in relief when a threatening spot on her chin receded, in her best gown and the new lace collar; all her excited hopes and happiness curdled to bile in her throat. She had to speak, though her mouth was dry. 'Master Verney, I am glad to see you again.' Thank God for manners!

'Mistress B-Bolsiter, the p-pleasure is mine.' Thank God for manners! 'P-pray you introduce me to your sister?' He'd got something right; the fat woman chuckled.

'Master Francis Verney — my mother, Lady Katharine Bolsiter.'

Kate held out her hand, smiling approval. A good-looking lad, or would be when he'd filled out a bit. A gentleman, and with some style; his suit was well-cut, of good steel-blue mockado slashed with black, only slightly padded, the cloak silk-lined, expensive but not

49

extravagant; his hose were of the new knitted worsted, his small ruff lace-trimmed, his shining buckles embossed silver. 'Master Verney, you're entirely welcome!'

The deep voice with its unexpected slight Scottish accent soothed Frank's nerves. He bent to kiss the dark hand, and as Kate rose, a tidal wave of crimson cut velvet and satin, light on her feet as in her younger days, he found himself drawn forward to be heartily kissed. 'One English habit I aye enjoy!' she chuckled. 'An' in especial when I find a lad wi' the inches that he's no need to climb on tiptoe to reach my lips!'

Frank let himself relax in her warmth. 'Lady Bolsiter.'

'Ha! I seldom let anyone stand on ceremony wi' me, an' never a handsome young man! Call me Kate, Master Verney. Lady Kate, if you must.' She chuckled again, a rich, warm gurgle that shook her whole massive bulk, and made Frank smile in return. 'Francis, is it, or Frank? May I call you so? After all, I'm old enough to be your auntie. An' big enough to be three o' them!' Dazzled, overwhelmed, amused, he suddenly felt happy again.

He turned to find Susanna smiling in relief. 'I hope I see you well?'

She was opening her mouth to answer, when the door latch clicked behind him. Instantly her face changed. A look of — what? Despair? Fury? Disgust? He swung round, alarmed, and stopped as if struck by lightning.

Kate sighed slightly. Ruth had gone out with friends; she should have been out of the way for hours. How like the besom, to come home early! Poor Susanna! 'Master Verney, Ruth. Frank, this is my elder daughter.'

She was beautiful. No. Divine. Her hair was palest gold, one adorable curl escaping from its pearled net to tremble on her ivory neck. A lace collar wired high as angel's wings framed an exquisitely lovely heart-shaped face. Her skin was pure, fine, perfect. Her eyes were oceans of speedwell blue. Her nose was delicately chiselled. Her mouth was a fraction wide, a fraction full, ideal, smiling, inviting — he gulped. She was offering him her hand to kiss. He couldn't breathe. Her gown was ice-blue silk, a wide, flowing skirt, a tiny waist under a bosom you could smuggle hedgehogs in . . . The joke he'd once thought hilarious shocked him, applied to this sublime goddess. He wanted to laugh, sing, fly . . . He suddenly realised he was gaping like a stranded codfish, still holding her slender hand, and hastily released it, fiery red. 'M-mistress B-B-Bolsiter.'

She curtseyed daintily. 'Master Verney.' Her voice was charming, light and sweet. She couldn't have noticed his hobbledehoy manners. 'It was you who so nobly came to the aid of my little sister yesterday.'

He shook his head. 'It was naught, m-mistress. And it was a gentleman, Sir Roger s-somebody, whom I had the honour of assisting.'

Her teeth were perfect pearls as she smiled. 'Sir Roger Frame. Such a dear man, so kind, to escort little Susanna to the play. Her very first time, and such an adventure! She tells a tale of high knight-errantry!'

'No, no! Your sister exaggerates. The only high th-thing was the lad climbing over the roof!' He glanced back at Susanna, and was surprised to see her staring at Ruth, white and rigid. 'M-mistress, are you ill?'

Susanna scarcely heard him amid the scorching roar of her hate. Ruth! Couldn't keep her greedy talons out of any man! God cast Ruth into the Pit! Please! She'd scratch the man-eating hag's skin off inch by inch with a pickle fork . . . What was that? Ill? She forced herself to speak, her voice strangled. 'Ill enough, sir, it seems.'

Kate was between them. 'Come an' sit down, my dear. You're a trifle pale. Frank, sit on the settle there, an' pass me a cushion. Ruth, there's wine on the sideboard, pour a glass for your sister. An' for our guest.'

Enthralled, Frank watched Ruth sway with notable grace to pour the wine. With pretty sympathy she gave her sister — er, Susanna — a glass. His turn next. He swallowed. Her delicate fingers touched his, and a fizz of prickling excitement rushed from his hand up his arm, to tighten round his chest and explode in his belly. She smiled. He took thought to breathe again as she turned to serve her mother.

Kate and Ruth, smiling, and Frank, grinning, filled the next hour with words. Neither Frank nor Susanna could have said what was talked of.

Susanna sat silent, smiling grimly, fighting for control. Balthazar the white cat came to her lap as usual; she should have chased him from her good satin, but she stroked him for comfort, till he purred and kneaded luxuriously. Be a cat . . . self-sufficient . . . dignified . . . She should have been prepared . . . been a cat . . .

When Kate signalled unmistakably, for the third time, finally, that it was time for him to leave, Frank gulped. 'Lady Kate, m-may I call again? And escort your daughter to — to anywhere?' To the ends of the earth . . .

Daughter. Ruth, of course. Poor Susanna . . . 'Of course you may call again, Frank. I never yet turned away a handsome lad. But —' Kate shook a finger at him — 'you'd no want my lasses to lose their reputation wi' you, would you?' Oh yes please . . . Her eyebrow rose as if she read his thoughts, and he blushed. 'No, indeed. So you'll no take either o' them out alone.' She smiled at his face, and patted his hand consolingly. 'But we're holdin' a supper party in ten days. If you care to, you may join us. Well?'

'I'll be honoured and delighted, m-madam.' The Spanish Army and the Earl of Leicester put together couldn't keep him away! He had a thought. 'But, Lady Kate, Sir Roger F-Frame escorted Susanna, alone —'

Kate rose, impressive and commanding, her smile and tone cooling. 'Sir Roger, sir, has been a friend o' this family for twenty year, long before my husband died. When you've known us so long, you may take the same small liberties wi' convention as I occasionally allow him.'

'M-madam, I shall study to b-become a f-friend of the f-family, and remain so f-for even longer than Sir Roger.' Her rich, forgiving chuckle rewarded him as he bowed to each in turn. 'P-pray excuse me, Lady Kate. M-mistress Ruth. Mistress — er — Susanna.' His unwilling feet took him out.

Moments later, an unwary rider passing a most respectable-looking lad was nearly unseated by an exultant Irish yell right under his horse's nose.

Behind Frank there was a silence in the parlour. Kate waited, one eyebrow raised in anticipation, for comments.

Susanna sat smiling faintly, stroking Balthazar to a steady purr.

Ruth prinked at her hair. 'A pleasant enough youth, I suppose.'

Susanna hummed non-committally. 'M'm.'

Ruth glanced over at her. 'Very gauche, of course. And that silly stammer — quite comical! But I rather liked him.'

'M'm?' Uninterested.

Frustrating. Gouge harder. 'I suppose one can't help liking a person who so obviously falls heels over head in love with one at first glance.'

'M'm.' Dismissive.

Forced into plain speaking, Ruth frowned. 'You don't mind, my dear?'

Susanna gently set down the cat and rose, one eyebrow up in almost perfect imitation of her mother, her face calm, her tone light. Be a cat . . . 'Mind? About a lad I met for the first time yesterday? Scarcely, Ruth.' She went out, smiling, and shut the door with silent precision.

Ruth was taken aback. She glanced at Kate, and laughed defensively. 'Sour grapes! She does care!'

Kate's lips quirked. 'Maybe so.' First point, naturally, to Ruth; second, against all expectation, to Susanna. Life was going to be much more interesting for a while; certainly for young Frank.

Robbery

An hour or so later Frank, trying hard to concentrate, was leaning on the river balustrade under Nonsuch House with Jack, who scratched rather less than he'd done the day before. 'Can you do it?'

''Ow should I know? Dunno the 'ouse, do I? Not in the city.' A strong condemnation. 'I'll nip out an' 'ave a look. An' you be there, see, 'bout sunset on Thursday. Keep off the road. I'll find ye. An' then we'll see.'

'What's wrong? Af-afraid?' Frank's tone was slightly contemptuous.

Jack looked at him in much greater contempt. 'Afraid? Ain't stupid. O' course I'm bleedin' afraid. 'Angin' if I'm caught, ain't it? Anyway, I'll do it. Will Feather, 'im as knows about locks, 'e's teached me a lot a'ready. 'Ere — bring some beef bones wiv yer.'

'What? B-bones? What for?'

'Dogs! Never 'eard on a 'ouse in the country wot din't 'ave no dogs. But feed 'em an' yer all right. So you bring the meat, see!'

Frank was about to protest that for a young man in fashionable clothes to carry a parcel of beef across London

54

was — well, it was ridiculous . . . But there was nobody to hear him. Jack was gone.

How many pounds was a few? Oh, beautiful Ruth . . . Would ten pounds of bones be about right? He must write her a poem. Ruth . . . Truth, of course; sooth; uncouth — oh, no, never! Youth, yes, good; tooth; booth; beef . . .

There were indeed dogs. Four huge mastiffs, bred and trained to bait bulls. Not the kind of pet usually found in Hackney, among the placid fields not three miles from London.

It was clear weather, dry for climbing, and the moon was nearly full, but a cold wind would keep any normal watchman inside. Couldn't be better. Jack perched in a beech tree just outside the high wall, and through the first new leaves studied Lord Vaux' house carefully. The house was new, with few handholds in the clean-cut corners and red and white brickwork. No helpful ivy or trees close by. But at the rear huddled the kitchen and stables. Yes. He sat back, satisfied. Once past the dogs, the house was his. With a bit of luck.

Among the stalls by Aldgate, he found what he needed: the broken end of a stout post about a yard long, and a snaffled coil of tough linen twine. When he examined it, he had over twenty yards of it. Ample.

In Thursday's twilight Frank was wandering dreamily along the road from the city gate. 'Of Aphrodite's self the living truth — p-proof? Truth, of course . . . No lovelier v-virgin — er — maiden lives than lovely Ruth. Can't repeat "living" and "lives". H'm. Breathes. Of Aphrodite's —'

'Oy! Wake up! Got the bones, eh?'

'Got what? Oh. It's you. Do you like p-poetry?'

Jack's eyes and teeth gleamed in the half-dark. 'Dunno. Never tasted it. Come round 'ere, so no cabbage-'ead yokels'll trip over us. Not like 'ome, wiv lanterns 'ung out so's ye can see where yer puttin' yer feet. Bleedin' cowpats! An' it's too quiet.' A vixen screamed close by.

55

Jack jumped at the unearthly screech. 'Gor, fair 'ates the country!' He picked up Frank's huge bundle by its string. 'Wot a pile! Gonner feed Burbage's bears, was yer? Now — oy! You listenin'?' Frank returned with reluctance from the realms of poesy. 'You gonner copy this letter when I gets it?'

'Oh! Er — yes.' Frank hadn't thought about this since he met Ruth. Ruth . . . Luckily, he always carried with him a small secretary case, with ink bottle, tiny silver pen and notepad. He coughed, trying to concentrate. He was supposed to be in charge here. 'You can get in, then?'

'Don't see why not. But you'll need to come some o' the way.'

'What?' Frank hadn't expected this.

'Well, I ain't climbin' up an' down wiv no letter in me teeth. Ain't sensible. Don't worry, I'll keep ye right!'

Half-starved to make them ferocious, the mastiffs followed a soft whistle to a quiet corner and pounced with gusto on half the big bundle of ribs, scattered from the top of the high wall. The lads clambered along to a respectful distance from the happy crunching, slipped down and scurried silently towards the house.

No lights or movement anywhere. 'Good. No visitors ternight. Come on,' Jack whispered. He started up the midden, carrying his wood, stepping carefully, but suddenly realised Frank was still hovering in distaste at the edge of the heap of kitchen rubbish and dung. 'Come on!' He snorted in contempt. 'Gentlefolks! So it's niffy! Come on, dainty-nose!'

Stung, Frank leapt up after him. His right foot landed straight on top of a pile of oyster shells, which slid and clattered under him.

Jack swore under his breath, grabbed Frank's wrist and hauled him up, gasping and squelching. The top of the pile was within three feet of the stable thatch; he pushed Frank up, up over the ridge, and down on his face just as a man came peering with a lantern. They lay flat, afraid he'd hear their hearts thundering, while he poked about. At last he turned back, calling in sleepy annoyance, 'Fox at the midden!'

Frank bit his lip. He'd nearly got them both caught. 'S-sorry!'

'Sorry don't mend no eggs!' The disgusted mutter reminded Frank of Phelippes, and he smothered a fit of half-hysterical laughter.

They worked their way along the stable to where it joined the wall of the house. 'As far's you come,' Jack murmured. 'Ye couldn't do the next bit.' He hoped he could. 'Wait 'ere. I'll lower the letter down ter ye.'

He slid quietly down to the corner and swung round onto a deep window-sill. He was on the gable end of the house, in full moonlight, open to any view; but who'd be out on a cold March night, and looking up? New-fangled glass windows towered above him. They were tall, like a church window, split by deep stone mullions into long vertical strips of small panes.

After a minute, Frank crawled down the roof to peer round the corner. There was no sign of Jack. A stout piece of wood lay on the nearest windowsill, a cord leading upwards from it. Frank's gaze followed the cord up, and he nearly fell.

Jack was five feet above him, his back braced against one mullion and his bare feet against the next, wriggling upwards like a caterpillar, inching his shoulders up, then his feet, then his shoulders again, moving steadily up the narrow, shallow gap. Definitely the best thief in London!

At the top, twelve feet up, Jack paused, scarcely panting. The eaves overhung him, slanting down a foot out from the wall and three feet above the top of the window, far beyond his reach. What now?

Jack pulled up the twine till the post bumped his heels, held firm with one foot and his shoulders while with the other foot he manoeuvred the wood into the gap, tapped it down to wedge it at an angle, kicked it hard to jam tight, and then simply stood up on its upper end, steadying himself with fingers tight on the stone.

Frank gasped in horror; Jack jumped in fright at the sudden noise. He clung unsteadily for a moment, till his heart calmed down. Bony! Bleeding idiot! Why couldn't he just do what he was told?

This was the bad bit. He untied his twine, tucked it into his shirt, and reached up to grip the fancy carved weather-boarding below the eaves. Frank nearly screamed as the lad swung free . . . But the new wood was sound and Jack was light, strong and agile. Grunting slightly now, he hauled up to get a hand to the tiles, and a foot, and hoist himself cautiously over the edge. After a moment he waved down, grinning, and disappeared.

Frank sat down on the roof below, his knees and hands trembling. He wasn't cut out for this. Even the thought of Ruth, called deliberately to mind, couldn't distract him. His ears strained for shouts of alarm.

At the back, the shutters of the second attic along were slack. Jack listened carefully; snoring . . . He eased in. Two big straw mattresses, where servant lasses slept huddled four or five together for warmth. Past, quick; just his luck if this was the night one of them had toothache and woke.

Down the stair, silently. A candle. That door there? Yes, but a servant snoring on a pallet outside it. Lean over him; try the door carefully. Locked.

He fished out the picklocks he'd bought from Will Feather. Hiding-place if the man woke? Over there; two steps and drop between a chest and a leather-covered chair. Alert for the sleeper stirring, he probed at the lock. Press here . . . No. Angle up . . . Down . . . Ah! The wards clunked back. The man grunted, rolled over, relaxed. After a minute, Jack turned the handle, pushed cautiously; no squeak, no shout of alarm; he stepped high over the man into the bedroom.

Light enough from the tall windows. The bed's curtains cosily closed. Steady breathing. The big cupboard? At the side there. Mind that stool . . . The carved top panel, slide it right . . . No. Left . . . Ahh. Another lock, on the secret drawer. Picklocks again . . . Well oiled, the lock moved readily, without a click. Gotcher!

Inside the shallow drawer, a handful of letters. He peered. Too dark to read them. Right — tie them all up and let young Bony sort them out.

After an aching year, a breathy whistle from above him made Frank jump. The letters were lowered. It was Jack's turn now to have idle time to worry. Would somebody wake? Or a messenger arrive? Or . . .

Trying to control his shivering, Frank untied the twine. Why had Jack sent all this bundle? Three letters in cipher. Page after page of his notebook as he copied, his hands so cold he was scared he'd drop his little silver pen. From the Earl of Pembroke, an invitation to dinner. A letter signed Tony B, thanking Vaux for introducing him to Captain Foscue — heavily underlined. Who was this Foscue, then? Or Tony B? Three florid pages said nothing else of any importance. Then why hide it? No address. Maybe Sir Francis would know. He blew on his fingers. Some accounts of money, mostly ordinary business, one from France — illegal; jot down a quick note. How long had it all taken?

Frank tied the letters together again and tugged the twine; it obediently vanished up into the darkness. Soon there was a scrape above Frank's head round the corner. Jack slithered over the eaves to dangle terrifyingly, groped with bare toes for the post, balanced onto it, tied on his twine again, braced himself on shoulders and feet, and kicked the wood free. Frank had expected him to descend faster than he'd gone up, and was rather surprised when he didn't. But at last he was safely down.

They had left the rest of the ribs above the midden, and tossed the bones to the far side of the stables. There was a rush of large paws, a snarling and crunching. In peace, the lads scampered to the wall, and over, and away down the lane.

They'd done it!

Jack was chirpy. 'Not bad, eh? A flash pad. But I never took nuffin'.'

'I'm glad to hear it.' In the reaction of relief, not just with cold, Frank's teeth were chattering. 'You left no sign you were th-there?'

''Cept as them dogs'll not want their meat termorrer. Gotter get back, though. Jess'll be frettin'. Me sister. On'y little, she is.'

Frank warmed to the lad; he wasn't as tough as he acted. 'My sister-in-law J-Jane doesn't like me coming in late, either.'

'Scolds yer, eh?' Jack's tone was sympathetic.

'No. J-just keeps complaining.'

Jack chuckled. 'Beatin's is bad enough, but whinin's murder.'

'Which does your m-mother do?'

'Mam's dead. Cholera. Two year ago, justabout.' Jack's tone was matter-of-fact. 'Arter me dad walked out. Jus' me an' Joe an' Jess now. Sal took us in. I 'as ter pay 'er fer our keep.' He bit his tongue to avoid telling Bony what he wanted. 'Don't your mam care if yer out?'

Somehow, it was easier to talk in the friendly dark. 'She doesn't know. She's ill.' Jack grunted in sympathy. 'M-my three little b-brothers died of plague last year. All the s-same day. And word came of my f-f-father's death. She's never recovered. J-Jane runs the house. My second b-brother's widow, thank God, or it'd be her house, and unbearable! M-mother used to sing for us, so happily.' He sighed. Self-pity. Change the subject. 'Look, there's the Tower!'

The gates were all shut, of course, but they warily followed the city wall round through the huddled slums to the path down to the river steps, dim-lit by a brazier, where a couple of boats waited, their oarsmen dozing in the hope of the double fare for a night journey. 'Oars, sir? Sculls? Up or down, sir? Tide's right fer the Bridge.'

He'd be home quicker with two rowers. 'Oars. Up to F-Fulham.' As the men of the larger boat stretched, and rattled their oars into the rowlocks with satisfaction at the good hire, Frank settled on the padded stern seat. 'Coming, J-Jack?'

Jack had been turning away, not expecting such consideration. 'Oo, ta, sir! Far's the Steelyard.' Grinning in frank enjoyment of the treat, he clambered in unhandily and sat down fast. 'Gor! Wobbly, innit!'

When the boat bumped the Steelyard steps Jack climbed out below the tall warehouses. 'Good night!' Frank said quietly. 'Tomorrow, same p-place, same time!' Jack nodded and waved as the boat surged off upriver again. He still had a five minute walk, but it was safer than landing at the Three Cranes Wharf. If Ivory Sal heard he'd been in a boat she'd ask questions.

He reached the tavern just as the last man on his feet wandered sadly out. Jess, in some distress at his lateness, was on her stool by the fire, a little live doll for the drunks to get sentimental over, or to buy drinks for. They thought it was funny when she was fuddled. Her face lit up when she saw Jack at the back door. 'Oo, Jacky!'

Ivory Sal's yellow teeth gleamed in her grin as he gave her two of the theatre man's shillings. 'Yer late, lad. Bad luck at the market, eh?'

''Ad ter pick the Lord Mayor's pocket fer ye, Sal,' he joked, smiling and winking down at Joe, crouched behind the bar as usual. Joe grinned back happily, and jingled his chain. He liked the noise. It made him feel safe.

Sal chuckled. 'That's wot I likes, a rogue wi' a touch o' spirit.' Her eye fell on her sons. 'Why can't you two speak up like 'im, eh? 'E never sulks at me!' Well Jack knew what would happen to him if he did; or to Joe, or Jess. He wished she'd stop; Billy wouldn't like this . . .

'The night's done, thank the Black Man. God's tripes, I'm stiff! Get them pots scrubbed, ye whoreson, afore ye beds down. Billy, roll them dead 'uns. Tom, sneck up. I'm off.'

While Tom barred the doors and shutters, and then lumbered off up the stair, Billy searched the clothes of the sleeping drunks, leaving a few coppers to prove they'd not been robbed, and bundled them into the straw to sleep it off. Jack lifted Jess and slid with her to his corner, hoping to get her settled out of the way. Billy was watching, however. 'Pots!' he snarled, sneering venomously. Billy was ugly, not so much in face, though he wasn't handsome, as in expression; he hated people, especially women. Even little Jess. Tom was strong, but Billy was evil. He slouched across the taproom to lift her from Jack's grasp, and leered down at the boy. 'Get yer work done, ye poxy bastard!' His fingers tightened on the baby's skinny arms.

Jess whimpered. Jack couldn't help ... except by getting the work done fast. He hurled himself at the fire, hauled the soup-pot off its hook and ran for the back door, paying no heed to its clumping against his ankles. In seconds he had the dregs of the soup out on the midden, and never mind saving any for himself and the others. The bottom was burned. A handful of straw and sand, to scour it. Water from the tub under the eaves in the corner, to rinse it. Not good enough, scour it again ... And pay no heed to the wails of pain, the crying, the screams, 'Oh, please, no! Oh, Jacky!'

Joe was grunting in distress, tugging at his chain, but no-one could help except Jack. When he was finished he could get Jess away. Sal never let Billy keep her too long — just till the work was done. Rinse the pot again. Clean enough. And the tankards. Rake up the ashes safe for the night ... At last he'd done. He reached too quickly for Jess, and got a kick in the belly that knocked him sprawling. 'Mind yer manners, starvelin'!' But Billy rose, and with a final vicious twist at Jess's fingers he tossed her on top of Jack, and slouched off up the stair.

Jack lay still for a while, cuddling Jess. He couldn't stand this much longer. His sister sobbed pitifully, clinging desperately round his neck. Some day soon he'd get her out of here. If young Bony came up to scratch . . .

As he rose, Jess whimpered. One of her fingers was dislocated. He straightened it while she squealed under her breath. It was nothing new. If she didn't have a bone broken somewhere, Billy was ill. It was one reason why she was so small, so wizened. Her frail little legs were bent with rickets, twisted sideways till her calves nearly touched the floor when she walked, but she was misshapen from Billy's torture, as well.

Jack picked her up gently and carried her to the corner behind the bar counter, where Joe was humming. He'd forgotten Billy already, and was playing again with the heavy chain that ran through the metal band riveted fast round his waist, and then up and into a deep hole between the beams of the wall, to fasten on a hidden hook far inside where Jack couldn't reach it. It held him there, a hostage, through the long, tempting nights.

Now Jack raked up the dirty straw on the floor to make a bed for them all. Cuddling her close, he hushed his little sister to quiet.

'Jacky . . .' she murmured.

'Aye? I'm 'ere.'

'I loves ye.'

'I loves you an' all. An' Joe, too. Now go ter sleep, Jess.'

She hushed, and her breathing slowed.

They all dreamed of heaven. Jess dreamed of warmth, and food, and no pain. Joe dreamed . . . happy . . . Jack dreamed that he'd kill Billy. Soon.

Next day Frank took his notes straight to Phelippes's office, and was invited to watch the master at work again.

Slate and chalk, damp cloth to wipe out, scratching and counting, sucking at his teeth and polishing the pink tip to his nose, Phelippes explained, 'A simple substitution code here, Master Verney. Write down the alphabet, you see, and under it the key word, and then all the letters not used in the key word. The trick is, of course, to find the key. But they are regular souls, these Jesuits. Here the key is Reclamo, a common choice. Then each letter in the script is replaced by the letter below it; so to decode the message, we simply seek out the letters in the lower line and lo and behold, there is the correct letter in the line above. So. You see?'

Frank admired the simplicity of it. Phelippes smirked.

'The second is a cipher, with signs for letters and some words. You copied it exact? So. Lo and behold, Master Verney!' With a flourish, he drew a paper from a shelf. On it, to Frank's astonishment, was a code with all the signs he had so carefully copied, and their meanings. Phelippes laughed silently, sucking away. 'Sometimes it is well, Master Verney, to give your opponents a little help. Provide the seed to hang themselves!'

He would explain no more, but turned to the third letter. 'Ah, a number cipher — but here stands the date, key to all the rest. Foolish, Master Verney! Fatal, Master Verney! Ah, here's a mistake. It should be 9801, not 9081.' Frank wondered if it was the Jesuit's slip or his own. 'Sir Francis will wish to see this at once. Come along, young sir.'

Sir Francis was in his office, dictating to a secretary at a speed that left Frank gasping in admiration of both Walsingham's clarity of thought, and the secretary's mastery of shorthand. As soon as the man was dismissed to make his fair copy, Sir Francis turned smiling to attend to them. 'Well, Phelippes? How have Master Verney and his boy done?'

Phelippes handed over the letters, and as Walsingham scanned them, Frank described what had happened.

Sir Francis rubbed his hands in approval. 'Now, let's see. What have we here? Wilhelmus filius Johanni — Sir William Johnson, the fool ... In nomine patris, etcetera ... What's this? Foscue has gone to see Morgan about the Enterprise. Morgan. Ahah!' He exchanged a private smile with Phelippes.

Frank cleared his throat. 'There was another letter, sir, which talked of a Captain F-Foscue. F-from a Tony B-B. He thanked V-Vaux most emphatically for an introduction to him. Nothing more, sir.'

'Did he so? Emphatically, you say? I know this Captain Foscue. A priest in disguise. He left for France three days ago. And the Enterprise, eh? A new plot against the Queen's Majesty, for sure.' He clapped Frank's shoulder, smiling. 'Well done, Master Verney. Well done indeed, both you and your light-fingered young friend. Now. Tony B. Antony B. A friend of Vaux ...'

'B-Babington?' Frank suggested. 'Sir Antony Babington, maybe.'

'A Catholic, yes. You know him?' Mr Secretary's eyes were piercing.

Frank shrugged. 'Not to say know, sir. He was a f-friend of my second b-brother, and v-visited us occasionally. I was at school. I've m-met him once or twice. I don't th-think he'd remember me.'

'H'm.' After a moment, Walsingham nodded accept-ance, and then again, more eagerly. 'This could be useful. Exactly what I need ... Yes, indeed. H'm ... Master Verney, how much do you know of your mother's history?'

'My m-mother? What has my mother to do with this? Do you insinuate —'

'No, no, sir, you mistake me! Your mother is a most respected lady. It is a sorrow for all her friends that she is unwell.' Unwell ... Frank winced, but controlled himself and bowed in acknowledgement. Sir Francis gestured to him and Phelippes to sit down. 'I'm going to give you something to think about, young man. Not a secret, exactly! But something of which you may be unaware.' He paused. Frank frowned. What was coming now? 'You know she was betrothed, before she met your father?'

Frank's tone was stiff. 'Yes, sir. To Gabriel M-Montgomery.'

'Indeed. A most handsome, honourable, courageous gentleman. Your mother's father was in the French King's Scots Guard, as was Montgomery. But after the king's death, his widow Queen Catherine wished to execute Montgomery.'

'But he escaped to England, with my m-mother's help.'

'And that of Mary Stewart, then wed to the young French King. Yes. It was in great part her doing that Montgomery was saved.' Frank wanted to applaud the Scots Queen, but prudently kept quiet. 'She would scarcely have helped, though, if she'd known both he and your family were Protestant! Indeed, your mother's own mother was murdered by a Catholic mob. Savages!' His thin lips twisted in contempt. 'However, since the whole family would have been arrested if the truth were known, your grandfather claimed that she had been killed by Protestants. And that is what the Catholics still believe. Now. When young King Francois died, Mary returned to Scotland in '61. What do you know of the Treaty of Edinburgh?'

'Edinburgh? Oh. Er — does it not say, sir, that M-Mary accepts Queen Elizabeth as true Queen of England? But she's never signed it.'

'True. The vile upstart thought — still thinks — she should be queen here! Now attend, sir! Queen Elizabeth sent ships to intercept Queen Mary, to hold her, as an honoured guest of course, until the Treaty was finally signed. But your mother, sir, interfered.'

'What! How?' Frank was enthralled.

'She has told you nothing of this? H'm. Very wise. She

felt that she owed a debt to Queen Mary, and — well, I need not go into details. She completely confounded Her Majesty's plan.'

Frank burst out laughing. He couldn't help it. His mother — his own mother — interfering successfully in the schemes of queens!

Phelippes sucked his teeth. 'It's not widely known, young sir.'

'No.' Sir Francis was displeased at the memory. 'We preferred to remain silent. And your mother has had the discretion to do so also. However, as it came about, she did not wed Montgomery. Do you know why?'

Frank nodded. 'Once she reached England, and was in his company for more than an hour at a time, sir, she f-found him totally b-boring. Nobly handsome as a Greek statue, she says, and a head as solid.' Phelippes was surprised into a snuffle of laughter. 'She had nothing but admiration for him. N-nothing at all. And her liveliness kept shocking him. His f-friend Sir Henry V-Verney was much more agreeable. They remained f-friends, though. They each danced at the other's wedding.'

'What became of him?' Phelippes asked.

Walsingham looked grim. 'I was in Paris on the dreadful day of Saint Bartholomew, when that she-devil Queen Catherine tried to massacre all the Protestants in France. I believe he was visiting his father, and just managed to escape.'

'Yes. He died in '74, Master Ph-Phelippes, in the F-French civil wars. Catherine caught him at last, and executed him.' Suddenly Frank's gaze sharpened. 'Sir F-Francis, did you know of this when you accepted me into your service? The help my m-mother gave the Scots queen, I mean?'

Phelippes sucked his teeth. 'Correct me if I'm right, young sir, but I'd guess that if Sir Francis considered this to be to your discredit, he would scarely have entrusted you with a mission last night.'

'Then, sir, why did you tell me this story of my m-mother's youth?'

'Why do you think?' Walsingham smiled as Frank worked it out.

'You th-think it may help me gain the confidence of the Catholics? Join their p-plots, discover their p-plans? Become a spy in very truth?' Frank was glowing with excitement, as Phelippes bobbed, teeth, nose and thin hair glistening, and Walsingham nodded gently. 'I'll do it!'

Sir Francis beamed. 'Your queen is deep in your debt, Master Verney!'

As Frank marched out, head high and brave, Phelippes sucked his teeth again and glanced slyly up at his master. 'Told us all John Franklin said was in the drawer. Ciphers, accounts, everything — and this extra letter John had no knowledge of, too. A good check. Oh, a sly one you are, Sir Francis! Catch more snails with honey than with vinegar. He seems a loyal lad. Honest, eager, sir. Obedient.' He sniffed. 'For the moment.'

'Obedient will suffice.' Walsingham's tone was dry.

Phelippes' was drier. 'Suffice whom, sir? You, or him?'

Sir Francis lifted a paper, his mouth firm. 'Suffice England, Master Phelippes. Send in a scrivener as you go. I have much to attend to.'

The Party

Susanna thought long and hard, in temper and not a few tears, and eventually was wise enough to ask Kate for help. 'Mother,' she said on the third of April, settling Balthazar comfortable and comforting on her lap, 'teach me how to attract people.' As her mother's mobile eyebrow rose, Susanna smiled wryly. 'Yes, all right! How to attract Frank Verney.'

Kate set aside her citterne and the sheets of new music she had been studying, and laughed. 'Well done, my dear! Aye be honest with yourself, however much ye lie to other folk.'

'What, me? Lie?' Susanna pretended to be shocked.

'Oh? When you wish Ruth "Good morning!" you truly mean it? Hah! You can't say you wish that she'd drop down dead, but you can aye hope for the best, eh? But never ever lie to yourself. Now. You want this one lad?'

'Have you any objection?' Susanna's tone was defiant. The lad was gentle born, perfectly eligible, if not a rich catch. But she didn't care; from the moment he'd spoken, she'd known this was the only lad for her.

Kate raised her eyebrows. 'I could get a titled nobleman

for you, lass, with your dowry and half my wealth to inherit later,' she tempted her daughter.

Susanna's usually soft lips were firm and determined. 'I don't want one, mother. I'm not Ruth. Well?'

Kate raised a pink-palmed hand in surrender. 'A fine young man, my dear. No doubt but he has a great future ahead of him. I've no objection in the world.' At that tone in her daughter's voice she was far too wise to argue. Susanna seemed quieter, but underneath, as Kate knew well, she had a steely resolution that made Ruth's rages look like a toddler's tantrums. When she was three, Susanna had refused to be cowed by scoldings, disgrace, even whippings, and had starved herself half to death rather than be looked after by a nurse who had accidentally killed her puppy. Opposing, trying to order or overbear her, would just set her mind even more obstinately on this lad. But other ways could be tried. 'You're certain sure, though, lass? It's no just spite at Ruth?'

Spite? That was a new thought. 'No . . .' It was the lad himself, with his shyness and stammer and great lanky legs, and the little quirk at the corner of his mouth when he was trying not to laugh, and the warmth that grew in her chest when she was with him . . . Susanna's lips, twitching in sweet memory, firmed again. 'No. There's nothing in the world I want more, mother. I'd go to him in my petticoat.'

Kate snorted in amusement. 'Huh! It would probably set him runnin'! An' there's no daughter o' mine chasin' a man in her shift, in any case, so you can put that idea right from your head, mistress!' They chuckled, at ease again together. 'Now, then. What advantages has Ruth over you?'

No need to think. 'She's beautiful.' The cat squirmed and hissed as the fingers gently scratching behind his ears poked instead of pleasuring.

'And?'

Susanna sighed in irritation. 'Isn't that enough?'

Kate snorted again. 'Aye, for a fool that's enough. Is Frank a fool?'

'No!'

'Be honest! Folly's no great drawback in a husband. An' it has little to do wi' intelligence.'

'Well . . .' Susanna considered. 'No. Not if he has time to think.'

Kate nodded. 'But Ruth'll no give him that time. She'll do as she aye does; play sweet an' sour, up an' down, come an' go, hope an' despair.'

Susanna gritted her teeth. 'And in the end she'll drop him for her earl she's aye bragging about, without a thought.' Balthazar spat again.

Kate reached over to soothe him. 'Aye. She doesn't care for him, which is a great advantage to her. Right, lassie. What advantages have you got?'

'Have I any?' Susanna tugged despondently at her lace collar.

'Don't be a fool! What can you do that she can't?'

'Nothing important. I sing well, but so does she. I can cook, but —'

'Don't underestimate yoursel' so! Look, lassie, she's pretty — no, be honest, she's lovely. She gets that from me, o' course. But you're a bonny lass too, even if you can't match her. An' her beauty's all she's got. You've a brain. Master Green says in Latin an' Greek you near match the queen hersel'. Madam there never opens a book. An' you're the practical one. You've run my house for the last two year, because it came natural to you. That must come from your father's side, for it's no my nature. You see to all — accounts, preserves, napery an' drapery, hirin' an' buildin'. You could have a better nose for wine, but that's the only thing I can fault you in. Your kitchen's a fair miracle. An' that's a great thing, for any seekin' woman. Men are slaves to their bellies an' their backs.'

Kate smiled at the dawning hope on Susanna's face.

Balthazar, neglected, mewed in complaint. 'An' you've more yet, lass. Though I hate to say it o' my own daughter, Ruth's selfish an' greedy. You're generous, in goods an' heart. She has the advantage that she doesn't care. You have it that you do. Let it show. Let him know you're glad he's there. There's naught makes a body happier than bein' liked. Ruth has her hooks in him now, an' you'll no get them out by deeds or words. Mind, now! Any word you say against her he'll take as jealousy or spite, an' it'll turn him from you, no from her. So never try to drag her down. Just make him happy, while she makes him miserable.'

'And in time, she'll show her true self, maybe?'

'Aye. Or if he's no fool he'll simply realise he prefers bein' wi' you to bein' wi' her. She'll drive him to you, if you can hold on long enough.' Maybe, maybe not; but it was as good advice as any.

'Long enough? Mother, I'll hold on till the Second Coming.'

'Good lass! An' be yourself. You saw he didn't like your hair curled up? So wear it down. Never heed the fashion. Be aye different, an' proud of it. Like me. Then your lad'll notice you.' And if Frank didn't, someone else would, that might take her mind off him. A better match, maybe. Thinking about which, 'An' you're old enough now to come down to my party.' Balthazar, as cats do, twisted in midair to land on his feet, hissing his disgust at being abruptly dumped. 'Aye, aye, never leap up so! Why no make yoursel' a new gown? Green suits you. I saw a bonny brocade in Master Van Damm's on the Bridge, an' silver tissue for an under-dress. You can have my silver chains with the beryls. I never wear them.'

Susanna, flushed and excited, kissing her mother, bouncing round the room in an ecstasy of joy and gratitude, stopped suddenly in horror. 'Only four days! Dear God Almighty! At least the food's well under way!'

She vanished in a howl of 'Peg! Peg, you lazy slut! Fetch my cloak — now!'

Balthazar sneered, washing disdainfully by the hearth. Such a disturbance! He was disappointed in the girl.

Kate sat back in her chair, laughing. Watch out, Ruth!

The supper party spiralled into a huge, glittering affair, as Kate's parties tended to do. Her guests were courtiers, soldiers and sailors, diplomats and lawyers, important merchants. People of power, of wealth and wit, action and reflection, beauty and culture. And two thirds of them, by Kate's special genius, men. Which pleased everybody.

When Frank arrived, nervous and shy in his best silk doublet and cloak, blue slashed with bronze, he found the whole street bustling, and already ringing with music. At least in this crowd he'd not be noticed. Or was that such a good thing? He didn't want to be completely overlooked . . .

As he entered, Kate seized and kissed him. 'Frank, the lasses are somewhere about. Just seek them out. I'll make time to speak to you just as soon as I can.' In the same breath, it seemed, she introduced him to Lord Howard of Effingham, Lord Admiral of England. 'This lad's brother sailed with Drake, my lord.' She whirled to the next arrival.

Howard snorted. 'Hah! Drake! Jumped-up slaver! Her Majesty allows her "beloved pirate" —' his tone was sarcastic — 'to go rollicking off to raid the Indies, while I can't get leave to take a trip over to Ostend!' Fortunately, before Frank had to answer, which he couldn't, a better audience claimed my lord's attention.

Gasping slightly, with shock and relief — the Lord Admiral! — Frank looked round for Ruth — ah, Ruth! He'd sat up half the night writing out his poem to her, and fastened a bunch of primroses into the ribbon — a pretty conceit, he was sure she'd like it. He set out through the throng to seek his beloved, the parchment burning in the breast of his doublet.

Kate was in her element. Her satin gown encrusted as a coral reef with crystals, garnets and pearls, she welcomed all her guests, danced gaily in her great hall, gravely discussed politics with statesmen in her gallery, slipped out to her parlour, with a wicked wink, to win thirty royals at dice, judiciously introduced eligible young men to eligible young ladies. She sang for them, her deep, rich voice intimate and caressing. Each guest was made to feel that this evening was planned for him alone, and all the others were there merely for his entertainment. Full of incredible energy, wherever there was dullness she appeared, swirling round her party like a carnation whirlwind, magnificently huge and bright even in that brilliant assembly, intriguing, commanding, more vital than any man or woman there, considerate of shyness and youth, ruthless towards pompous stupidity; wherever she went, laughter and joy and life surrounded her.

Ruth enjoyed herself, too. Her cream silk gown, unboned and supple, chosen specially to go with the colour of any man's clothes, was fresh and dainty as well as elegant. While she flirted, charmed, fluttered from one man to the next, accepted compliments with pretty modesty, Frank found that whenever he approached her she was dancing, or talking with a partner of such high rank that he couldn't interrupt. From a distance, she smiled and waved and blew him kisses, and with satisfaction watched his frustration. Not that she particularly wanted him; but he'd been Susanna's.

Kate shrugged; it was Ruth's nature. Foxes killed chickens.

Eventually, Frank managed to speak to her. 'Mistress Ruth! Your b-b-beauty overwhelms me!' God's belly! Had he not practised it over and over?

Ruth gave him her kiss, smiling sweetly at his rapture. 'Master Frank — such a crush! I'm faint for lack of air, and parched with thirst!'

He leapt at the chance. 'Some w-wine? I'll be honoured

74

to f-fetch it for you!' And then he'd have a chance to give her his poem. At her smile and nod, he dashed off into the crowd again to the long gallery next door where the wine was being dispensed. A glass — back to where he'd left her, his hand reaching into his doublet for the parchment . . .

She was dancing with Sir John Hawkins.

He drank the wine himself. A feeling of hopelessness grew in him. How could he compete with the wealth, the rank, the power of her other suitors? If he'd known it was going to be such a great occasion he'd not have come.

Dejected, he turned towards the door.

A short, sturdy figure danced towards him, holding out her hands in warm welcome, calling, 'Frank! This is the first proper party I've been allowed to come in to. Isn't it fun!' Susanna smiled sunnily up at him, pleased with her gown finished that very morning, her borrowed jewels, her smooth hair, her timing. Though it had been hard, she had held back unseen, watching him mooning about, sympathetically angry at his unhappy frustration, till at last Ruth let him down; cheers! Now it was her turn — her chance! 'Oh, how happy I am to see you! I've been so busy, and I thought I'd missed you, and I was so disappointed!'

His heart wasn't in his smile, but it was cheering to be greeted with such open pleasure. He couldn't go on moping with that bright face smiling at him. He bowed over her hand, and was tugged forward to be heartily kissed. 'Now, now! Don't treat me as a stranger! I don't kiss every man, but you're a friend! Will you dance with me?'

He blushed in mixed surprise and pleasure. 'Willingly, m-mistress — though is it not supposed to be the g-gentleman asks the lady?'

As if she hadn't known! 'Oh, dear! Never mind, I'll soon learn!' She mimed cheerful dismay, her eyes bright with mischief. 'I don't know anybody else who might ask me. Except Sir Roger, over there. And I'd much rather dance with you!'

He couldn't help grinning back at her. 'You look so f-fine tonight, you'll have the men queueing up to be introduced, M-mistress Susanna!'

'Thank you kindly, Master Francis! I'm glad you approve!' She curtseyed, pretty in her pleasure. She didn't notice that several other men were watching her. Frank did, and felt a small glow of pride. 'But I pray you, partner me this time. I'm so nervous!'

Dancers were moving onto the floor for the next dance. Frank bit his lip; Ruth was led out by a merchant whose gold chains, he thought jealously, would moor a galleon . . . His spirits slumped again. He wished he'd not seen Susanna, had just gone straight home . . . Hadn't come at all . . .

Susanna, her lips tight as she checked where his gaze lay, pulled him into the fast, running steps of the coranto, and in attending to the movement he cheered up. When the dance ended, before he could fall back into the dismals, she tugged him off to the side and kept him involved as she gave directions to an elderly steward who was organising the setting-up of tables in the gallery. 'Is that too close to the wall, do you think, Frank? Yes, I thought so too. Move them out a little, Master Slim. That cloth's wrinkled. Now, spread all out as I told you, well mixed — does that look right, Frank? More pasties over there? And the benches . . . Good.'

A stream of servants was carrying up dishes of roast meats of many kinds, beef, goose, heron, quails, venison, larks, capons . . . pies huge and tiny, creams and custards, salads, bright jellies, cakes. Frank's nose was caressed and intrigued by the sweet and savoury scents wafting past him. He sniffed heartily, his interest in life reviving sharply, and Susanna smiled with satisfaction. Just as her mother had said; this was her advantage.

She stepped away to check a dish. 'What a f-feast,

Master Slim!' Frank remarked to the steward. 'I hope it tastes as good as it smells.'

'Indeed, young sir. Mistress Susanna's a marvel.'

'Susanna?' Frank looked startled. 'You m-mean she cooked all this?'

'Oh, no, sir.' The old man smiled up at him superciliously. 'That would be scarcely fitting! But she orders all. Master Danby, now, the chief cook, he's a master with roasts, and his pastry coffins are adequate, but he's niggard with spices. And less idea of pretty kickshawses than the cat. And Mistress Ruth may be dainty and fine, and Lady Kate a great hostess to all the court, but they're neither of them any hand as a housewife. 'Tis young Mistress Susan runs the household.'

Susanna returned to find Frank staring at her. Puzzled, she happened to catch Slim's eye. To her surprise, he winked, with a fatherly nod.

Ruth was flirting with three men when she noticed Frank dancing a volta with Susanna, tossing her high in the great leaps that gave the dance its name, laughing. What? A duty dance was well enough; but to stay and enjoy himself apart from her? It would do her important admirers no harm to be ignored while she paid some attention to a nobody. She excused herself prettily as the dance ended, and slipped through the throng to appear unexpected at Frank's elbow, her blue eyes deeply apologetic. 'Oh, Master Verney! I do beseech your pardon. You were so kind, and I so longed for the wine! But a Hawkins, you know! So masterful! Pirates all!' She smiled dazzlingly. 'I must make up to you for it — but how?' Frank hadn't the chance to think, let alone speak, before the idea clearly struck her. She clapped her slender hands. 'I know! Pray escort me to supper! I promised Lord Hugh, but —' she twinkled wickedly — 'if he fails to attend me, he can scarcely complain that I find someone more attractive!'

Frank's heart rose and swelled. Breathing was hard.

She preferred him to this Lord Hugh . . . 'Your arm, sir!' Mesmerised, he raised his arm for her to lay her pretty, imperious hand on his wrist. Tingling at her touch, he led Ruth towards the tables with not a glance at Susanna beside him.

Susanna drew a deep breath. Don't make a scene. Don't tip a jelly over her head, or rip her gown to ribbons, or pull all her hair out. However much you want to. Be a cat. Land on your feet when you're dropped . . . She found Slim watching her with concern, and managed a smile. 'More wine up at the far table, Master Slim. And salmagundy by the fire.'

A little later, Frank felt a twinge of guilt. He hadn't excused himself from Susanna. Bad manners. He'd apologise later. He saw she had an escort. Good. Several escorts! Good. Well, yes, good . . . Then Ruth, lovely Ruth, reclaimed all his attention, and he returned to bliss.

Suddenly he remembered his poem. 'M-mistress — I have a small gift f-for you.' As Ruth looked encouraging, he fished inside his doublet for the folded parchment, holding it out with a shy smile till he saw Ruth's hesitation. He looked down. The once-crisp envelope was limp, stained by the damp stems of the broken and wilted primroses. Scarlet with humiliation, he wished the earth would open and let him sink to his grave.

He was crushed. Revive him . . . Ruth opened it, cooed like a charming child. 'Oh, Frank! A poem! To me? How wonderful!' Her smile was stunning, her scent of honeysuckle dizzying . . . He was transported with delight. Up — and down . . . She smiled maliciously. 'Dear Frank, pray read it to me? Now?'

He gulped. 'No, no, M-mistress Ruth. Truly, it's not w-worthy. Not among all this company!' But she smiled, nodding, insisting . . . He started in a mumble.

'Speak up, Frank! I can't hear you! Gentlemen, I pray you, silence for a moment! Master Verney has written a sonnet to me — pray let me hear it!'

A circle of quiet spread round them. In abject misery, Frank stammered and stuttered miserably through his verse.

'Alas, th-that all my days I sadly p-pass
M-mournful and b-bleak, recumbent on the grass
In dreams of one whose hand I dare not touch,
F-f-for th-that my hand doth love her hand too
    m-much.
If I should touch, I could not help but hold,
In w-w-wicked kidnap, impudent and b-b-bold,
Too greedy for my angel's p-presence near,
Too j-jealous to release her f-f-fingers dear.
If I were less in l-l-love, I'd dare to lay
M-my hand upon her hand, and even say
How much my adoration f-falls below
Her worthiness, as f-f-far too well I know.
Of Aph-Aphrodite's p-p-power the living truth,
No l-lovelier m-maiden b-breathes than l-lovely
    Ruth.'

There was a pause. Frank kept his face lowered, waiting for laughter. It was pretentious, clumsy, childish, obvious, unoriginal . . .

Someone began to clap. Others joined in. He looked up, scarcely believing it. Susanna, smiling brightly, was leading the applause. How kind — but what did Ruth think . . . Ruth started clapping too . . .

'Your first love poem? Not bad, Frank!' Kate's deep voice chuckled beside him, her hand warm on his shoulder. 'She's had a sight worse!' She'd had others? That fairly dented his pleasure. As Kate had intended.

Ruth took the parchment from him and in front of them all kissed it. 'I'll treasure it always, dear Frank!'

Life had no more to offer.

Susanna held grimly to her temper.

Babington

Frank took a room in a lodging house called 'The Garden', in Holborn, to be near Whitehall. From seven till noon, he was set to summarising letters and reports. His afternoons were to be spent in improving his French and Spanish, swordsmanship and general fitness. He wished that he had the nerve to call on Lady Bolsiter — on Ruth — more often than every second day. It was only just across the river now . . .

In the middle of April, Walsingham sent for him. 'You are prepared to shed your blood for your queen, Master Verney, if necessary?' He chuckled alarmingly at Frank's nod. 'You may yet get your chance. Meanwhile, I have a small task for you. Tomorrow, in Finsbury Fields. You will shoot round the rovers course, alone, and arrive at the tenth target, the one nearest the Moorgate road, at exactly one hour before noon, to meet a man.'

'How shall I know him, sir?'

'Never fear for that. Just wait there. He'll come to you.'

'And what shall I do then, sir?'

'Do?' Walsingham's smile was smug and provoking. 'Do whatever seems best to you.' Frank felt apprehensive.

All men had by law to be able to use the longbow, to defend the realm against the French or the Scots. The Council provided archery butts at the Artillery Ground, just outside the Moorgate, and, on Finsbury Fields nearby, a more interesting rovers course with targets at varied distances and directions, and all different — a wooden post, a face roughly cut on a treetrunk, a mossy straw-stuffed dummy peering out of a bush. It was a popular summer pastime; sheep and passers-by on the course ran some risk.

Out of practice, Frank found his arms soon began to ache, even firing only four or five arrows at each target. Riders and wagons passed the windmills by the Moorgate road a hundred yards away, but as he reached the ninth target, there was no-one close by except a gang of bravoes going round the course after him, passing round a leather bottle, singing and squabbling. Who was he to meet?

An arrow flew wide, within twenty feet of Frank. He called, 'F-fore! W-ware before ye!' in a friendly way. One of the bravoes, his face somehow familiar, swore at him. He shrugged and started to walk past to the tenth marker. They turned after him, cat-calling. 'Doesn't like our shooting, eh? Don't like his face. Got to shoot! Keep out the damned Papes! Disloyal dog! Papist hisself!' Another arrow flew, closer.

The meeting would have to wait; no-one could face half a dozen drunken ruffians alone. Frank walked faster. They followed. He started to run. Cries of triumph behind him. 'Run, rabbit, run! Sic 'im, Rover! Proper rovers, this! Blood 'im, Will! Stick the Papist!' An arrow thudded into the ground by his feet. He was gasping already. Could he outrun them, reach the road and help? No, the bully boys were fitter and faster than he was. He set his back to a tree and with trembling fingers set an arrow to his bowstring. He wished he had a sword.

They surrounded him, tough, hard-eyed, sniggering, jeering. 'Not runnin' no more? Gonner fight, pretty boy?

Ooh, I'm shakin'! Skinny, inn'e? I thought Papes was all fat as swine!'

A cracking thud. A shaft stood in the treetrunk by his ear, still and solid. Frank jumped and yelped. Ashamed of himself, he yelled breathlessly, 'Leave me b-b-be! I'll f-fell one of you, at least! G-go away!'

The bullies jeered at his stammer, drunkenly imitating him. 'Leave me b-b-be! G-g-go away! Lay an egg, ch-chicken! Cluck, cluck, chicken!' They started to circle him, waving knives. Mouth open, panting with fear as much as running, he stood at bay. Another thud by his side; another arrow. Their shouting was changing into a chant. 'Papist pig! Stick 'im on a stick! Papist pig! Stick 'im on a stick!' To his horror, he found himself whimpering, and angrily clenched his teeth. God's belly! He wasn't a hero, he'd run if he could. But he'd not be a coward!

Somebody called, 'Now!' A fierce, jerking agony in his right leg. An arrow had pierced the flesh of his thigh, pinning it to the tree behind him. 'Papist!' they yelled. 'Papist pig!' They advanced, grinning, shouting, their blades bright.

Desperately, he loosed his arrow at one bully, and heard a scream. Got one, at least! Oh, to hell with them! Had he shouted it? He reached down, snapped off short the feathered shaft of the arrow in his thigh and kicked his leg forward off the broken stump, ignoring the stab in his sudden fury. Drawing his knife, he leapt out to face them, but his wounded leg gave under him and he fell, still trying to slash upwards. His tormentors jumped back in surprise at the unexpected attack, but then lurched forward —

In a rattle of hooves, four horsemen crashed through the bushes, swords swinging. A pistol cracked. Yelling, the bravoes fled.

Three of the riders followed them, driving them away. The fourth leapt from his saddle to take Frank in his arms and urge him, 'Lie still, sir! You are safe! Magnificent! An act of the theatre! Achilles in the flesh! Indeed, indeed, sir, my heart burns in admiration for you!' He slapped a beringed hand in emphasis on the chest of his violet doublet.

'Oh. Th-thank you.' There didn't seem to be much else to say. Frank's head was spinning. Achilles? Oh, yes; he was wounded in the heel. Who was it who had been filled with arrows like a pin-cushion? 'Nearly S-Saint S-Sebastian,' he muttered.

His rescuer cried out in delight, clutching Frank to his bosom again. 'I knew it! When I heard what the villains were shouting, I knew I must rescue you. We of the True Faith must stand together, sir, must we not? What good fortune that I was summoned back to town unexpectedly, else you might have been sore hurt! Providence works in mysterious ways, indeed!'

Frank, half smothered by purple wool, suddenly started to giggle. He knew where he'd seen his attacker before; outside Phelippes's office. Providence? This was Walsingham's doing, all of it — the archery, the careful timing, the bravoes, the loud and repeated yells of Papist, the slight wound. Probably the summons back to London, too. This dandy here, this foolish, foppish Catholic, was the person Sir Francis had planned for him to meet. With the best of all recommendations — being martyred for the Faith! Spend your blood for Her Majesty, eh? Never use bravoes if you can help it? Sly old fox. He lay and chuckled.

His rescuer gasped in respect. 'Sir, I honour your fortitude! Antony Babington, at your service, sir! Entirely at your service!'

Within ten days Frank was Babington's bosom friend. After Sir Anthony — 'Call me Tony! An old friend of the family, am I not? Forgive me that I failed to recognise you instantly!' — after Tony had carried him home to the exclamations and complaints of his sister-in-law Jane, he had had to lie up, with the hole in his leg throbbing. But Tony called with dried fruits and a bottle of brandy, to set Jane tutting. And they talked — Tony talked — with an alarming lack of discretion. Walsingham would have been horrified. Or pleased.

Frank pled interest but ignorance of the Roman Faith. Tony, brilliant in egg-yolk yellow, clasped his hand joyously. 'You shall soon know more, Frank! We know that your father reared you as a heretic, but the heart of your mother's son must yearn for the Truth!'

'My m-mother's son?' Frank, in dressing-gown and cushioned armchair, his leg and head showily bandaged, pretended to be puzzled.

'Why yes! For your grandmother was murdered by Protestants, and your mother herself, may God soon return her to health —' he crossed himself. Hiding his shock, Frank copied him. Joyously, Tony clasped Frank's hand. 'You shall soon return to us! Your mother, God bless her, was lady-in-waiting to both Queen Catherine de Medici, and the martyr Mary of Scotland, whom she once saved from captivity! I am informed about you, you see!' He was proud of his astuteness. 'You are born and bred one of us, dear Frank!'

Exactly what Walsingham had predicted.

Sir Anthony was delighted with his new disciple, but he didn't lose his head. He hesitated fully eight minutes before promising, 'Yes, I shall introduce you to a priest, Frank, for instruction. Yet you know that if priests venture here, their heads are forfeit, and those of any who shelter them! We must take great precautions against discovery. Spies are everywhere, dear Frank!' Indeed.

As soon as he could walk, Frank made his way quietly to report to Walsingham. The great man himself was away at the queen's favourite palace of Nonsuch. However, Phelippes welcomed Frank into his bright, baking-hot cubby-hole. 'Master Verney, our sacrificial lamb! We felt for you, as Abraham for Isaac, sir!' His beaming face didn't show much pain. 'But our stratagem succeeded! There you are, like a worm in a grub, ready to destroy horrible treason before it comes to flower! We apologise, sir, we pour salt tears over your pains. But set against the safety of the realm, sir, I ask you, would you have risked spoiling the plan by telling yourself about it? H'm? Secrecy, Master Verney! Surprise, Master Verney!'

Frank had to laugh at the little man's glee. 'It was indeed a surprise, sir! I th-thought for a while my life was in danger.'

'No, no!' Phelippes chortled. 'A fright, merely! Two drops of blood!'

'F-fright?' Well . . . But the memory was already fading, overlaid by the warmth of success. 'Master Ph-Phelippes, what do I do now? Sir Anthony will p-probably —'

'Certainly, young sir! Almost certainly!'

'Certainly, then, invite me to j-join any p-plan he's m-making. But I f-feel I mustn't be seen anywhere near Sir F-Francis. Or you.'

'Such discretion, young sir! But there is no difficulty. You are not the only young man to know both Protestants and Catholics! You have claimed, as always, that you work for Master Poulter, Clerk to the Treasury here? There are so many departments! St James's swarms with offices as a bee with honey!' Phelippes sucked his teeth, glowing. 'Now, you know what we need? Names, dates, meetings, hidden weapons, and of course the details of the devilish scheme itself when they open it to you. In the meantime, you will simply be friendly. You know what I mean? Do not push, young man, or they will bolt the bridge against you.' He hesitated. 'I shall tell you no more. You must — must! — act the innocent, Master Verney, which is more convincing if one is indeed innocent. Or at least ignorant. For now you are in deadly combat against the whole might of kings!'

Frank's heart throbbed with pride, heroism, excitement. Watching him, Phelippes felt a sudden unexpected pang of pity.

The very next day, Sir Anthony appeared again, to hale Frank away in spite of Jane's wails about Frank keeping his leg up to rest it after going about on it too soon, which sped his departure in case Babington asked where he'd been. However, the young lord was as usual too full of his own plans to inquire. 'We must hasten, Frank, for my friends await you!'

In the parlour of a house in Holborn, warm and scented with apple-wood smoke, the men waiting were for the moment a blur of new faces and names. 'My dearest friend, Chidiock Tichbourne, whose house this is. He studies law with me in Barnard's Inn, as does Tom Barnwell here. My good friend Thomas, Lord Salisbury — we're planning a trip to Italy, eh, Tom? Edward Tilney, one of the queen's own guard, Frank; we move in high company here!' They all bowed, laughing, murmuring welcome.

Father Vernon, a Jesuit hiding in London, would instruct Frank in the Faith. Frank bowed in gratitude. But if Jane ever found out . . .

They chattered lightly enough, probing gently. Frank knew enough law to satisfy them. 'I'm no j-jurisconsult, sir, but I know a writ of p-praemunire from one of novodamus.' They laughed again and relaxed.

The talk moved to the Queen of Scots. Frank's ears pricked. They waxed indignant over her illegal, dishonourable imprisonment. Queen Elizabeth was much to blame for her cruel persecution of the martyred lady.

Babington mentioned that there were many abroad who would be glad to see Mary on the throne of England. 'Where she should be, Frank. For Catherine of Aragon was still alive when Elizabeth was born. King Henry's divorce was illegal, of course. Therefore Elizabeth has no true claim to England. It should have gone to her cousin Mary on the death of Mary Tudor twenty years ago. And,' Tony tapped the side of his nose significantly, 'there are some who seek to make it so despite the Bond of Association!'

Innocent didn't mean stupid. 'That's the oath all the

nobles swore after Ridolfi's p-plot last year that if Queen Elizabeth is attacked again, they'll slay Queen Mary without any f-further trial? Then surely you — er — we p-put her life in danger, by our v-very attempts to help her.'

Babington clapped his shoulder. 'A sharp observation, Frank! But I'm sure no move will be made without full preparation!' That didn't sound urgent. Babington wasn't finished, though. He murmured bashfully, 'I have myself been of some slight assistance to Her Majesty.' He pretended modest reluctance, but was clearly dying to talk. Frank listened eagerly. Was this the great plot? 'Some five years ago, I delivered some letters from the French Ambassador to a secret messenger who took them to Queen Mary.'

Was that all? Frank seemed less than overwhelmed, so Tichbourne added another daring exploit. 'Tony once carried a priest secretly to Derbyshire in his carriage. He could have been executed for it.'

That was true. Frank praised Babington, who blushed proudly. 'Do you still carry letters? Or p-priests?' There must be something!

Babington shrugged, shook his head and sighed. 'I have a packet of letters here,' he admitted, 'but since Mary has been moved to Chartley, with that unyielding Puritan, Paulet, as her jailer, all communication is cut off. I shall await further instructions from Morgan, her agent in Paris.' Aware that it sounded weak, he crossed himself. 'God will aid this unhappy princess in His good time.'

'Amen,' they agreed piously, and turned with relief to cards.

Frank reported faithfully. 'But in truth, I think they're small th-threat to the realm. Windy, f-foolish dreamers all.'

Walsingham was unconvinced. Frank was instructed to continue to visit. 'Patience, patience, young sir!' Phelippes advised him. 'Trust Sir Francis. He knows more than he says. He'd not ask you to do this for nothing, oh, no. He'll put pepper on their tails, in his own time.'

So Frank went to lectures with them, drank in the Three Tuns with them, rode, shot and fenced, played cards and dice, bowls and skittles and backgammon with them, and was accepted as one of the group. And then, one morning, his landlady called him early. 'Sir, there's a lad here desperate to see ye!'

Jack thoroughly enjoyed being rich. In his new orange velvet, whose fleas were now accustomed to him, he strolled the streets instead of the roofs, with the confident assurance of honest intent; and of course, since he had no need to steal, purses fairly threw themselves at his fingers.

He paid a Yeoman Warder a penny to see the lions fed in the Tower. He visited, and watched for a change, several plays, an execution and a bearbaiting where he won five shillings betting that the great Harry Hunks would kill a man — that was the best show of all. He cheered on a pitched battle between the boys of two grammar schools, the Pigeons of Paul's against Anthony's Pigs, and quietly carried off two satchels full of books in Latin and Greek. Ikey offered him only a groat for the lot, and in disgust he threw them in the Thames. That'd teach Ikey!

There were some tasks for young Bony, house raids again, but all in town, where the windows could be reached from a neighbouring roof. Simple. Once, he took the time to follow Bony home to the house in Holborn; better know all you can about who you're dealing with!

He watched the great Livery Companies, the Merchant Taylors or Fishmongers, parading to church behind their banners. He cheered himself hoarse among the loyal crowd as Queen Elizabeth herself started out on her annual Progress round the south of England, the Royal Barge leading a fine regatta down to Greenwich. He lounged in St Paul's Church, watching young gallants and masked ladies meet in secret among the busy, noisy stalls in the porch. Like a gentleman he tossed farthings to the cripples begging round the north gate, displaying their bleeding ulcers and distorted limbs to passers-by, and passed on, glad it wasn't him.

Jess and Joe were thrilled by the sweetmeats and raisins, pies and nuts he brought in. He was careful to offer Sal and her sons a share first, of course. From the flea market he bought a shift of red flannel for Jess, and sturdy brown breeches and shirt and a leather jerkin to replace Joe's rags; and, for himself, a tan linsey-wolsey shirt. Billy sneered, and beat them all, but left them the clothes.

One day Jack found he needed to change a gold coin into silver, to pay Ivory Sal. Quietly, in case Sal found out. No problem! Shortly, he was apologising elaborately to a bookseller, proffering a gold angel. 'I does regret, sir, givin' such a vallyble clinker, but 'Er Ladyship 'adn't no silver 'andy. No, it don't matter, any o' them books'll do.' Annoyed by the bookseller's sneer, he didn't notice Ikey's malicious face behind a bookshelf. He came away with nine shillings and eightpence in silver, and a fourpenny book of poetry. He'd give it to Bony, he liked that stuff.

That evening the taproom was crowded. Jess was by the fire as usual. Joe and Tom weren't there — they must be out. Billy was behind the bar, and Sal was serving, swinging round with the jugs, filling leather jacks and joking with the customers. 'Drink up, Jonas Peabody! Yer wife'll be in for ye soon! Keep yer mucky 'ands t'yerself, Amyas, or I'll break yer arm! Somethin' wrong wi' yer brandy, me bully? Here, lemme taste!' She lifted the horn cup and drained it in one swift gulp. 'Nought wrong wi' it as I can see!' The smoky chimney set them coughing. 'Ye dry ducks! Wet yer gizzards, an' quack wi' some spit an' spirit!' Her huge ivory beads and bangles rattled as she jested round the tables.

'Well, Jacky? 'Ow's me little jackdaw done today, eh? Good lad. I knows as 'ow I can trust ye, innit right?' She sat down smiling in a spare seat on a settle by the fire and held out her hand.

Jack could feel a tension in the air somewhere, but couldn't identify it. He shrugged. Imagination. 'There y'are, Sal. Two shillin'.'

Her stubby hand slid forward like a snake striking and clamped round his wrist. 'Now, I thanks ye, Jacky lad. But ain't ye thankful ter me? Or is it a lie, eh?' Her smile was still full, but didn't reach her eyes.

Jack knew better than to struggle, with his wrist held in those short steel-trap fingers. ''Course it ain't a lie. Sal. Right thankful, we is, all on us.' Gor, what was wrong? His heart was thudding against his ribs.

'Ain't ye got naught else ter say ter me? Oh, Jacky boy!' She shook her head in reproof, and her grip tightened painfully. 'An' me treatin' ye like yer mam.' Her voice rose, to draw the attention of the customers. 'Sad, sad it is when a lad as ye've raised from a babby cheats ye. When yer mam died, did she not say ter me, "Sal," she says wiv 'er dyin' breath, "Sal, look arter me babes fer me!" An' like me own, ye've been!' Jack shuddered. Whatever it was, it was always worse when she started this way.

The vicious grasp on his wrist tightened till he yelped. It twisted, wrenched him down on one knee. She leaned forward, her face only an inch from his white stare. 'Oh, Jacky, Jacky! Wot a bad lad, ter 'ave gold, see, an' buyin' books, an' never givin' 'is old Aunty Sal 'er share!'

'Gold? Gold? An' books? Wot the 'ell d'e want wi' that trash?' Exclamations of surprise and outrage rose all round.

'Aye! Books!' Her free hand ripped at his doublet, and the little volume of poetry fell to the straw. Casually, she tossed it into the fire. How did she know? Jack felt sick.

Jess was trembling, staring blindly. That was what had been wrong; she hadn't smiled at him. She could have warned him! No, she couldn't.

'Now, Jacky. Say as yer sorry.'

'I'm sorry, Sal!' he sobbed. His tears might satisfy her. They didn't.

'Oh, it fair 'urts me to the marrow o' me old bones when ye 'olds back on me. An' me doin' me best for ye an' yer sister 'ere, an' Joe, see?' A blow crashed onto his ears with every phrase. 'Oh, Jacky, me 'eart's near breakin'!' She twisted his wrist again.

God, how could he escape? Jack forced a ghastly grin. 'It's me arm as is near breakin', Sal. An' 'ow can I bring ye the gold if I can't climb fer it? It's 'igh up, 'idden. Fer ter give ye a surprise.'

Her smiling lips and her nostrils were white as his cheeks. 'A surprise? It's that, all right. An' one fer you too, ye bastard.' She stood up, still holding his wrist. 'Now, Jacky. 'Ere's wot yer gonner do. Ye'll tell me first 'ow much gold ye've got?' He hesitated. She twisted hard. He screamed. He was acting, but not much. 'Don't dare lie, ye devil!'

'Three angels, Sal.' It wasn't enough to satisfy her. 'An' two sovereigns. An' some silver as I spent. Wot I din't give ye, anyway.' He dared to argue. 'I give ye the two shillin' every day, Sal! Din't I?'

Again his arm was cruelly wrenched, till he yelled. Jess whimpered, and was kicked to silence. There was some murmuring among the audience — well, if the lad had paid his agreed shot . . . Sal bent slowly till Jack could feel her beery breath on his eyelids. 'One more word!' she hissed. 'One whisper, an' yer sister there, she'll be on the fire wi' yer book!' Jack's hair crisped. She'd do it, too . . . She straightened, and glared down at him. 'The gold, Jacky. Fetch it. Now.'

He had to. As fast as he could, he scrambled up to his eyrie. How much had he said? Two sovereigns and four angels? No, three. He fished them out, and then remembered he had changed one — there'd only be two left . . . In an agony of terror for his little sister, he raced back to the inn.

The taproom was empty, except for Sal and Billy. No Jess.

'Where is she, Sal?' he begged. 'You ain't 'urt 'er? 'Ere's the coin. But where's Jess?'

The tall woman smiled slowly. 'Upstairs, Jacky. An' she'll stay there, until I knows as I can trust ye.' She took the gold, looking at it curiously. Then she nodded to Billy. 'A treat fer ye, son.' And Billy gripped him, smiling at his mother, and hurt him . . .

When Billy was finished, Jack could scarcely move. One eye was closed, and he was afraid a couple of his ribs were cracked. But he turned his bruised face painfully up to Sal. 'Sal,' he whispered, 'can I go up an' see Jess? Please?'

'Be thankful I don't set Billy on ye again!' She picked him up by one arm, slapped him again, and threw him out into the yard. It was raining. He spent the night huddled in a pile of rags in one of the sheds, aching. And next day, and every day, he had to find two shillings . . .

After two days, half recovered, he tried again. 'Sal, can I see Jess?'

She didn't even pause to consider it. 'No.'

'When can I see 'er, then? She's me sister, Sal! I gotter see 'er!'

Her eyes slitted. 'Ye'd dare demand? O' me?'

'No, no, Sal! But 'ow do I know she's all right? Alive, even?'

'Ye'll 'ear 'er scream, that's 'ow ye'll know! An' yer brother too!' Her sudden, hissing rage was frightening.

He cowered away in genuine fear and dismay. 'No, Sal, please! Don't 'urt 'er! Nor Joe!' Billy loomed behind Sal, and Jack turned and fled.

He had to see Jess tonight! The most likely place for her was a cupboard in Sal's own room. His ribs ached fiercely, but he'd manage. Best go now, while the tap was busy to keep Sal occupied. He clambered wincing up to the jutting roofs that sagged over the yard, up to the window at the end of the top storey. The shutter was barred inside. No problem. A thin knife blade through a crack to ease it up . . . In seconds he was swinging into Sal's bedroom, landing light as a snowflake despite his hurts. The cupboard door was locked. He whispered, 'Jess! Are ye there?'

A whisper. 'Jacky! Oh, Jacky, I'm mis'able!' She started to cry.

'Sh! Ye'll 'ave Sal up!' Her whimpering stopped instantly. Will Feather's picklocks had the door open in seconds, and he reached to take Jess in his arms. But she moaned softly, and at the feel of her he stiffened. She felt all wrong. He drew her over towards the faint light by the window, and nearly screamed. 'Wot's she done t' ye? Oh, Jess! Wot's she done?' His voice was harsh and choked.

The little girl's left arm was bent up, twisted behind her head, and held by straps. In a while, if she wasn't released, as she wouldn't be; if the straps were tightened daily, with no thought of her pain, as they would be, and the arm forced further and further over, she'd have both arms on one side of her body, and her young bones would set in that shape for ever.

Sal was giving Jess a trade, as she had promised, by making her into a cripple, to earn her keep as a beggar in St Paul's. As long as she survived. But such children didn't often live long. Even if they didn't die of the twisting, as many did, their owners usually killed them off without a second thought when they grew too big to be appealing, cheap to feed, easily manageable. His little sister . . .

He wiped away her tears, holding his stomach muscles rigid in case he vomited. 'Shush, now, Jess! I'll look arter ye! I aye does, don't I?' She nodded; sideways. He cuddled her awkwardly, not knowing how best to hold her so that he wouldn't hurt her.

She was parched with thirst. 'Jus' be a minute. Don't go away, now!' She couldn't smile. It took only seconds to climb down, find a piggin and fill it from the rain barrel. But it was horrible to see how well she had already learned how to use her left arm over on the right side of her head, both hands working together to hold and steady the little pail at her lips.

He couldn't rescue her, even if he could have carried her down over the roofs, even if Joe wasn't a hostage. For one end of a chain like Joe's was stapled firm to the doorpost and the other held round her neck, not by a padlock that he might pick, but by an iron bar, thrust through two links and bent into a loop by Tom's enormous strength. He couldn't free her.

He couldn't let Sal know he'd been here, or she'd punish Jess for it; so he couldn't even unfasten the straps, for he'd never have been able to tie her up so tight again when he left.

He stayed for over an hour. She lay on his lap, restless in her pain and his, while he nursed her, whispering cheerfully. At last she fell asleep in his arms. He must go, before Sal came up. He eased her down on the mouldy straw. One last touch at her hair, and he climbed out, barring the door and shutter, taking the piggin, leaving no trace that he'd been there. He hoped.

There was nothing else he could do. Not tonight.

But he'd find young Bony in the morning. Time to ask for help . . .

And he'd kill them, some day. Sal, and Billy. Some day soon.

The Rescue

'Ye said as 'ow ye'd 'elp me when I asked ye. Well, sir, I'm askin'. Ye've gotter 'elp me get Jess out o' there, afore Sal kills 'er an' Joe both!'

When Frank thought of that child twisted so mercilessly, his stomach heaved. He knew it happened, but . . . 'Of course! We'll save them, J-Jack!'

Jack's eyes suddenly filled with tears. He rubbed them roughly away with his sleeve, ashamed to show such weakness. 'Right, sir. I'm yer slave fer this, as God's me witness! Wot'll we do?'

'Do?' Frank cleared his throat. 'Er — could I f-free your sister's chain, do you th-think?'

Jack spat. 'Ain't nobody could unbend that iron 'cept Tom. Need a chisel. An' they'd 'ear that. Same's wiv Joe; Sal's got bells all over in the 'ole where 'is chain's 'ooked up. Joe's too un'andy ter reach in an' un'ook 'isself, even if 'e could understan' wot ter do, an' my arms is too short, an' when I tried ter reach in wiv a stick I 'ad a bell down in 'alf a blink, an' Sal were down in less'n that, an' she beat Joe summat dreadful. Din't dare try again.'

'So we m-must get them all out, somehow. A f-fire,

95

maybe? No, of course not. No guarantee we'd get your sister f-freed in time. H'm.' He couldn't see what to do. 'What's the inn like?'

Jack considered, looking round the pleasant little parlour of Frank's rooms. 'Bigger'n this. Door that side out ter the lane, an' the stairs up in a corner. Two floors above, wiv beds fer sailors an' such, an' Sal's room where Jess is. Bar's 'ere, wiv Joe's chain right next it, by the back door ter the yard.' He looked slyly sideways at Frank. 'Great fer smugglin', Sal. Brass, window glass, needles, gunpowder, loot goes out. In, it's wine, olive oil, lace, furs, sugar, anythin'. There's a pend atween two ware'ouses runs down ter the river right aside us, an' a deal o' stuff goes up an' down wivout Customer Smythe knows about it, inter Sal's cellar. Not the one under the taproom, the secret one in the yard. Best 'id cellar in Lunnon, that is. Smythe's men's 'unted fer it a dozen times. An' the sheriff. Never found a sniff on it.' He was quite proud of it.

Frank sat up. 'That's the answer! We w-wait till there's something worth f-finding in it, and tell the sheriff. He'll arrest Sal and B-Billy and Tom, and we can just walk in to get J-Joe and Jess. That's it!'

'Tell the sheriff?' Jack's voice was high with incredulity. 'Me?'

'Don't worry! He'll not j-jail you, not when you're helping him!'

'That's it! That's bleedin' it! Splittin' ter the sheriff! Ain't — ain't right!' Nark? Even on your worst enemy? Never!

Frank finally lost his temper. His fist banged on the table. 'You care more for Sal than your own f-family!' Jack's face crumpled. 'You want my help? Well, I need your help. Do you or don't you want to rescue Jess? Then this is what you must do. Or do I f-forget it?'

At last Jack had to agree to the appalling novelty of helping the law. 'B-bring me word here, then,' Frank told him. 'That's nearer than the "Golden Cock", isn't it? I'll be here at noon every day, but I m-may have to go out again after that. Right?' As Jack stood up to go, Frank asked casually, 'Where will you take Joe and J-Jess? Once you've got them out?'

Jack shrugged, still upset. 'Dunno. Think o' summat.'

'Come home with me. To F-Fulham.' Frank blinked. Why had he said that?

Jack's face lit up. 'Gor, yer a real gent!' Then he hesitated. 'But — gotter warn ye. Sal — she's dangerous. Are ye sure, sir?'

That plucky generosity made Frank's mind up. If a little guttersnipe could risk losing shelter for himself and his family out of consideration for a friend's safety, then a gentleman could do no less. 'Of course I'm sure. Th-that's settled.' What would Jane say? He clenched his teeth. He was a man, now. He could bring his friends home if he liked!

The gratitude was spilling out of Jack, spluttering and near tears yet again. But there was something more. 'Look 'ere, sir. I can't go stealin', not if I'm watchin', an' maybe liftin' letters fer the Privy Conk.' Happy enough to make jokes, he grinned engagingly. 'I needs silver fer Sal. Can ye change a royal fer me?' He chuckled at Frank's exasperation.

With the gate shut, no-one could see what was going on in the inn yard, for no windows overlooked it. But the roofs were Jack's home ground. The inn's old thatch was mouldy and moss-grown, damp and prickly to lie on, exposed to every cold wind and April raindrop in the sky; but it was a perfect vantage point. Jack was wedged behind a chimney for warmth before the sun rose next day, and still there at sunset. Nothing. Not in nor out of the cellar. He climbed down stiffly, shivering and yawning, to hand over two shillings to Sal as if he'd been honestly thieving.

The day after, he was up on watch again. And the next day; and, near despair, the next. He slipped in to visit

97

Jess every evening, while Sal was busy in the taproom. The visits comforted the child, but were a torture for him. Every time, her arm was further over, her head dragged lower down beneath the straining armpit, and setting harder. But until the right time came, he couldn't help her.

At last, an hour before noon on the fifth day, Billy crossed the yard to throw the gate open as hooves rattled on the stones outside. Five donkeys laden high with bales of straw trotted along the back lane, and the driver turned them expertly through to the yard. In seconds the gate was barred again. Jack came alert. They had straw a-plenty. Could this be it?

The straw was dropped and tossed aside, to reveal long bundles. Tom came out to help unload and stack them by the sheds at one side. Jack peered eagerly. Metal tubes, about four feet long, as thick as his wrist, four to a heavy bundle. What could they be?

Two bundles were unloaded from each of four donkeys. Then, as Tom lifted two smallish sacks from the last beast, a stone turned under his foot and he fell. One sack split with a ringing clatter, and spiky metal things the size of your hand skittered all over to set the donkeys kicking. Cursing, Tom and Billy dived after the tinkling objects. Jack suddenly recognised them; locks for arquebuses. The tubes were the barrels. Sal was smuggling firearms!

Within ten minutes the straw was innocently piled over the ironware, and the donkeys trooping out of the yard again. As soon as there were no outsiders watching — as far as she knew — Sal whistled Joe out of the house and rolled up her sleeves. Her arms were skinny and white as leeks, but Jack knew her muscles were strong as the Three Cranes themselves.

The four of them started to heave at one of the sheds. It was tumbledown, half full of rags in old baskets, apparently no different from the other sheds around it. But with the strength of Sal and Tom, Billy and Joe each at a corner, the posts drew up like bad teeth out of deep sockets between the cobbles. The whole body of the shed was lifted and carried aside. Then the floor, a wooden platform covered with earth, strongly pegged together on runners like a sledge, was heaved to the side of the yard with the light baskets of rags on it; and below were steps down to the best-hidden cellar in London.

They started passing the arquebus barrels and fittings down the steps. The moment that their eyes were safely down on their work, Jack wriggled stiffly back out of sight, and ran. Could he reach Holborn before noon?

Frank was actually walking off down the street as Jack panted to the eaves above him and breathlessly called, 'Oy! Bony — er — sir!'

It took Frank a second or two to place the shout and peer up at the silhouette against the pale sky. 'J-Jack! Have you news?'

'Think I'd be 'ere else?' Monkeying down half-holds on the jutting house beams, puffing and grinning, Jack was too excited to be tactful.

Catching him as he dropped the last feet, Frank got a good ripe whiff. A whisper in his mind said, 'Jane'll go crazy!' Then he heard Jack's words. 'Arquebuses? Just the metal? Of course, w-wooden stocks can be f-fitted wherever they're going. M-maybe to the rebels in Ireland! That's treason, Jack! Come on! We m-must get to the Tower at once!'

Oh, Gor! 'You go, sir,' Jack begged desperately. 'I daresn't! Bleedin' kill me if they suspects, Billy 'n Sal! I'll get back, an' mark the shed, put a red rag on its door, see? An' open the gate. But I can't be seen, not wiv the soldiers, case summat goes wrong.' He didn't stop to argue, but vanished into the crowds like one bee in a swarm.

Frank was left open-mouthed behind him. He shrugged. Well, the lad had every right to be scared. It made two of them.

He braced himself to force entrance to the Tower, to insist that he was Walsingham's man, with news of treason! It turned out to be incredibly easy. By good fortune, the sheriff himself was there, received Frank with flattering speed and turned rich, ripe plum with joy. He knew Ivory Sal by reputation, and his serjeants all knew her personally. Every one of them had, at some time, searched the inn in vain, frustrated and furious. They readily agreed to allow Master Verney to stay in the background, and almost came to blows about who would have the pleasure of making the arrest.

Back at the inn, Jack climbed to the highest neighbouring roof, to watch for a boat full of soldiers. Bony might be a long time — he had to row down to the Tower, and then get a search party organised. He was biting his nails with tension when at last he saw an eight-oar barge glinting with armour draw in to the Three Cranes Quay. Must be him. Oh, Gor! Time to go! Check, very carefully; no-one at any of the windows to see his tell-tale actions. He placed the red rag, unbarred the gate, leapt for the cracked wall that was his ladder to the roof, and was hidden again in ten seconds. So far so good . . . Anxiously peering over the thatch, he waited to see the gate swing open.

Billy came out to the midden.

Would he notice the rag?

No; but he saw the opened bar. Suspiciously he jerked the gate wide. Jack's heart nearly stopped, but the lane was still empty. Grunting, Billy shut the gate firmly, jammed the bar tight and went back inside.

Jack bit his nails even deeper, his belly churning with fear. When Bony and his men arrived, if they had to break in, they'd alarm the whole house. He could open the gate again, but if he was seen, Sal would be warned, and maybe escape anyway, and know it was him . . . Gor! He had to!

He slid down, ran over and swung the bar just as a hand pushed outside. The gates opened quietly. Holding his breath, he flattened out of sight behind them.

'Well oiled, eh, corporal?' one soldier muttered as the men crept in.

'Aye. Don't want all the neighbours to know when ye've visitors!'

'But who left 'em open for us, eh?'

'Ask Walsing'am! Dobber, Jacob, on guard by the door. The shed wi' the red rag, the younker said. That one! Right, lads! Ready? Lift, quiet!'

Meanwhile, Serjeant Thanksgiving Palmer and two of his men were stamping through the front door of the inn into the taproom. 'Bless the day, Tom,' he boomed heartily. 'An' you, Joe.' Joe, raking out the filthiest of the straw, knee-high in disturbed fleas, grinned.

Tom straightened up from tapping a barrel. 'Come ter search again, serjeant? Ye won't 'ave no more luck nor last time. 'Ere, you, Joe, get movin' again, ye block!' He stomped over to the foot of the stairs and yelled up, 'Billy! Mam! Sheriff's men again!'

Palmer shook his head. 'Ye'll not 'ave yer brother an' yer mam to 'old yer 'and on the Day o' Judgement, Tom.'

Tom swore at him. Billy's heavy clogs clattered down the stair. 'This all we pays taxes fer? Nuffin' else ter do? But don't let me stop ye wastin' yer time, serjeant!' He grinned, sneering. ''Ere, 'ave a stoup. On the 'ouse!'

'Bless yer generous 'eart!' There was a thud outside the back door. As Billy started to turn, Palmer leaned forward. 'There's a lighter unloadin' at the wharf back there, Billy. Sweet wines out o' Bordeaux. Any down yer cellar? Without payin' Customer Smythe 'is dues?'

Tom laughed. 'Look away, serjeant! Yer welcome ter all ye finds!'

Billy frowned at him, and took a step towards the back door.

'Ye said a stoup, Billy?' The serjeant clapped his hands and rubbed them in anticipation. 'But not if ye can't afford it . . .'

Insulted, distracted, Billy snarled, 'Fill us a jug, then! Joe!' Joe stared, and slowly started to move towards them. 'Oh, stan' still, arse'ole! I'll do it meself, afore we all dies o' thirst!' He poured a tankard, and grinned again. 'One stoup, I said! Between yer!'

'God bless all as deserves it!' Ignoring Billy's sneer, the serjeant and his men passed the heavy tankard round, clearing their throats, clunking the mug on the counter, shuffling their feet, grunting thanks and appreciation, making noise and time for the men in the yard to do their work without interruption. 'Fine stuff, this! I must congratulate yer mam. Where is she, then? Allow me to pay me respects to the lady o' the 'ouse!'

'Be down in a minute,' Billy said shortly. 'Where d'ye want ter start, then? Attics or cellar?'

A man appeared behind him at the yard door, saluting with an ear-to-ear grin. Two more followed, carrying something long and heavy. Serjeant Palmer sighed in satisfaction, wiping ale froth off his moustache with a happy hand. 'We-ell, I thought we'd 'ave a change today, lads. We started without ye. In the yard.'

Billy reacted fast. The back door was blocked — men with some of the gun barrels; more entering by the front at the serjeant's whistle. While Tom was still gaping, Billy slapped up the tankard that Palmer held against his chest, to bang hard into his face. 'Run, Tom!' He vaulted the nearest table and charged for the stair. Tom, finally waking up, was only a yard behind. They were nearly at the first turn when the soldiers caught them by the legs, hauled them down and fell on them like threshers at harvest.

It was a brisk little fight, up and down the stairs and across the taproom. Tables and benches splintered, and an ale cask was dislodged by a wild kick at its support to crunch down, booming dully, on a soldier's foot. The soldier screamed. His mates shouted. Tom roared, 'Mam! Mam!' as he fought. Billy snarled like a wolf under the flailing cudgels.

The neighbours clustered round the door and the yard gate. 'Shouldn't we do summat?' 'Nar. Ivory Sal don't take kindly ter nosey parkers.'

The last thing Joe had been told to do was to stand still. He did so, his wooden rake dangling in his lax hand, chortling in excitement at the din and violence that raged round him leaving him untouched in the middle like a tree in a dogfight.

Upstairs, Jess trembled at the noise.

Outside by the gate, Jack bit his knuckles in suspense.

At last the crashes and shouting died away.

There was a pause.

A very battered troop trickled out into the yard. The serjeant's nose was purple and swollen, dribbling blood like a leaky ale-tap. There were four broken fingers, one dislocated jaw and the crushed foot. Two men had been stabbed. All of them had bruises or cuts from Tom's fists or Billy's knife and clogs. But they still looked heartily pleased with themselves.

Tom and Billy were dragged out, thoroughly battered, their hands tied. The soldiers didn't treat them carefully. They were shoved over to where the entrance to the cellar lay open to the spectators' fascinated gaze. Serjeant Palmer gently mopped his nose, pointing to the steps down into the dark. 'Well, lads? We fou'd it, id the edd. Arquebuses, Billy! Treasod, Tob! See you od the gibbet! You add yer buther. Rowse! Where's Ivory Sal?'

The corporal was coming out of the inn, shaking his head. 'She ain't there, serjeant. Can't find 'er noplace. She's gone.'

Palmer's roar rattled the chimneys. 'God? How cad she be god? They said she was 'ere! Up the stair! Dab this blood!' One of his men gave him a shirt from the washing-line and he did so.

Behind him, Jack cursed quietly. He'd known something would go wrong! Goddam that Bony! Nothing but trouble since he first showed his long face!

'She bust be 'id! Rowse, 'ave ye searched every roob?'

'Aye, serjeant! Nothin', 'cept this!' With a showman's flourish, he pointed to where one of his men was carrying out Jess, stiff with fear, the staple swinging at the end of the chain that still hung round her neck. 'Look 'ere, serjeant! Them God-forsaken villains! She were chained up there. Look at wot they've did to 'er!'

The other men crowded round, exclaiming in pity and disgust, till Jess's nerve broke. She started to scream, 'Jacky! Jacky! Jacky!'

Oh, Gor! Jack had to move. He pushed nervously through the crowd. 'Lemme 'ave 'er, sir. I'll quiet 'er.'

He was too late. A bellowing made the soldiers leap aside, lifting their cudgels again to defend themselves. Joe had stood smiling, jingling his belt, vaguely watching the men, but at his little sister's screams he charged out in his immense strength to rescue her, roaring, rake swinging.

Jack jumped forward, yelling as loudly as he could. 'Joe! Joe! 'S all right! Calm down! Stop, Joe! Stop!' Gor, they'd half-kill Joe if he hit one of them. They'd have to, to stop him. 'Joe! Stan' still! 'S me, Joe, stop! Jess is all right! Quiet, Jess! Joe! Calm down, both o' yer! Joe, stop!'

Joe stared round. Jess was there, and Jack. Jess was crying. But Jack was holding her. 'Joe, stan' still! 'S all right! Stan' still!' He knew the voice, and the face. He knew how to stand still. Jaw drooping in bewilderment, he stopped. Jack gulped with relief; so did the soldiers.

It took another four or five minutes to get matters sorted out. Tom and Billy were dragged away. Tom stared back in bewilderment. 'Where's mam? She were upstairs —' he started to bleat.

Billy kicked his feet from under him. 'Blabbery gooseturd!' Tom stared back as he was hauled to his feet and hustled off, but he went silently.

Palmer waved the men back in. 'You 'eard 'ib! Look everywhere! Floorboards, walls, everywhere! That bitch bust be 'id sobewhere!'

There was a sudden wail behind him. Jack had cut the straps off Jess, talking soothingly to Joe all the time, and had tried to straighten her arm out; but it hurt her. Joe grunted in sympathetic distress. Jack hastily stopped pulling at the raised arm and cuddled his sister to quiet again. Palmer glared. 'Who're you? Ad whadd'ye wad?'

Don't be cheeky, not when the man's nose is sore. 'Jack, sir. Jack Downie. I've come for me brother an' sister. Jess, 'ere, an' Joe.'

Palmer grunted suspiciously. 'The crazy lad?'

'Ain't crazy, not really!' Jack protested. 'Just when 'e's upset!'

'I doticed!' Palmer agreed. 'No wudder they chaid 'ib up at dight.'

'Strong, see, 'e is, but not in the 'ead. Can work, but not talk.'

'Useful!' Palmer commented, sniffing carefully. 'What about you, eh? What do you do? You cad talk!'

Oh, Gor . . . But suddenly Frank was there, acting quietly official. He'd rather have stayed hidden among the spectators, but if Jack was actually imprisoned as Sal's accomplice, it would be harder to slip the children away. 'S-Serjeant, it was the lad here who inf-formed us, and opened the gate. No w-word of it must get out, you understand!' He grimaced significantly, and Palmer looked wise. 'Have one of your men f-find tools to cut off these chains, and we'll be away.'

It surprised him again how readily he was obeyed. 'There ai't dobody 'ere'll go agaidst Bister Secretary Walsigab. Dobody. God's sword o' truth agai'st the Papists, 'e is, 'ib ad Burghley both, God strengthed 'eb.' There was a general mutter of agreement. Cautiously, Palmer blew his nose. 'Ah, that's better. We'll cut 'em free, an' you can have 'em.'

The corporal came in, nervously, and Palmer looked grim. 'Well, Rowse? Ivory Sal? Where is she?'

The man saluted. 'Serjeant, there's a door in a corner,

see? 'Idden. Into the 'ouse next door. Sal's gone.' Palmer was puce. Rowse went on fast, 'While we was fightin', sir. We was all in 'ere. An' all needed, too, sir.'

Though angry at the escape, Palmer couldn't argue with that. But Jack's heart lurched. Sal, free. Did she know about him? What would she do?

With surprising sympathy a soldier chiselled through the bar holding Jess's collar, but there was a difficulty with Joe. He liked his solid, half-inch-thick metal belt with the jingling rings. It was his, it was special to him, and he refused to let the soldiers touch it. He moaned unhappily, backing away, starting to grunt in anger.

'Proud of it, 'e is. Best leave it on 'im,' Jack suggested urgently.

'Yes, do so, Serjeant P-Palmer.' Frank urged the young-sters towards the door. 'I thank you f-for your expert assistance, and your discretion. Be sure I'll mention b-both to my m-master.' Jack handed Jess up to Joe to carry, and they left the serjeant in a glow of proud dreams of promotion.

The spectators settled down to wait. Some filtered over to peer into the cellar; some eyed the guards speculatively. There must be a fortune in gold hidden somewhere. And the soldiers would have to leave sometime . . .

The Crane

Joe happily shambling alongside, Frank and Jack walked through the busy crowd towards the boat steps at Three Cranes Wharf. They had to watch out for swinging nets of ten-gallon winecasks, three to each load, which the forty-foot jibs of two of the cranes were hoisting from a small lighter by the quay. 'Leavin', eh, Jackdaw?' called a man from the line of dockers trundling casks into a warehouse. 'Don't blame ye! Good luck!' His friends agreed. 'Take care o' yer sister! Nasty, that! But Joe's welcome back any time! They ain't got Sal? Watch out fer 'er!' Jack nodded. He intended to.

Jess whimpered softly, frightened by the light, the noise, the bustle. 'It's all right, lass!' Frank assured her. 'We'll take a b-boat upriver to F-Fulham — that's where I live.' And so did Jane . . .

Jack felt numb. He looked up at Joe grinning vaguely out across the river beside him, Jess cowering in his arms; and he gulped. 'We're away! Done it! Oh, thanks, sir! Never could'a did it wivout yer!' His eyes were watering with sheer relief. 'Oh, Joe! Oh, Jess, lass, we're safe now!'

A sweet voice sang, 'Master Verney! How pleasant to see you again!'

Frank stopped dead and swept off his hat. Jack sniffed in no surprise at his foolish grin as a beautiful young lady floated across the dock from an open warehouse door and held out a tiny hand to be kissed. 'Are you here to buy wine, sir?' She shuddered delicately. 'Pray you disperse the beggars. I cannot abide their stench. You should not encourage them.'

Frank flushed. Jack didn't care. Joe didn't notice. Jess whimpered.

Ruth gave a soft cry of dismay. 'Oh, dear! That child! What a dreadful sight!' Relieved by this compassion, Frank smiled at her. 'Drive her off, for God's sake! I can't bear her near me! Disgusting! And the clown! Away, oaf! Here — take this, and go!' She tossed a coin on the cobbles.

Kate's deep voice, not at all amused, rang from the open warehouse door. 'Ruth! Will I have your name called in church for unchristian lack o' charity?' An accusing archangel in Turkey red silks, she glared at Ruth.

'I am charitable, mother!' Ruth protested. 'I threw him a penny!'

'I feel sure that Master Verney and his friends stand in little need of it.' Susanna was frowning beside her mother. She knew that small lad.

There was a sudden shout from behind the ladies, and a plump, short figure pushed out onto the dock. 'God's oddikins! That's him! The thief from the theatre! And —' Sir Roger Frame whipped accusingly round on Frank, his cloak flaring — 'and you helped him escape! I was right!'

Jack glanced at Frank, but he was rigid with shock. No help there. Right. Run. But Joe, and Jess . . . Come back for them! He swung round. A tall woman with a concealing shawl over her head was watching him, only ten feet away. Sal! Ivory Sal! She knew about him, that he'd betrayed her and her boys. She'd kill him! If he ran, alone, she'd catch him. If he stayed, the man would have him arrested . . . He was trapped . . .

He hadn't eaten for twenty hours; he'd been excited, exalted, terrified, all in an hour. His face was paper-white. 'What's wrong wi' the lad?' the black lady called. 'Watch, he's faintin'!' Jack could take a hint as well as the next. It was a way out; they'd maybe not hit him if they thought him unconscious. With a sigh, he rolled his eyes upwards and collapsed.

Susanna moved first. She knelt down by the boy, ignoring Ruth's cry of protest, carefully feeling his skull. It gave her time to think while Sir Roger ranted about the loss of his watch to the dockers thronging round them. She had an excellent memory for faces. This was certainly the theatre thief. But Frank was protecting him. So she must do so too.

She tutted at Sir Roger still sputtering and spouting above her. 'Come now, Sir Roger! Peace, I pray you, or you'll have to apologise to Master Verney all over again!' Frank stared at her, very pale. She smiled at him.

'What? What's that you're saying, Mistress Susanna? Apologise?'

'Indeed!' Her tone was kindly amused. 'This is never the thief, sir! I grant you, I thought so also for a moment. There's a general likeness, but this boy is shorter, and two or three years younger.'

Astonished, Jack grunted, and moaned to cover it. Joe, hovering unhappily beside him, grinned in relief, and Jess called, 'Jacky! You better? Wake up, Jacky!' He opened a cautious eye, to find a pretty girl smiling down at him. 'Lie still, now!' He knew the face; the lass from the theatre! But she was smiling. He lay still, wondering, feeling sick.

A black hand offered a damp handkerchief and a glass of watered wine for him to sip while the girl held his head. There was some discussion above him. Then Bony's voice. 'J-Jack, how d'you f-feel?' He didn't bother trying to answer. 'We're going to lift you down into a b-boat. To carry you home as quick as we can.' He was getting away with it.

A docker lifted him. He tried to peer round for Sal, but relaxed. No sign of her. The girl came and waved to him as he was carried down the wooden steps that ran down past the pilings of the wharf. Had she winked?

Urged after him, Joe was unsure of what to do, but Jess knew. She tugged at his collar. 'Go with Jack, Joe! That way! Follow Jack!' she piped in his ear. At last he started forward down the narrow steps.

Someone shouted, 'Ware! Ware kegs!' A docker. Joe knew the voice. Four treads down, he turned to look.

The nearest of the three cranes was turning the wrong way, away from the wharf, pivoting faster and faster under a raging thrust on its counterweights, jib swinging round, out over the river and in towards the crowd again, load of wine kegs flying wide at the end of the rope, reeling out, aimed at the head of the steps to smash into the milling crowd there, or split the net on the pilings and crush everything below in an avalanche of hundred-pound barrels.

Susanna, by the top step, froze, her legs suddenly pithless, helplessly watching the battering-ram kegs swinging directly at her. On the steps in front of her, Joe was holding Jess. Jack was just below them in the boat. The kegs would strike directly on them, and kill them all four.

By the crane, Sal melted back into the crowd, her face shadowed under her shawl. The cranemen, a gold angel in each man's pouch, could carry on now. Goodbye, Jackdaw . . .

The nearest dockers reached the crane, grabbed the control ropes and hauled back. The crane jib whipped like a fishing rod, groaning with strain over the screams of the watchers. It slowed, stopped. The net-load of kegs kept swinging.

Frank grabbed Susanna, thinking fast, no room in the

110

yelling crowd to drag her aside to dodge the swinging barrels, no time, he didn't try; he pushed, hard, right off the edge of the wharf, down eight feet into the river.

Joe didn't think at all. He set Jess down on the wharf edge behind him. Then he braced himself and leaned out, reaching to catch the impossible, unstoppable impact of three full kegs of wine, swinging in fast as a thrown stone. The net, hard with sharp, heavy edges, crashed him back against the top edge of the piling.

It didn't burst. It bulged, strained — and stopped as the crane jib sprang back. Slowly, it seemed, the load of kegs drifted away. It unreeled gently into the river, joined by the cranedrivers escaping their angry mates.

The whole thing had taken less than ten seconds.

Ruth fainted gracefully.

Everyone else looked in horror to see the lad, crushed by the kegs.

Rubbing his belly, Joe grinned up at them. The half-inch-thick iron ring of his belt was flattened to an oval four inches deep.

Susanna laughed fit to split, once she'd got her breath back from the smack into the river. The boatmen had pulled them in easily, but the water in her wide petticoats weighed her down. Lumbering up the steps, she grinned up at Kate peering anxiously over the wharf edge above her. 'Elegant as a pregnant hay-wain, mother! Give me a hand, then!' Kate, her alarm relaxing to a smile, reached to haul her daughter up to the wharf, where she collapsed onto a bollard, coughing and spitting and giggling helplessly, her face pink with laughter and excitement, her hair lank and shiny with wet, while little green rivulets trickled all round her.

Frank followed her, dripping and drooping in scarlet humiliation. Nothing is more embarrassing than a public act of heroism which turns out to be unnecessary. Especially when it lands you in muddy water in front of the lady of your dreams. Then he was smothered in Kate's hug amid the dockers' cheers. 'Frank, ye're a hero! My lass could have been killed. We're deep in your debt, my dear!' Ruth, daintily recovered, murmured agreement, but his eyes and ears were still too full of embarrassment, water and Kate's thanks for him to hear her.

Peg and their other servants were fetching out cloths to dry them, cloaks, brandy. Frank was glad of a glass, but Susanna refused. 'Have I not just drunk half the Thames? Oh, Frank! What a waste of your noble deed!'

'Indeed, sir!' Ruth finally managed to push in, her blue eyes full of hero-worship. 'You risked your life! Dear little Susanna might well have been killed, and you, too! Oh, thank God you are safe!'

Frank shrugged modestly, pleased, recovering fast at his darling's admiration. 'Oh, it was nothing, m-mistress. As your sister says, it was a f-foolish waste of time.'

Kate cried out in protest. 'Never think it, son!'

Susanna was even fiercer. 'I never said that, Frank! Saving my life a waste of time? Huh!' She struggled soggily to her feet, reached up to throw her arms round his neck and pulled him down to be kissed heartily. 'It truly was a noble deed. Quick thinking, and brave action — oh, thank you!' The dockers cheered again.

'Oh, Frank!' Ruth was taking his hand worshipfully. 'I've never —'

Kate interrupted briskly. 'Come by, Ruth! The pair of them must quit these wet things before they catch their deaths of cold. You can drool over him later.' Ruth's smile tightened a fraction, but Kate ignored her. 'Come over to Southwark with us, Frank. We'll find you dry garments.'

'It's the least we owe you, for your heroism!' Ruth was enthusiastic, but took care not to brush against his wet clothes. Taffeta stained so easily!

Susanna nearly pushed her into the river too. Whose hero was he?

Their mother sniffed. 'Huh! It's the big lad there you

should be praising as a hero, Ruth. If he'd not stood to hold back the casks, the net could well have burst an' killed us all with kegs, includin' you.'

Ruth's eyes widened in a momentary alarm, but she shrugged it off. She couldn't really have been hurt. 'I doubt whether he knew what he was doing, mother, a dolt like that! Though I'm very grateful to him too, of course.' She smiled to Frank. 'I'll give him another penny. Are you ready, Frank?'

However, this was the first Susanna and Frank had heard of Joe's astounding feat of strength. They didn't move away, but gazed at Joe, who had picked Jess up again. He was standing grinning, humming vacantly. Frank stared at the squeezed belt. 'My God! Look at th-that! J-Joe, did you hold back the casks?' Joe just grinned. It was Jess, beside his ear, who nodded shyly. 'My God!' He gaped in wonder.

'God's oddikins, look at it!' Sir Roger noticed Joe trying to ease the belt. 'It's near cutting him in half! What can we do?'

The porters knew. They quickly ran two ropes through the iron belt, squeezed them to front and back and queued, laughing, to take hold in two teams like a tug-of-war to pull it out again. Puzzled but co-operative, Joe stood in the middle, still holding Jess.

Rather worried, Susanna stepped forward, holding out her arms for the child. 'Come to me, my dear! Oh, your poor arm! Come along, sweetheart!'

Ruth squeaked in alarm. 'Susanna! Your gown! It'll be filthy!'

'Don't be daft! It already is, Ruth!' she snapped in irritation, and turned back to Joe. 'Give her to me — Joe, is it, Frank? Let me hold her, Joe. In case you drop her.' Joe wouldn't have dropped his little sister if a house had fallen on him, but Susanna coaxed till Jess leaned forward to the pretty lady with the smile, and obediently Joe yielded her up.

Frank was frowning as Susanna gentled the poor child. Surprised, she wondered why, and then with a leap of her heart realised that it wasn't at her; Ruth was stepping back, away from the distorted baby, her lovely face showing her disgust. Susanna waited hopefully; what would he say? And would Ruth lose her temper at him? Please, God?

But Sir Roger was looking round importantly. 'Ready, men? One! Two! Heave!' Cheering, the dockers leaned back to take the strain, and Frank jumped to lend a hand. The ropes tightened, Joe was tugged a few steps this way and that, and gradually the narrow oval was stretched out to a comfortable egg shape. Joe grinned, scratching his bruised belly.

Oh, well. Susanna sighed. Maybe next time . . .

Frank leant over and waved reassurance to Jack, who was staring up from the boat below, wondering what was going on. 'Don't w-worry, Jack! We're j-just coming.' He turned to Kate. 'Th-thank you for your invitation, ladies, but I must get the children home with me as soon as m-may be.'

'What? You're never taking these filthy ragamuffins with you? To stay? In your own home?' Frank's face stiffened. Rather late, Ruth realised she wasn't showing at her best. But what a strange idea! What kind of young man was this, indeed, carrying about with him hideous children and idiots and thieves — she didn't believe a word of what Susanna had said! However, hunting instinct died hard. She laid a gentle hand on his arm. 'You must come home with us first, Frank!'

Susanna hid her pleasure as he firmly refused, beckoning Joe to the steps again. Improve the moment. 'Ruth, don't forget the penny you promised the lad!' She watched Frank watching Ruth's care not to touch Joe's hand. 'Here you are, then, Joe! Here's your little sister!' She passed Jess back, to cling in some relief to her brother; the lady was nice, but the one you know is best. 'I thank you also, Joe!' She smiled warmly to him, and gave him a hug. Oh, the joy, to see Frank noticing the sour look on Ruth's face!

Gently, Susanna kissed Jess's cheek, ignoring the jutting arm. 'Poor child! I wish you all —' she cast a single glance down at Jack fidgeting apprehensively below — 'every one of you, happiness in your new home.' She kissed Frank again as he descended the steps, when his face came level with hers, delighted when he blushed, and waved brightly as the boat pulled away from the wharfside. What an hour! It had been worth the ducking!

Jack lay still as long as he decently could, but Jess kept worrying over him. Eventually he decided it was time to sit up. Jess squeaked, 'Jacky! Jacky!' and wriggled to sit with him. He put an arm round her, smiled at Joe and Frank, and tried to relax. Ivory Sal was behind them; the girl had kept quiet, for whatever reason. They were safe, for the moment.

None of them talked very much as the boatmen rowed them up the broad river. Joe had nothing to say. Jess, who had never been outside the city before, clung to her big brother as Jack pointed out the huge noblemen's houses on the Strand, the palaces of Westminster, St James's and Lambeth, the green woods, fields and little villages of Battersea and Chelsea.

Frank sat mostly in silence. What would Jane say? What would Ruth think of him? Susanna had taken her ducking very well — she could have been angry; but then, she was always fun and friendly to be with. He coughed and shivered in his wet clothes. The breeze over the river was chilly.

At last the boat turned in towards a landing-stage by another village. 'F-Fulham. Only half a m-mile now,' Frank assured them, paying off the boatmen. 'It's not so f-fine as the mansions in Chelsea, mind. We've never had gold to rebuild in the modern style. No f-fancy brickwork and Italian plaster. But we've chimneys to all

115

the f-fireplaces, and glass in m-most of the windows, and m-mother relaid the gardens. Look, up the path through the trees there. That's V-Verneys.' His voice rang with pride and affection.

The cobbled path, barely wide enough for a carriage, curved round a rambling old manor-house, extended so often that it looked like a dozen houses stuck together. Bright-eyed dormers peered under raised eyebrows through the steep red tiles, thatch or slates of the many-layered roofs. The tar and whitewash on wood and plaster, and the green painted shutters, were fresh and clean. At the front, a porch sheltered a wide oak door above three broad steps. Plenty ways up to the roof here, Jack thought — but he'd not need to climb round this house, surely!

Jess clung even tighter to Joe's neck, and Joe was treading on Jack's heels. Turning to reassure them, Jack tripped on the steps. Frank, almost as nervous, tried to laugh. 'Be easy, all of you! You'll get something to eat in a m-minute, J-Jack. Come along!' He nodded to the porter opening the door for them. 'Davy, where's M-Mistress J-Jane?'

'In the still-room, Master Francis. Did her blackcurrant cordials not ferment and blow up like mines, and the still-room like a slaughterhouse? Rebottling the lot she is, and her hands and temper red as murder. She said not to disturb her for less than the queen.' Davy eyed the three youngsters with no enthusiasm, and Jack's temper itched. 'She'll not be best pleased.'

Frank shrugged. 'When is she ever?' He wasn't unhappy to put off introducing the children to her. Looking at them, and sniffing them, and seeing Davy's face, his heart sank. Then a door at the rear of the hall opened. With relief Frank pounced on the small, angular woman who entered, her plain, dark gown neat, her apron and collar dazzling white. 'Hepsibah, thank God! The very person! Heppy, I need your help.'

'Dear Lord Almighty!' She was already reaching for

little Jess, her lined face full of pity and concern. Jack, who had bristled protectively, relaxed at the woman's next words as Joe did at her manner. 'Sweet lambkin! That's never natural? Done on purpose? Never! Oh, the villains! But the Lord will punish them in His own time. Come then, my dawtie, come to old Heppy!' She gently lifted Jess from Joe's arms, clucking and motherly. Jess shrank back at first, but slowly relaxed against the woman's breast.

'Heppy.' Frank coughed. 'You know my good-sister. If she sees them now, w-well . . . But if we could get them tidied up . . .'

She tilted her head and tutted up at him. 'Master Francis, Master Francis! Was there ever a week you didn't bring some starveling into the house? And I aiding you . . . Well, then. I suppose I've not changed neither.' She flustered as he planted a kiss on her wrinkled cheek. 'Away with you, good-for-naught! You needn't think to butter me up like that!' She suddenly realised — 'But you're all damp, Master Francis!'

'It's nothing. I f-fell in the river. Not the f-first time, eh?' She tut-tutted at him again, in loving scolding. 'I'll go and change. Will you see to J-Jack, here, and Joe, and this is J-Jess?'

The old woman puffed in resignation. 'A bath first, then.' Jack looked thunderstruck. 'And clean clothes, and away with those rags.'

Scowling, Jack opened his mouth. Frank clamped a hand on his shoulder, before the lad said anything unforgivable. 'F-food f-first, Heppy.'

Hepsibah had seen Jack's face too, and she had a lot of experience with boys. She nodded. 'Foolish of me. Aye, well, Master Francis, supper's in two hours, but I'll find them something.' Jack's face cleared like magic. Hepsibah beckoned a man. 'A fire, Wilkin, and hot water to Master Francis's room at once. Now, Master Francis, into a hot bath with you, spit spot, and I'll send you up a horehound infusion or you'll get an ague, sure as eggs is eggs. Off you go, now, before you visit your mother.'

Frank, nodding and smiling reassuringly, saw Jack ushered away to the back of the house, and then turned with a sigh and a cough to the stair.

A bath, in April? Heppy had some very odd ideas. As he stripped, two lads carried in good rough linen towels, a brazier of glowing charcoal and a bucket of hot water from the kitchen. A wash was ample. He was soon clean, dry, rubbed red and warm, and dressed in fresh clothes. When the horehound and honey cordial was brought, he made a face but gulped it down. It did soothe his throat, and anyway, he hadn't the heart to send it back.

Right. The next thing to do was to visit his mother.

The Lark

On the landing, Frank paused to draw a deep breath. He tapped, pressed the latch of his mother's door and walked quietly in.

It was a friendly little bedroom, warm and cheerful, panelled in light oak, carpeted with dry lavender and woollen rugs. Daffodils sprang bright to the eye in a silver bowl, their clear yellow matching the bed hangings. A new window with large panes of glass looked out over the garden behind the house, where a man and a boy were busy planting out young cabbages.

The little maid sitting sewing by the fire rose quickly and bobbed a curtsey, smiling. Frank nodded to her. 'Sarah. Any change?'

She shook her head, regretful. 'No, Master Francis. Not yet.'

He sighed, and turned reluctantly towards the window and the chair which rocked, rocked there, regular as any pendulum, in deep grooves worn into a thick green rug. The cushions of the chair were embroidered, neat as the small lady who sat there, rocking, rocking, her brown dress tidy and clean, her face a smooth cream, her eyes

119

empty as they had been since the day her three babies died together in the same hour that news came of her husband's death. Frank walked over and knelt beside her, taking her hand. 'Mother,' he said quietly. 'M-Mother, I'm back.' Her face was still and blank, changing no more than the rhythm of the chair, rocking, rocking.

Once he knew that the old gossip wasn't going to try washing him, Jack was quite ready to follow her, tugging Joe behind him, along two twisty passages, down three steps, along another passage, and through another door into a cavernous room, swirling with clouds of steam and smoke like a vision of hell, except that hell could never smell so delicious. Roast meat, honey, onions, sage, costmary — he gave up trying to identify them. He just followed the woman to a table, sat on the stool she pointed to, and as mindlessly as Joe, as gratefully as Jess, he seized the thick slice of cold pork pie set before him and stuffed it into his mouth with both hands.

After a while, though, he took time to look round him. Along one long wall was a row of fires and ovens, with huge pots swung on iron cranes, and spitted, spitting roasts. Piles of meat and vegetables lay on the tables down the centre of the room. Half a dozen cooks and a dozen scullions and kitchen drabs, half naked in the heat, were hard at the labour of preparing the day's dinner for all the ninety folk of the manor and its farm. But in spite of their work, they still had time to peer at the strangers, stare at Jess's arm, whisper, sniff, sneer. Jack's temper started to itch again.

Suddenly the passage door slammed open. A young woman marched in, her high-rolled sleeves of fine indigo wool showing arms and hands as stained with cordials as her apron. Hepsibah drew in front of the children, as if to hide them, but the lady strode towards them, her heels clicketting across the tiled floor, and waved the old servant aside with a crimson hand. Her pretty face was sharp with annoyance.

'This is beyond all! Master Francis has no consideration! Lodgings in Holborn, forsooth, as if this house
wasn't good enough, in and out at all hours, no pattern
nor reason, coming and going, no warning, and are these
the friends he makes in Westminster? Gutter brats! Put
your hand down, you, child!' She sniffed. 'What's that
stench? Oh my Lord Almighty, it's them! Lord knows I
never complain, but really!' Jess shrank. Jack glared. Joe
grinned greasily through a mouthful of pork. 'Stop that
grimace, clown! Who are you?' Her whine was in danger
of being drowned by snarl.

Hepsibah tried to defend them, to explain. Under cover
of the argument, Jack slid from his stool. Bitch! Damn
young Bony! Welcome, eh? 'Come on, Joe! Keep by me!'
He picked Jess up and turned towards the door.

'Come back here, you!' the whiny voice snapped.
'Stop!'

'Come on!' He ran, tugging Joe after him. Small, agile,
even carrying Jess he slid like an eel through the crowd,
as he did in Cheapside market; but not Joe.

Passing the fires, Joe tripped, and joggled a cauldron of
soup to scald a scullion's feet and flood hissing, red-hot
ashes over the floor. Venison ribs and a dozen chickens
cascaded to patter and skid under the feet of his pursuers.
Among growing screams and curses, a basket of duck
feathers was kicked to snow white down over all the
food. A bowl of eggs crashed in yellow ruin; piles and
pyramids of cabbages and onions tumbled and rolled; a
knife slid to stab a girl's toe; a side of bacon ripped off
its hook; a tray of custards in pots teetered and smashed
to the tiles; a rack of spits rattled down to snare unwary
ankles; a pile of pigeons bounced, for the kitchen cat to
snatch one and leap with it to a shelf where badly-stacked
wooden platters toppled and clattered. Screams and oaths
boiled up as the children struggled through the smoke to
the door and out to the passage.

Where now? A door opened at one end; daylight

beyond. 'This way!' They charged out, cooks and scullions swarming after them. Trees, grass, seed-beds, flowers. Walls; a walled garden, not the yard. A gardener's lad was yelling, on his knees clutching a trug before them, tumbled backwards by their rush, while fat seakale stems rolled and squashed underfoot. Jack slipped on them and dropped Jess. As he staggered, the cooks caught up.

What could he do?

For Joe, nothing. Ten men were clutching the big lad, battering at him with spits and ladles. He roared and fought to wade on through them, but even he couldn't escape so many. Nobody had a cleaver, thank God. Leave him, and come back later for him. Where was Jess?

Terrified, the child was fleeing down a brick path between little low hedges of lavender, grey and dull in the April sunshine. She ran straight down the knot-garden, too frightened to stop at his call, too panic-stricken to turn aside, her twisted feet twinkling under the red petticoat, her left hand waving helplessly high beyond her head. She wasn't strong, nor used to running. She wailed, 'Jacky! Jacky, help! Oh, Jacky!'

Above, in his mother's room, Frank had sent off the maid and taken her chair over to the window. His mother sat staring out, rocking gently, nodding slightly, almost as if she was listening while as usual he told her all the events and thoughts of the day. 'I w-wonder why Susanna didn't say anything about J-Jack,' he mused. 'I'm deep in her debt. And I ruined her gown, but she j-just l-laughed. She's always happy.' His mother hummed and rocked steadily. 'You know, mother, it's good in one way to have someone I can talk to, who never replies. I can say everything in my m-mind, even about W-Walsingham and — and Ruth. Without being af-afraid you'll sneer, or call me a f-fool, the way Harry did, or complain like J-Jane. But, oh, I wish you were back with me again! I miss your laugh, and your singing, Mistress Lark!' He sighed. His mother's chair rocked, rocked.

'Well. The doctors say we must keep talking to you. What else can I say? Ruth — I was — I didn't — I wasn't happy at what Ruth said about the b-baby. It's a p-pity she's so delicate, so spiritual. She can't b-bear to see anybody hurt. She has to p-protect herself. It makes her look hard and selfish, if you don't know how sensitive she is in her heart.' He sighed. 'Tomorrow I'll — what's that din?' Shouting echoed from the garden. 'God's p-Peace, what's that lad at now?' He jumped to the window.

Jack caught Jess and snatched her up, leaping aside to dodge the gardeners appearing among the trees. Someone opened a window above him and leaned out, yelling. Bony. No time to stop and chat! He twisted and turned, seeking a way out, a gate through the high wall. There wasn't one. He escaped one group by leaping over a smouldering fire of weeds, played tag with some scullions in and out of a row of espalier apple trees, dodged right between a pair of gardeners who collided with a yell behind him. Three cooks slammed after him through a hedge of roses, shouting apprehensively even before they hit the thorns.

It was no use; he was finally cornered in an angle of the walls back near the kitchen door again.

Even among the shouting, gesticulating crowd it took Jane only a few seconds to make herself heard. Jack crouched, hugging Jess, bent over her to protect her from the rakes and rolling pins. Would fainting help? No, not with this bitch. A beating, then, for him and Joe, and probably Jess, too, but they were all used to that; and then they'd be thrown out. But it was worth it, they'd had a good meal, and they'd still be free of Sal. Resigned, he waited for the woman to stop ranting, to get it over with.

Jane fairly roasted the children, and with them, Frank, who had run down the stair to their defence. 'Filthy, stinking beggars! Will you stop that brat screeching, I can't hear myself speak!'

'Well, you're the only one!'

She wailed right over him. 'That appalling child's arm! Look at them! They're alive! Lice and fleas and all kinds of vermin! I know all about Christian charity, thank you, Frank, you need not presume to lecture me on the subject! I never complain, as you well know, but this is too much! You had no right to bring them here. I'll have none such in my house!'

'In whose house, did you say, Daughter Jane?'

The shouting stopped. The sticks stopped. There was a general indrawn breath, and all the faces turned as one to look up at the speaker. A small woman, brown and neat, holding onto the open windowframe above their heads.

Jane flushed as red as her hands. Her mouth sagged open.

It was Frank who broke the silence, with a cry of sheer joy. 'Mother! Oh, m-mother! You're back with us again! Mother! It's a m-miracle!'

The servants burst into a chatter, a roar of noisy pleasure, wonder, congratulation, rejoicing. 'Mistress Lark! She's well again!' They cheered, danced, capered with delight. Jane's face was pinched and white.

Two minutes later, Lark smiled at Frank in her room. 'It's spring, is it not, my dear? April? Never, surely? Six months I've sat here? It seems only a day or two.' He pointed silently to the furrows her chair had worn in the rug. 'Oh, dear!' She shook her head in dismay.

Jane took her arm, smiling, urging her towards her chair. 'Sit down, Mother Alice! You'll be tired. Let me send you up a hot posset, while you rest. I'll see to all. Come now, sit you down!'

The grey, featureless tide of depression lapped at the edge of Lark's mind again, urging her to agree, give in, not bother, leave all this noise and trouble till later, let Jane take it on herself if she wished . . . But she straightened her back and forced the flood away. 'No, I thank you, Jane. I've done that too much already.'

'Well, if you're sure —'

'I am. I must stir myself to attend to my own affairs again.'

Jane stiffened self-righteously. 'Are you saying I've done wrong, Mother Alice? I've taken too much upon myself?' She sniffed. 'What state would this house be in if I'd not been here while you were ill, may I ask? Have you any idea of the trouble your son has caused? Or the impertinence and laziness of your servants? And the storm that lifted the thatch right off the cow-byres, and the well freezing? I've done no more than my duty by your household, Mother Alice, and I don't expect thanks for it, but to be scolded for it — well, I never thought to see the day! Modern times, modern manners, I suppose! My mother always told me, "Jane," she always said, "a true Christian should never expect gratitude," she said, "for she'll not get it," and it's true as God's Word —'

Lark, hand raised in defence, finally managed to stop her. 'Daughter Jane, for all your care and attention during my illness I am grateful indeed. But now, I pray you, the hot posset you offered, of your kindness.'

Justified, almost soothed, Jane hurried out. Lark exchanged a rueful glance with her son. At her gesture, he turned her chair firmly away from the window, and she sank into it with a sigh of relief, gathering her strength again to study these odd children her son had produced.

In front of Joe's bulk, Jess was clinging desperately to Jack's hand. He wasn't quite sure what was going on, but this sweet-faced little lady had stopped the men beating him and Joe, and scared off that bitch who wanted rid of him. But she was so clean! He was suddenly aware, as he had refused to be before, of the dirt on his family's new, 'good' clothes, their stink of dung and sweat, vomit, stale beer and mouldy straw from the inn, the filth matted in their hair. But the lady's smile was gentle, and her voice kind as she beckoned to Jess, saying, 'Come here, child.'

Jess whimpered, a tiny breath of sound, as Jack urged

her forward. Then the lady's hands smoothed the little girl's cheek, and she held out her arms to Jack to lift Jess onto her lap, lice, dirt and all, and started to rock and sing softly and sweetly to the child, an old lullaby, while Jess sat rigid and trembling.

After a while her shivering stopped, and she breathed more easily.

At last she turned her head and smiled timidly for a second.

Lark smiled back.

Frank sighed. God's love, he'd never dreamed that this could happen! He was near tears as he watched and listened.

His mother glanced up. 'Hepsibah, tell the lasses to fetch hot water and soap, and clean clothes. We'll start easing this arm down, while the child's in a hot bath.' Jess looked frightened. 'Hush, now, my dear. It'll not hurt, only a little. You'll be a brave girl and not cry, and you'll soon be straight again.' She smiled at Jack and Joe. 'There's naught to fear now. You are all very welcome here.'

Joe just smiled. Jack glowered again. Hot water, and soap? But he'd not show he was afraid. Not to any woman.

A week later, on May Day, Lady Alice's recovery was celebrated with the finest feasting that Frank could remember. Jack had never seen anything like it, except the Lord Mayor's Show. Joe thought he was in heaven.

Long before dawn every soul in the manor and the cottages around it was up and dressed in their finest, creamy linen gowns and smocks, tunics and doublets, brilliantly beribboned and embroidered. 'Come, my dawtie!' old Hepzibah told Jess, carrying her among the giggling, joking crowd. 'Come, wash your face in the may dew just as the sun strike ye, and ye'll be prettier yet all the year!' To please Hepzibah, Jess leaned solemnly down to a damp froth of hawthorn-blossom, and lifted her cheeks freckled with ivory petals just as the first sunbeams glinted. The women cooed, even the hardest-hearted charmed by her shy, sweet smile and huge dark eyes.

They scattered into the woods to gather blossoms and not a few kisses, and joyously trooped back at noon, many rather rumpled, singing lustily to the accompaniment of two shawms and three bagpipes, a viol, a fife and two drums, in the old traditional tune, 'Summer is i-comen in!'

All the manor folk were gathered at the front door, Lark laughing, Jane determinedly smiling, to welcome the procession with eggs, primrose cakes and ale. Frank poured lavishly, filling quart jacks like thimbles, while the may boughs were ceremoniously brought in and hung round the hall.

Jane sniffed acidly. 'Who'll be your May King, then? Him?' She nodded at Joe where he stood beside the head gardener, Elijah Parry, who had taken kindly to him. Joe grinned happily.

'Bless you, Mistress Jane,' Parry called jovially, 'maybe he do knock over everythin' in the house, but now he's learned how to dig, I can set him to a row an' leave him to finish it.' He grinned. 'If I ain't there to turn him at the end, though, he'll go straight on across the county!'

At length a stable lad was crowned King of the May, chose a giggling dairymaid as his queen, and led the first dance round the old maypole in a field beside the house. It had been brightly repainted and garlanded, and a young bullock, not the more usual sheep, was slung on a spit over a firepit near it to roast slowly through the day.

There were gipsies, who strove mightily with the local musicians to outplay each other. Among the morrisses and jigs and roundels, time after time young men and women, and older ones too, disentangled the ribbons of the maypole and danced it, men one way, women the other. The red and white strands wove in and out, over and under, back and forward as the steps of the dance were called, twining and plaiting the ribbons till at last the dancers came together to the centre, to shut their eyes, turn and kiss the dancer behind them. As time and ale ran on, the tangles grew worse and wilder. Joe was led through the steps, to end up kissing Elijah Parry.

At one side of the field the gipsies displayed their acts — jugglers, dancing dogs, even a fire-eater. They rigged a tightrope head-high between two trees, and a girl younger than Jack, in a red skirt no longer than her knees, with a pole for balance, danced in the centre of the rope to the music of the gipsies' guitars and the whistles of the lads. Her father bet that no-one could copy her. 'A groat to a penny, sirs! Tree to tree! Walk across, to win!' A dozen lads lost their coins, wobbling and crashing among their friends' laughter.

For the honour of the house, and for fun, too, Jack stepped forward. 'Lemme 'ave a go!' Amid cheers he climbed the ladder to balance at one end, his back supported by the tree trunk behind him. The rope felt odd to his bare feet, springy but firm, twisting below him. Run it? No. 'Gimme a 'old o' that pole, then!' he called, and tossed it so that he was holding it by the centre, as the girl had done. Gradually, he straightened off the tree.

It was much the same as on a roof. Don't look down, feel with your feet. Look ahead; move the pole, not yourself, to counter any wobble. The rope swung queerly under him, but he kept up, as if a string tied his hair to the sky, flat step by step by step, down a slope, a long, slow waver, stop, wait for balance again, and then on and up. Gently he put out a hand to the trunk of the other tree, tossing the pole high with a whoop of delight. 'Dunnit! Gimme me pence!'

He had half expected trouble here, but the gipsy paid him promptly, amid applause and a queue forming to try. 'Well done, lad! Join us next year!' Jack glowed as he saw Bony and the old lady clapping too.

128

A third set of musicians and dancers appeared — the Morriss Men from the village nearby, visiting all the local manors in turn with their special costumes, handed down over the generations from times when their meaning was known; Snap the dragon, the Betty, the Fool. 'Idolatry!' Jane muttered. She was ignored; everyone knew she was a Puritan, and they wanted to stop everything that folk enjoyed, even bear-baiting!

Towards noon the scent of the roasting bullock drew a constant stream of folk, helping turn the spit, basting it, and at happy last chewing on juicy brown slices of beef. There were tuns of ale, a cask of wine; old women had cakes to sell; Lark had wide baskets brought out, piled with pasties for everyone. Even Jane, wincing at the cost of the celebration, was seen to nibble a prune pie and smile.

During the meal the gipsies told fortunes. Jack had his palm read by a dark, thin woman who told him that he held a queen in his hand; but when he asked what she meant, she shrugged, laughed, and spouted what he knew was stock rubbish about danger of fire, sudden wealth, long life . . . A queen in his hand? He looked at his grubby palm with interest.

The young folk, rested, started again. In Hoodman Blind, it was odd how well some of the blindfolded lads could pick out the prettiest lasses. Lark gave them a ten-week-old piglet, thickly greased, and free to whoever caught him, but after a wild chase he escaped into the woods leaving his tail in a man's hand. The May King led them on a crazy follow-my-leader, right round the bounds of the estate, over ditches and fences, whooping and cock-crowing along the tops of walls. One lad fell into the duckpond. Pairs of lads, mounted pig-a-back, armed with bags of straw tied over the ends of hay-rakes, jousted with each other to win ribbons for their lasses. Jack, mounted on Joe, won one, which he gave to Jess. A cock was tied to a stake with a long string; they all stood round in a wide circle, pelting it with stones, and the old woman who finally killed it with a lucky throw won it for her dinner. In a quarter-staff contest Frank was ignominiously beaten in the first round and nearly lost a tooth, to his conqueror's profuse apologies. He had to beg a leech from Jane to lower the swelling on his lip, but later he repaired his damaged prestige by a very pretty display of fencing with a visiting friend. Lark beamed.

As dusk fell, the entertainment moved indoors to the decorated hall, for dancing and singing till near midnight. But at last, reluctantly, the party started to break up. The gipsies were thanked, paid, and carefully seen off the estate. Lady Lark was heartily cheered; the last folk trooped out, and the great door was shut. But many folk, lost in a soft melancholy, sat on by the red embers of the roasting pit to sing quietly, and finish the last scraps of the bullock, and sing, and empty the last ale-cask, and cuddle in the dark glow, and tell delightfully shivery ghost stories, and sing ... and gradually drift away, in ones and mostly twos, to homes and hay-sheds, firesides and sheltered corners ...

And May-day was over.

Escape

Next day, Frank called in on his mother before he left for London. She smiled up at him, still tired from the day before, but cheerful. 'Your mouth looks better, my dear. Will you be back for supper?'

He shrugged. 'I don't expect so. I'll p-probably go to my lodgings. But I might, j-just to enjoy seeing you well again. I don't know.' He chuckled. 'That's what annoys J-Jane so much.'

'Don't worry, my dear. We'll feed you if you come. Your duty to your master comes first. Walsingham, isn't it?' She sighed, leaning back against her pillows. 'It's strange. I can remember you talking to me. But at the time it seemed quite unimportant. Too far away to bother answering you, or doing anything about anything.' She patted his hand to reassure him. 'Never look so worried, my dear, I'll not slip back into the dumps. I have so much to catch up with. Jane has looked after the house excellent well, but she has no idea at all about the garden. And these children I've to see to. Jess — what a sweet-natured babe! Her arm is better already, and with boneset poultices and oil rubs, and good food, we'll soon have it and her poor little legs

131

straight.' But then her fond smile died away. 'She is happy here, and Joe seems to be settled in the garden, too. But the middle child, Jack — I fear me he'll not stay.'

Frank grinned. 'I never expected he w-would, mother. J-jackdaws are town birds! But I'm glad you like them. Glad I f-found them!'

He repeated it to Jack on their boat down to Westminster through the pearly dawn mists. Jack grinned. 'D'ye 'ear me complainin'?' He hunched an uneasy shoulder. 'But I gotter get clear, sir. That many females cooin' round Jess, rubbin' 'er arm, cuddlin' 'er when she cries . . . Gives me the 'eaves. She don't need me.' Glancing up, he saw Frank's amusement at the jealousy that he was trying to hide, and had the grace to give a rueful grin. 'Well, were only 'er an' me an' Joe — aye, well. Joe's fine, too. That 'Lijah Parry, yer gard'ner, 'e'll look arter 'im. Good man, 'e is. Jus' right fer Joe. An' 'e likes it, Joe do. But — well . . .'

Frank laughed. 'Not to your taste, J-Jack?'

'Not likely.' Jack was gloomy. 'Lose all me spark. No place fer a Lunnon lad, that. Slow an' —' He glanced at Frank. 'Peaceful.'

'You mean dull. Too quiet, you said once.'

'Quiet?' Jack snorted. 'You 'eard them birds at sunup? Bleedin' din, worser'n Three Cranes! Oh, well.' He shrugged with a forgiving grimace. 'Fulham's country, innit? Not like the city.' He glanced down at his new dark green worsted doublet and trunks. Quality stuff, but a bit dull for his taste. Better be polite. 'Yer mam's right gen'rous. Grand, this. 'Ave ter watch out for me own pockets, 'stead o' pickin' other folks's!'

The boat was approaching Westminster Stairs already, after the quicker run downstream. 'What are you going to do, J-Jack?' Frank asked.

'Find out wot's 'appenin'. Wiv Sal, an' them. Gotter find 'er afore she finds me. An' then back ter business, eh? 'Ave ter watch out where I climbs, though. Never do ter 'ave 'alf the town pointin' at the young gennelman leapin' about the roofs!' The boat bumped against the jetty, and Frank climbed out. Jack looked up at him. 'Leave word fer me same's afore in the Golden Cock.' Frank chuckled at Jack's lordly air as he leaned back snootily on the cushions and waved a languid hand to the boatmen. 'Queen's 'Ythe, an' lean on them oars!' Then he spoiled it by sitting up with an anguished yelp. 'Oy, 'ang on! Sir! Oy, sir! Got a sixpence fer the fare?'

In the long office where his desk stood among forty others, a message awaited Frank; Master Verney was to attend on Master Secretary Walsingham. Instantly. His fellow-clerks made consoling faces over their pens as with trepidation he hurried along the corridor.

The great man was reading letters. He scarcely glanced up. 'Master Verney. Yesterday the Sheriff of London thanked me for my assistance, mentioning your name. I dislike surprises, however gratifying. Your explanation, if you please.'

It was disconcerting that the older man continued to read and make notes about a series of papers, while listening to the story and asking some pretty sharp questions. When Frank had finished, Sir Francis sat back. Frank quaked. Had he done wrong in using Walsingham's name at all?

However, Sir Francis nodded briskly. 'This Jack Daw — he intends to remain a thief? He is not seduced into honesty by the easier life in Fulham? No? H'm. I have an addition to my reputation as omniscient, and helpful to the sheriff; I also have my thief. Good. There are loose ends. Bad. This fugitive, Ivory Sal. The Bolsiter girl. Keep them in mind, young man. Loose ends tend to trip one up later. The fewer, the better. But on the whole, fair. Aye. Fair.' Frank beamed in relief. 'For a beginner.' Frank controlled a grimace of resignation. 'You are well regarded, I am told, Master Verney, in your work. You can relate facts from various sources, and have an insight into the truth behind the actual words of a report. You may well have a great future ahead of you.' Frank blushed with pleasure. Walsingham waved a dismissive hand. 'You may return to your desk.' He shook his head as the young man left. So easily led . . . Had he ever been so young? He doubted it. He certainly couldn't remember it.

Jack changed back into his orange suit with satisfaction, partly at the style, and partly at the familiar stink. No more soap! No more women! No more fussing! Pity the fleas were hungry again, but you couldn't have everything. A rub of dirt on face and neck, and he dropped home to the middens of the lane, a returning hero among his ragged friends swarming out of the dark, dank tenements to go to their daily work or theft. They crowded round him, demanding news of Joe and Jess and the nob who had taken them away. He spun a great tale; 'Joe 's off ter the Indies on a ship ter make 'is fortune, Jess's adopted by the Earl o' Suffolk. Me? The queen wanted ter marry me, but I says no, can't leave the Vintry. The comp'ny's that 'igh-class!' They screeched with laughter.

With Ivory Sal away, everybody was delighted to chat to him about her; but nobody had anything to tell him.

In the inn, he exchanged cheery greetings with the sailors and their doxies yawning down into the taproom for their breakfast ale. Caradoc Jones, who had taken over by force of fist, was naturally worried about Sal's return. 'You finds 'er, Jacky, you tells me, I gives yer a shillin'!' Jack nodded obligingly, and spat behind Craddy's back. A shilling? Cheapskate!

An old couple on their way to market paused to gossip. It was hard to know which was which, they were so alike with their tattered gowns, huddled shawls, wrinkled lips, echoing each other's breathy voices. 'Aye, she's off! A 'ole inter Black Annie's 'ouse, an' off she steps down 'e stair an' out 'e door an' away, shawl on 'er 'ead like Moll Slut, an' norra sign on 'er since.' He — or she — chomped toothlessly.

'Norra sign. Norra 'air on 'er 'ead.' The other, equally ancient at forty-five, hawked and spat. 'An' where's all 'er gold, eh? Eh? Norra inch on 'at 'ouse not been searched.'

'Norra inch. An' nuffin' found. Norra lead token. Nuffin'.'

'Nuffin'. So where is it, eh? Eh?' She — or he — sniffed resentfully.

He gave them a farthing. 'Where's Sal gone ter, gammer? You 'eard?'

'Where is she now, eh? 'At's askin'! Where, eh? Eh?' They cackled, enjoying the thrill of his worry, sorry to have no news for him. 'Aye, ye'd best find 'er, eh? Eh? Afore she finds you!'

'Norra soul's 'eard on 'er. Off safe, fer sure, livin' soft on all 'er gold, norra care in 'e world. But 'er boys is safe 'eld.'

'Newgate Jail, eh, 'at's where 'ey is, big Tom an' 'at devil Billy.'

'An' Sal sittin' meek 's a church mouse, an' be damned to 'em.'

Jack knew better. Sal might be safe somewhere, but she'd not forgotten her sons. Nor him.

The old couple were half right. Sal was indeed safe, living in a room she had hired long before in Southwark, padded to seem plump, grey hair dyed dull black under a cap, ivory beads and bangles hidden away, her dress meek and drab, the most respectable woman — the only respectable woman — on the stair.

At that moment, though, she was talking to Billy. In the wall of the Newgate Jail there was a barred opening to the road through the old city gate, where prisoners crowded to beg from passers-by. There were charity endowments for fresh straw, water and bread, but the seldom-paid jailers kept the money. Prisoners with coin paid for food and water, straw mattresses, blankets and firewood, and had to defend themselves during the night from theft or even murder by those with nothing.

However, Tom and Billy were not yet weakened by starvation or jail sickness. Although his ankles were linked by three feet of heavy chain, Tom's huge fists could still hold back the crowd to let Sal hand in some silver and speak to Billy in near-privacy.

'Soon, lad, soon, never fear.'

Billy glowered. 'Aye, but when? Ain't no bleedin' palace in 'ere!'

She hushed him. 'Ain't easy out 'ere, neither. Them damned arquebuses. I knowed as I shouldn't never 'ave touched 'em. Don't want me in there aside o' ye, does ye? But I'll 'ave ye out anon.'

He snarled viciously. 'Ye'd better! Or else —'

'Or wot?' Her eyes snapped from the shadow of her concealing shawl. 'Or else wot, eh, Billy boy? Forgot where y'are, eh? If I just walks away, wot'll ye do? Ye'll 'ang, Billy! That's wot! 'Anged, drawed an' quartered fer treason, that's wot ye'll be! So mind yer manners or the last ye'll see o' me's me back!'

Abashed by a ferocity even greater than his own, he hung his head 'Aye, mam. But when? It's drivin' me crazy, shut up in 'ere!'

His submission calmed her. 'I knows, I knows, son,' she soothed him, patting his hand. He was always her favourite, her baby.

He paid her no heed. 'I can't stand it! I gotter get out! An' then — that — Jack.' He was hoarse with tension. ''Im an' 'is sister.' His hands twisted at the bars till the rusty iron tore his palms, but in his frenzy he didn't notice it. 'I'll get 'em — I'll find 'em — an' I'll — I'll —'

'Quiet! Keep yer voice down, ye tomfool!' But Sal was speaking to herself. Billy had swung round away from the grating, lurching across the cobbles past Tom. As he moved back, the other prisoners pushed forward. Sal saw one bump into Billy. In relief, almost, her son's fists exploded into a blur of blows. The grating filled with pleading faces and clutching hands, and cries of, 'Alms! Fer the love o' God, alms, mistress!' drowned the brief scream behind them. She turned away without a glance. Billy'd calm down soon. There was no profit in revenge, anyway. She'd already wasted money on bribing the craneman. But given the chance, of course ... That woman on the wharf. Kate Bolsiter, the big black bitch. She lived not half a mile from Sal's room. She'd maybe know where Jack was ...

That was for later. First, Billy must be got out of danger. And Tom.

She wasn't short of money. Gold, too, not mere silver. Smuggling, dealing in stolen goods, the inn, all made a good profit, and none of it wasted on drink or fancy living, neither. It was all invested with the Lombards, under the name of Mistress Banks — easy for everyone to remember. How could she best use it? Rig the jury? Bribe a judge? If all else failed, an armed attack as they were brought out to be hanged?

Try the easiest way first. Where did the jailers go for their ale ...?

Jack, naturally, spent his time looking for Sal, lurking hour after hour, day after day, on roofs over all the markets in London and the Liberties, with no success. He asked all his friends; stallholders and beggars, knifegrinders, thieves, butchers, bakers and watersellers, housemaids and horseholders, doxies and dockers. But no-one had seen the tall, skinny, strong woman with the white hair. He didn't know whether to be glad or scared, and ended up having howling nightmares alone in his hidden loft, till the beadle of the Plumbers' Hall swore that the old place was haunted.

A fortnight later, though, he was walking home though Cheapside market one night when he felt a tug at his elbow, and whirled. 'Bessy! Stupid cow! I near put me fist through yer teeth!'

She shrugged a hasty apology. 'Jacky! Tom an' Billy! Vey're dead!'

Jack, still recovering from the shock of a hand on his arm that wasn't grabbing him, didn't understand for a moment. Then his jaw dropped. 'Wot? Dead? 'Ow? Who done it? An' 'ow d'ye know?'

The girl was pleased to have such good news for him. 'I been diggin' out old graves in St Sepulchre's, right by Newgate. Puttin' ve bones an' skulls an' vat down in ve crypt, see, fer ter leave room fer more bodies. An' I seen ve jailers loadin' ve death-cart. Not ten yards away, vey was. Eight deaders terday, checked off on a list. Tom an' Billy Taverner, jail fever. I 'eard 'em. An' —' as Jack was about to interrupt — 'I seed 'em bein' loaded. Not many as tall 's wot 'em two was. An' ve jailer, 'e says vere'll be anuvver ten dead ternight — a bad summer it'll be, 'e says, startin' so early.'

Jack shook his head. 'Both on 'em? On the same day? No, Bessy.'

She was huffy. 'Go an' ask Jem Gutbag iffen ye doesn't trust me!'

He wanted to, so much! But he couldn't. 'I ain't sayin' as yer lyin' ter me, Bessy,' he hurriedly explained. 'But Sal's worked summat. She's got 'em out. Some'ow. I dunno 'ow, but she's done it!'

He was quite right.

The night before, in the dark before dawn, Jem Gutbag lay sweating in the Newgate guardroom. He couldn't forget the cold eyes that had stared him down from under the woman's shawl in the alehouse. 'Ten angels 'ere an' now — an' other ten after. More'n ye've ever seen.' Short fingers had pincered his wrist. 'Ye'll not think o' cheatin' a poor widder woman? I'd call down the wrath o' 'Eaven on ye — an' it'd come, be sure o' that. It'd come.' The blasphemous threat was less chilling than the eyes. It was for them, more than for the gold for his old age, that he was taking the risk this night. If he was discovered, he'd lose at least the gold, and maybe his job. Or his head.

His mates were snoring solidly at last. He rose, took a lantern and the ring of keys and opened the iron-strapped inner door to the prison.

The cells and passages were carpeted with men and women, sleeping but not silent. They snored, muttered in their sleep, wept, tossed and yelled in nightmare, rattled their chains, lying huddled on their straw mattresses, if they could afford the weekly penny, heedless of the stench or the rats running over them. Jem clutched his cudgel nervously. If the wrong man woke . . . Cob Ironsmith, who'd seen his wife die of starvation yesterday, he'd like to catch a jailer alone . . .

Tom was snoring like a boar in his cell, a good dry one, paid for with Sal's silver, about twelve feet square, airy from a barred window high in the wall and with only five people in it. Billy was awake, tense and twitchy; as Jem unlocked the door and shoved it open Billy was already up on one elbow, watching. 'Jem Gutbag. Wot the 'ell d'ye want? The trial's not fer three days yet . . .' Then, listening to his own question, he sat up with a jerk. 'Is it — Sal?'

The jailer hushed him urgently. 'Quiet, ye tom-fool! Ye want ter wake the 'ole place? Aye, it's 'er. They's two corpusses down stairs as us'll fetch up 'ere, an' ye'll go out, see, an' they'll be found termorrer, an' who's ter say as they ain't you?' In the corner, the blanket stirred; the litle girl who slept there with her parents murmured sleepily. He hefted his cudgel . . . but whether he'd heard or not, her father settled her down again. There'd be no trouble there. 'Stick out yer feet, I got the key t'yer fetters. Now come on, quiet-like. I needs a 'and.'

Stretching, Billy glanced at Tom. 'No, no!' Jem beckoned him away. 'If they's an alarum an' I 'as ter put ye back, 's only one set ter fasten on.' The old man didn't see the glare in Billy's eyes. Put him back . . ?

They picked their steps among the sleepers to a stair with a slimy green trickle of water from the gutters down one side. 'Down 'ere, see. Don't slip. Now in 'ere — mind yer 'ead!' The black stink almost smothered the candle, but after a minute Billy could make out Jem beckoning him. On the far side, a corpse lay at his feet, already stripped by its stick-like neighbours of its poor blanket and clothes. ''Im. Don't let 'im fall.'

''E'll not bruise!' Billy grinned.

'Don't want no din!' The body was stiff and awkward, but light; a skeleton bundled in parchment. 'Dies like flies down 'ere. Fever, see, an' the water. Just gets wot runs down the steps 'ere.' Jem's comment was quite matter-of-fact. 'Got no coin, see, fer vittles ner nowt. So they dies. Nobody'll miss 'em. Drop 'im on yer bed, an' us'll go fer the next un.' He was happier now that he was half done. Two dead men, two big men in one day; that was what he'd been waiting for, and the woman's eyes colder every day, till at last he'd been too scared to wait longer. So now they had to collect the second body. Which wasn't quite dead yet.

That was no trouble.

The second man was heavier. Jem gave Billy a hand on the stair, and was puffing by the time they were at the top again. 'Gutbag!' Billy jeered.

Jem glared in the dim light. 'Gutenberg!' At the snarl, one of the men sleeping in the corridor started to sit up, mumbling, 'Whassa' . . ?' Jem daren't hit Billy; his cudgel cracked the man's skull.

Billy punched Tom awake, while Jem unlocked his fetters. In two minutes the corpses were chained in place of Sal's sons, who were creeping behind Jem back down the stair to the outer gate; and from a shadow stepped Ivory Sal, waiting these past five hours for her boys. She seized Billy and hugged him. Tom breathed deeply in the fresher air, stretching in freedom at last before he shoved

Billy aside and lifted his mother bodily, to nuzzle into her hair. 'Oh, mam.'

Billy watched, sneering. Over Tom's shoulder Sal glanced aside at the wizened old jailer, and jerked her head significantly. Billy grinned crookedly. 'Jem Gutbag.' His voice was soft. 'Wot ye waitin' fer?'

Jem was already scuttling in and shoving the gate, locking it with little care for silence; and safe inside, leaning against it, wiping the cold sweat of fear off his forehead. But he'd got ten gold coins in advance, hidden in his fireplace, and though he'd hoped, he'd never really expected to get the others. He'd come out not bad at all . . .

Outside, Sal linked arms with her sons. 'Now, lads, din't I say as I'd get ye out? An' ye're dead. Official! Ye're free!' Tom hugged her again, and she slapped his shoulder. 'There's a lot ter do, now. I got it all planned. Ye'll dye yer 'air, same's me —'

'Jackdaw first.'

She frowned. 'Leave 'im be, Billy. We'll get oursel's settled first.'

Billy grunted in dissent. 'Nar, mam.' Tom stiffened; nobody argued with Sal! 'Jacky. 'E's been splittin' me 'ead fer days. I been in 'ell acos on 'im. Jacky first.' The moonlight gleamed white in his eyes.

She didn't hit him, or swear. By sheer force of will, she stared down his glare. 'You 'ears me? I says no! You gonner counter me?' His mad eyes sank resentfully. She could feel the tension trembling in his shoulders, and gave him a sop to his pride. 'Not yet, son, but soon. We'll get yer damned little Jackdaw fer ye soon.'

Among the huddle of unsavoury tenements behind the Gully Hole in Southwark, Sal knew one house that stood alone in a high-walled yard with a narrow gate. A single visit from Billy and Tom was enough to convince the owner of the house that he'd be glad to sell it, cheap. That same afternoon the deeds were signed — even lawyers moved fast when Billy smiled at them — and a builder moved in, with stone and beams, a host of workmen, and Tom glowering to speed the hammers. By the middle of May Sal had a fortress, impregnable to anything except a full-scale assault, just as she had planned it.

Her bankers in Lombard Street were told that Mistress Banks intended to invest in a ship, a collier, to bring coals from Newcastle. 'A growing trade, mistress, with the rising population, and demand from the new brass foundries and glass-works for the filthy, stinking stuff. Do you not agree that for a private house, pear-wood scents most delightfully?'

'Mistress Banks' smiled, her greyish teeth shining and her breath sweetened with enough peppermint to make a horse cough. 'Aye. Gimme five 'undred gold angels, an' a 'undred royals. I'll be back fer more. But that'll do me fer now.' The gold was counted out into a strong bag, and given to her clumsy lout of a servant — Tom — with a penny and instructions to carry it carefully in the breast of his leather doublet. She was ushered out with smiles, bows, and eyes rolled to heaven in horror behind her back.

'Right, now, lads!' That evening she settled herself into a chair behind a wide oak table in the small room above the front door. Her back was to the panelling, and through the window in front of her she had a clear view of the gate and the narrow passage up to it. 'This is my room. The gold's 'id be'ind the panel next door, an' it stays there till I says ter bring it out, Billy. Nobody goes in nor out o' this room while ye're carryin' it, neither, so's nobody ever knows where it's kept. Tom, I'll get a couple o' mastiffs from Burbage, off the bears. Beat up, they'll be, but all the more vicious fer that. Keep 'em chained by the sentry-box beside the yard gate. Ye'll stand guard there. Keep the gate barred till Billy gives ye the word from me ter let folks pass, in or out. Ye'll 'ave a cudgel, an' the dogs, an' see 'ere!' With a flourish she produced two double-barrelled pistols. 'That'll please ye, eh?'

Billy sneered as Tom's heavy face split in a grin of joy. 'By, mam!' He picked up the weapons, each two feet long and over ten pounds in weight, and tossed them gently and lightly in his huge hands. He loved bangs.

Sal slapped his shoulder. 'There's powder an' ball aplenty. An' if ye needs more 'elp, call on Billy.' More help! He chortled at the idea.

'I'll start out lendin' at ten per cent a month, till we've drawn customers wi' the low rates, an' I'll up 'em ter a penny in the shillin' every week. Good business, eh? An' you'll see as 'ow nobody don't skip off wivout payin', eh, lads?' They grinned. Billy rubbed his hands.

'But 'ow'll we get customers, mam?' Tom wondered.

'Never fear, son,' she reassured him. 'I've spoke ter the sheriff 'ere in Southwark. Word'll get out.'

It did. Soon she was one of the biggest money-lenders in Southwark, paying ten gold angels weekly to the sheriff for protection. She grudged it, but it was better to pay than have the law after her. Tom and Billy kept off her rivals. She was happy. Who'd know her here, in Southwark, with her hair dyed and her sons known as her servants? They could retire in a few years, and move to Bristol. She came from near there, it'd be nice to go home, buy a big house like a lady, and find a bride for Billy — there was bound to be somebody who'd think his money was worth his temper . . . Tom too, of course. But her baby, Billy, was the one she dreamed for.

Hands twitching, Billy dreamed of Jack.

The Enterprise

Jack always kept an eye open for Sal while on his errands
for Frank and Walsingham. He even visited the other side,
Southwark, where the girl lived who had denied knowing
him. But there was no word of the tall, thin, white-haired
woman. Maybe Tom and Billy were really dead, and she'd
gone away, or died of plague, or somebody who hated her,
and no lack of those, had cut her throat some dark night
and thrown her in the river . . . He dared to relax and
enjoy himself.

For fun, he started to practise the walking on a rope that
the gipsy girl had done. It wasn't too hard, once he got the
knack. His pals cheered when he put on a show for them,
running and dancing across the street above their heads.
Better than a fair, they swore! It was useful, too; with a
rope and a grapnel he could cross surprising spaces, and
ease even quite bulky loot through a window and out into
the open night.

His secret nest in the Plumbers' Hall grew full of pretty
things, lifted from all over London and carried up over
the roofs simply for him to enjoy. An embroidered stool,
a fur bedspread — he was proud of that, he'd lifted it

off the sleeper under it — a carved chest, a brass pot set under a gargoyle for a water supply, a silver-mounted dagger, a good pewter cup, even a small carpet. With his new Fulham clothes, and knowledge of how to behave, he could go to richer places, be seen more often and less suspected, and his pickings grew vastly. Money or goods, he stole what he wanted, when he wanted, and with no rent or protection to pay, he didn't have to sell the surplus unless he wanted. Ikey was very obliging these days.

Every couple of weeks, Jack took a boat upriver to Fulham. Lark always welcomed him. 'Oh, Jack, how pleasant to see you again! How are you? Prosperous, I see! Another gift? Oh, you shouldn't!' She always took it, hiding her doubts about where he'd got it, and sent him quickly from Jane's disapproval up to the nursery and Jess.

The little girl had been adopted by the entire household, in gratitude for bringing back their mistress to health. Her arm, and even her legs, were almost straight again. Only a habit of holding her head over to one side recalled the dreadful straps. She was quite the young lady, in her new broadcloth gowns and miniature farthingales.

She'd smile rather doubtfully and then remember him. 'Oo, Jacky! Got a present?' He always had — marchpane, or an orange, or a carved toy. She thanked him prettily, as Hepsibah taught her, and boasted about her new achievements. 'See my sewing! Look at the stitches! All straight! And my hornbook!' She'd peer at the letters, and read, with slow pride, 'The Lord our God is one Lord; and thou shalt love the Lord thy God with all thy heart, and with all thy soul, and with all thy mind, and with all thy strength.' She was learning to bake, too, and sometimes had a scone or cake to impress him.

He wanted to stay, to play with her, but this world scared him. It was too clean, too orderly . . . And Jess was growing away from him. Well, she was only little, and a girl. She was better off here, he knew. He just wished she didn't turn to old Hepsibah quite so readily as soon as he said he must go . . . He sighed as he went out.

Hepsibah shook her head over him. Poor lad!

Oddly enough, big Joe, labouring with mighty goodwill out in the garden and home farm, knew him better. The moment Jack's small figure appeared round a hedge or gate, Joe would heave up with a huge bellow of joy from his hauling or barrowing, shovelling or digging. He'd drop his tools and surge across to lift Jack up bodily, chuckling, hugging him till Jack yelled breathlessly, 'Oy! Put me down, Joe! Down! Gor, yer bigger'n when I last seen ye! 'Oo's been feedin' ye beans, eh?' Joe, understanding less than half, would grin and bob and grunt as he dumped Jack on his feet again, and they would hold hands and laugh from sheer happiness.

Elijah Parry gave a good report of Joe. He was settled well, with a bed above the stables among the other garden lads, and was holding his own against their rough, natural teasing. 'They learned fast, young Jack. Cares naught for words, your brother, they can say what they like, but if they push him too far, trippin' him or stealin' his dinner from under his nose or whatever, he finally loses his temper. He's no skill at fisticuffs, but he just swings out with those great hands, and anythin' he hits flies into the next county. And all forgotten instant, as soon as they leave him be. No, there was some bad feeling at first, but I spoke to them, that it was their doing, an' now they respect him for it. They're proud of him, even. Strongest lad in five parishes. He can lift any four o' them together, and carry them across the room. Never seen a lad as strong. Set him to haulin' against a Shire horse, and I'd not care to bet on the winner!' He roared with laughter. 'They'd break the rope!'

Jack always returned to London easy in his mind about his family. They were happy. And he was having the time of his life. With all the money he could steal, and keep, now, and spend freely, he treated his friends from the

Three Cranes to all they could eat and drink in the local taverns. They cheered him, praised him, thought he was a hero. They all loved him.

He couldn't be lonely, surely?

In real gratitude, he pressed Frank for extra work. Phelippes was surprised and delighted. 'What a paragon indeed! I'd not have believed it! You cast your bread upon the waters, young sir, and it has returned to you a bed of roses! Well done, Master Verney! But tell your young friend to be patient. This is the lull before the ill wind. We shall have work enough for him soon, I swear. Sir Francis has much in mind these days. He is confident of a plot. Treason, Master Verney! Treachery, Master Verney! Its foul stink is on the wing!'

Frank was doubtful. 'I can f-find no trace, Master Ph-Phelippes. Sir Antony speaks f-freely to me of all that comes into his head, and most often of v-visiting Italy with Lord Salisbury. That's his dream, not p-plotting.'

Phelippes sniffed. 'But things may change rapidly, young sir! No, you must remain heart in glove with Sir Antony, visit him often, profess conviction. Though you're in no danger of being converted, I trust? That would lead to a different kind of conviction!' He sucked his teeth juicily.

Only two days later, on the second of June, Frank left Susanna's house. He took boat to Blackfriars Steps as usual, and headed for his lodgings in Holborn near the Fleet River, already starting to stink in the summer warmth. When he arrived at the Three Tuns, he found his friends making wagers on which of two crows would win a dead eel they were squabbling over. Both dropped it, and a cat ran off with it, to everyone's laughter. Frank was about to call for a pasty when a man tugged his sleeve. 'Yes? Oh, S-Simon. What's the excitement? '

Babington's man shrugged, panting. 'Dunno, sir. Two men come, an' my master, 'e told me to run find 'is friends, sir, you, an' Lord Salisbury, an' Master Barnwell, quick as winkin', an' beg you come to 'is rooms wi' all speed. You're the last, sir.'

Frank shrugged. 'V-very well, I'll come.' In some puzzlement he followed the man towards Hern's Rents. Two men?

Babington opened the door himself. 'My dear Frank! Come in, come in quickly!' While Frank greeted Tichborne and his other friends, Babington himself was getting rid of his servant. 'Simon, here's a shilling. Make yourself scarce for an hour or two. Just don't return drunken!' He checked that the man had left and the stair was empty before shutting the door. 'We must be wary, dear Frank! It has come at last!'

'What has?' Why was Tony so nervous? As if he was afraid someone might be spying — Dear God! Was this what Walsingham had been expecting?

'Meet John Savage, Frank.' A tall young man with an open, stupid face bowed with awkward friendliness. His brown doublet was heavy homespun, badly worn at the elbows and cuffs. A poor relation, maybe? But before Frank had fully risen from his bow to Master Savage, Babington was tugging his sleeve, drawing him aside, gesturing proudly to the other guest. 'And this gentleman, Frank, is known as Captain Foscue.' Frank bowed, and nearly fell over as he recalled the letter in Lord Vaux' house. A Jesuit!

'Captain Foscue' was only of medium height, not as tall as Frank or Babington, burly and high-coloured like an outdoor man, swaggering his gold lace and long sword bravely as any bully soldier. He clapped Frank's shoulders with approval. 'Sir Antony tells me that you are deep in our counsels, sir, and may be trusted as much as himself.'

Frank bowed again, trying not to blush or tremble. What was happening?

Babington answered the thought as if he'd heard it. 'Captain Foscue is a messenger of gravest import! His

148

true name is Ballard; Father Ballard. Yes, Frank; a priest! In disguise! He doesn't look it, does he?' Well, that was the idea, Frank thought. 'And he has a matter of vital concern to discuss with my closest and secretest friends! Amongst whom I count you, dear Frank!' Babington's voice hovered between dread and delight. 'Father, we are all here. I beg you to give us your message.'

The big man beamed round at them. 'It is great news, my children! And you must swear by the True Faith to keep it secret!' They swore it, crossing themselves eagerly. 'Our salvation is at last at hand! The Kings of France and Spain are ready to join with us to rescue the blessed martyr of Scotland, Queen Mary, to set her in her rightful place, and expel the usurper Elizabeth and all her heretical pirate supporters! Thomas Morgan, the Queen of Scots' man of affairs in France, sends me to all the loyal men of England, to confirm their help for this our glorious enterprise!'

Enterprise? Frank felt as if he was suffocating. God's Body! Walsingham was right all along! Not that he'd ever doubted him . . .

Ballard clasped Babington by the shoulders. 'And to be our leader, you, Sir Antony, are specially recommended to me by Morgan himself!'

Babington swallowed. 'Me?' His voice was almost a squeak. 'Why me?'

'Her Majesty remembers the help which you have already given her. And relies on your loyalty and courage to accomplish her cause!' Babington's jaw and eyes were equally wide. Passing a couple of packets of letters, and hiding a priest — and now this! Ballard beamed round. 'All of you! You shall bring about the redemption of your country!'

It was Salisbury who asked, 'How?'

Ballard's voice deepened significantly. 'There are sixty thousand men, under the Dukes of Guise and Parma, ready poised to strike!'

Absurd! Frank suddenly found his mind working clearly

149

again. Sixty thousand? He'd heard his brother complaining bitterly about the difficulty and expense of maintaining a troop of fifty soldiers. Sixty thousand? Poised ready? And not a hint known? He didn't believe it.

The rest did, though; but to Ballard's dismay they rejected the idea emphatically. Lord Salisbury was again first to control his jaw. 'Strike? Strike here, you mean? Invade? England? No! It's impossible!'

'Indeed, sir! The Spanish Ambassador, Mendoza, has assured me of it! In person! Sixty thousand men, both Spanish and French, are already under arms, awaiting our word where they will be most welcomed!'

'Welcomed? They won't be.' That was Tichborne.

'Who'd help an invasion?' Barnwell was insulted.

Salisbury was appalled. 'Enslave us to foreigners? Never!'

Frank was glad they opposed this terrifying nonsense. He was no expert; it might be true, some of it, at least. The Spanish Ambassador? Invasion? He judged that Ballard believed it. Find out more. Argue, like the others. 'It wouldn't be enough, anyway!'

Babington pulled himself together, agreeing with Frank. 'We have our dreams, father, but this would be an impossible solution.' He shook his head, sighing, resigned and relieved. 'Impossible.'

But Ballard set an arm round his shoulders. 'Be of good cheer, Sir Antony! All things are possible if it is God's will! I assure you that there are as many good Catholics promised to aid us, here in England!'

Even Babington disbelieved that. 'Full sixty thousand? I can't credit it. No, no, Father! While Elizabeth lives, usurper or no, there is no such dissatisfaction as will make men rise for us.' The others nodded.

'You are right!' Ballard surprised them. 'But the excommunication of the Princess Elizabeth is to be renewed, to free all from their allegiance to her. And there is more!' He leaned close, beckoning them all to gather round, whispering. 'You said wisely, "While Elizabeth lives." But there is an instrument at hand, to free us of her presence!'

Frank found it hard to breathe. Invasion? No, he'd not credit it. Babington, foolish, vainglorious Tony as the leader of a rebellion? Huh! But to murder the queen — that was possible. What would the rest say to it?

To his relief, they were as shocked as he was. 'Kill her? No! It would be — monstrous! Wicked!' Salisbury protested. He looked sick, his short beard almost trembling over his ruff. 'And then to let our country be invaded — to help the invaders, even — no! No, I'll hear no more! I vowed silence, Tony, and I suppose I'll keep my vow. But this — no!' He marched out, Barnwell at his heels. The two voices exclaiming in disgust could be heard all the way down the stairs.

Frank wondered if he should go with them and report at once. No; he must stay, to discover all there was to know.

Chidiock Tichborne broke the silence. 'I must say, Tony, I agree with them. I'm sorry, Father, but invasion — and murder —'

'If it were indeed murder, no man of honour could set hand to it!' Ballard was fierce. 'But in defence of our sacred faith, to return this suffering land to the true love of Holy Mother Church, to save the Queen of Scots, we must do what in any other cause would be abominable. Think, Master Tichborne! To save a man with the stone, a surgeon must cut with a knife into his body. For any common man to do so without such cause is unlawful, and rightly so; but in this case, it is the sole cure, despite all the risks, and so is licensed. And so we do also. The soldiers who will come are our friends. They wish to help us! To save the souls of all Englishmen, mistakenly taught, all presently doomed to eternal hell-fire for heresy! Some blood will be shed, of course, but it is the only way! The only way to rescue your country! And those whose souls you save will thank you for it, in after years. You will be heroes!'

Babington brightened slightly, but Tichborne, normally the sunniest of souls, was still unhappy. He glanced at Frank for support to go on arguing. 'But — killing the queen — murder — treason —'

'It's not murder!' Ballard reassured him. 'It is the execution of one who has taken up arms against her lawful sovereign, Queen Mary, and by force and treasonous guile usurped her throne, held her in captivity for twenty years, and plans her death! For how long will it be, think ye, before Elizabeth finds some reason to execute her?'

Well, that was true, Frank thought. If Walsingham had his way.

'Whose is the treason? Ours, in supporting our lawful Queen Mary, though uncrowned here? Or Elizabeth's, in seizing the throne to which she had no right?' His voice softened, as Tichborne still looked doubtful. 'My son, if it could be done without her death, it would be. But you must know that her followers will continue to fight for her sake as long as she lives. She would be a constant danger to our true queen. She must die!'

Frank nodded. That was exactly what Walsingham said about Mary.

Babington looked questioningly to him. 'What do you think, Frank?'

He hesitated. Lord, what should he say? Approve, and urge him into treason? Condemn, and perhaps be excluded from any future plans? 'I scarce know what to th-think, Tony. I hate the idea of an invasion, as any man m-must. But if it's truly the only way —'

Ballard took his hand. 'Sir, you have the marrow of it in you. Thanks be to God that one man at least can see the truth!'

Babington bit his lip. 'Dear Frank, I have come to rely on your good sense. If you recommend it — yes. I can see . . . As you urge, it is indeed the only way . . . I think.'

Frank tried not to look confounded. He hadn't thought he sounded so very keen on the idea! Babington swung back to Ballard. 'But what is this instrument of our deliverance, father?'

The hobbledehoy youth, John Savage, lounging casually on the window seat, grinned. 'Me,' he said.

With a rueful smile at their surprise, Ballard nodded. 'John here will free us from the rule of the usurper.'

'What? How?' Tichborne got it out just before Babington.

'I'm going to kill Elizabeth,' Savage said helpfully. They gaped. He nodded. 'I swore I would. Last year. In Rheims. I thought I'd study to be a priest, but they said I could do more good this way. So it was my duty. So I swore. So I will.' He smiled, quite satisfied that he had explained himself reasonably.

Ballard cleared his throat. 'It may seem unlikely,' he murmured. Well, yes; Savage's elbows were poking through his sleeves. He'd not get to Court like that, Frank thought with a spurt of hysteria. 'But John is a most reliable young man. He was a soldier, before he turned to the Church. His martial skill and dedication will bring us victory in this battle. He has enrolled to read law at Barnard's Inn, as a cover for his true purpose, while we prepare our part in the enterprise.'

Frank felt full of energy. Enterprise? Battle? Murdering the queen, he meant! But he'd be stopped! Frank would see to it!

They discussed the matter for some time, and Babington slowly convinced himself. 'The laws grow constantly more severe. You know, father, the latest statutes say that simply to be a Catholic is to be a traitor. And it must grow worse. This deed may bring dishonour and desolation on our country. But in inaction equally there is desolation and extreme hazard for us all, and yet no way to better our state. Aye, we must act.'

Chidiock Tichborne was still doubtful, but willing to go along with his friends. He suggested, 'We'll need to hurry, if we're going to rescue Queen Mary. She's been ill for months now, poor lady.'

'Well thought on, Master Tichborne!' Ballard agreed. 'Once she is crowned Queen of England, Mary can make her brother-in-law, Henri of France, heir to her throne, and England will remain Catholic. But if she dies first, by illness or, God prevent, by execution, Elizabeth's next heir is Mary's son, James of Scotland, who is unfortunately Protestant. We should lose all benefit of our actions. We must indeed make haste!' Chidiock looked slightly flummoxed. That wasn't really what he'd meant.

They agreed on two actions. Babington would stay in London, to gather a group together to rescue Mary and support Savage, who assured them, 'Leave Elizabeth's death to me, sirs. Whenever you say. Tomorrow, if you like. Get me into the queen's presence, and I'll carry out my oath; no more to be said.' He was even rather huffy at the idea of anyone helping him.

Frank cleared his throat. 'But Queen Mary must be safe f-first!' Tony agreed, hastily, in relief. Savage shrugged accommodatingly.

Happier to talk about planning the rescue of his dream princess, Babington declared he would approach Salisbury and Barnwell again. 'And with your arguments, Father, and for love of their faith, and for my sake, also, I know they will help us in the end. We have you, dear Chidiock, and you, Frank. Then Charles Tilney and Edward Abingdon. They are in the queen's — the Princess Elizabeth's bodyguard, Father, but good Catholics.'

Ballard was delighted. 'I know one or two others. But they must all be sworn to secrecy first, Sir Antony, before you open the plan to them!'

'Of course! I am no fool, Father! We are all here experienced in intrigue!' Frank had trouble controlling his expression.

Meanwhile, Ballard would travel north to Norfolk and

Yorkshire, the Catholic counties, to find out what help the Catholic gentry would guarantee for the invasion. Babington would pay his expenses. 'Excellently efficient!' Ballard praised them. 'Our enterprise is well begun!'

Savage left for his lodgings by Barnard's Inn, and the priest retired early, since he had to set out next day early. Chidiock, Sir Antony and Frank were left sitting silent in the growing gloom.

At last Babington stretched and sighed. 'How easily one is caught up in affairs!' He rose and poured fresh wine for them all. 'Such a great adventure, of such immense import. Danger, and machinations, and the fate of nations hanging on our swords. Shall we be remembered with honour or loathing? And only yesterday ... I wish — I almost wish I could still be simply planning to visit Italy.' He heaved another sigh. 'But when a gentleman is called by his faith and his queen, he must answer. I feel like a knight of olden days, my queen's champion!' Cheered by the thought, he rose to his feet and raised his glass. 'Drink with me, Chidiock, Frank, my dearest friends! To success in this quest for our queen, and a happy outcome of our enterprise!' Chidiock drank the toast with him, smiling.

Frank didn't move. He knew how Tony felt. He'd felt just the same ...

Suddenly all his keen excitement had vanished. If this was all true, and not the dream it almost seemed to be, then his report would save Queen Elizabeth's life, but these young men, his friends, foolish Tony, cheerful Chidiock, Tom Salisbury, Barnwell — and that idiot John Savage — they would all die. He sat still, shivering, till Tichborne cried, 'Frank! How remiss of me! It grows chilly! I'll call Simon to light the fire!'

At that Frank dragged himself out of his dark thoughts. He had his duty to do, whatever he felt. 'No, no,

Chidiock! No need for me! I'm on my way home directly!' He raised his glass almost defiantly. 'To success, and saving the queen!' He tossed off the wine in one gulp, spluttered as it caught his throat, and the moment of tension passed in laughter and coughing and back-patting.

Gifford

A fortnight later, Walsingham rose from the desk where he had been working in the June sunshine, to pace the panelled office of his house in Barn Elms. 'Let me be sure I understand you, Master Verney.' He was in his shirt sleeves, playing with the cords of his open collar while Frank, fully and formally dressed in brown wool doublet and starched ruff, sweated with nervousness as well as heat. 'Some Catholics, led by Babington, plan to kill the queen. True? Others whom Babington has sounded out will not help, but have not reported it, and are thus concealing a plot against Her Majesty's life. True? They plan foreign invasion to set Mary Stewart on the throne. True? Yet you claim that their real desire is to go abroad. Rubbish! Lord Salisbury may indeed have offered you, as a Treasury officer, four hundred pounds to help them get a passport. But not, I think, to avoid the evil deed. They wish to be ready to escape if they are discovered!'

Frank bit his lip, flushing in embarrassed defiance. He knew Tony and Tom. He didn't think so, but what could he say? 'They're so incompetent!'

Idiotic boy!

'Incompetent? I am glad to hear it! You would perhaps prefer me to wait for regicides to succeed before I act?'

Frank winced. 'B-but. sir, I'm sure they're no real threat to Her M-Majesty, save for the m-madman J-John Savage ...' He broke off under Walsingham's baleful glare.

'You, a half-fledged apprentice, you will bandy words with me?' The snarl softened. 'Come, Master Verney! You are new to these matters. I pray you, accept that I must know more of them than yourself.' His voice was suddenly confiding, almost kindly. 'You consider these young men fools — and you are right. Yet a fool can pull a trigger as well as a sage. They pity their 'martyred queen'. Hah! When she was seventeen, she calmly watched scores of French Protestants tortured to death. At twenty-four, she enticed her husband, Darnley, to return to Edinburgh, for her paramour Bothwell to murder him. Your plotters were in the nursery then!' His energy, his conviction were overwhelming. 'They did not see Queen Mary Tudor, Elizabeth's sister, try to force the nation back to the arms of the Pope. Hundreds of true martyrs upheld the Protestant Faith unto death! Hundreds! And if this wily Jezebel were to gain the throne with a Catholic army to support her, hundreds more would do so! The monster would bring us the tortures of the Inquisition! The massacres of Saint Bartholomew's Day!'

He slapped the table. 'Believe me, sir! Babington and his friends are indeed mere fools. I agree! But I know the sly minds in France and Spain who are using them! You think there is no danger of foreign invasion? I tell you that it is at hand! In Spain the ships of invasion are even now being built! Why do I not prevent — nay, sir, why do I encourage Drake and his piratical friends to seize the ships which bring gold and jewels from the Indies to Spain? I know the ungodly purpose for which this treasure is intended! And it is through such as these young fools that the first, the vital blow will come, if we, you and I, do not prevent it!'

He sat back, his fists unclenching, his voice dropping to almost a pleading tone. 'So obey me, Master Verney. Trust me! Lead these foolish birds into my net, to prevent ruin to our realm and religion! My task is to save the queen, not her foes. I must and will strike at them where they are weakest, not strongest. Is that not good sense? Well, then. Do you aid the queen, or her enemies? Can we trust you, Master Verney?'

For a long moment, as Frank still wrestled with his conscience, Sir Francis feared he had misjudged it, but at last Frank nodded. 'Yes, sir.' His voice was almost inaudible. Poor foolish Tony!

Walsingham hid his pleasure. He hadn't lost the lad's willing loyalty. No need for — other pressures. 'Very well. Now, this is what you will do. You will suggest to Babington that Ballard's word is not sufficient authority for such a dreadful action. It is in any case his own feeling in the matter? Aye. You will encourage this, urge him to demand written instructions from someone in unquestionable authority. You understand me?'

'Yes, sir. But whom can they ask for this p-proof? M-Morgan in Paris, or —' He broke off and gazed at Walsingham. 'Ph-Phelippes sent Gifford a letter f-from Mary. It's not Babington you want, at all. It's M-Mary.'

'Have I not just been saying so? She is my quest of the Holy Grail, my heart's desire!' He coughed; he seldom showed his feelings so much. 'Your duty, young man, is to put the idea into Babington's head. And together, Master Verney, we shall scotch this treason, and save England from civil war, murder and invasion. Now — to work!' He motioned Frank away.

But Frank made one more plea. 'Sir, will you not speak to B-Babington yourself? He might well tell you all, without f-further trouble.'

With some difficulty, feeling a warning twinge in his

gut, Walsingham stopped himself exploding in fury. He forced himself to consider. It might indeed be useful — and if it would keep Verney happy ... Nursing the boy along like this was ridiculous, but an agent of such youthful promise was not to be wasted for want of a little patience while his shell was still soft. 'Very well. If he offers, I shall accept his services.'

'Th-thank you! I knew you'd be f-fair, sir! Thank you indeed!' Frank beamed in delight and relief, bowing himself out.

Walsingham wiped his face with his kerchief and sat gazing at the door for a moment. Fair? Was the young man really such an idiot? He might have to reconsider ... He sniffed; the Lord's Will be done.

Poor Frank's time was more than fully occupied. He wasn't excused his morning work at the Whitehall office just because he was involved in one of Mr Secretary Walsingham's schemes, and also he had to be in constant contact with Babington — not that these two were difficult to combine, for Babington never rose before noon. But in addition, there were reports to write for Phelippes, orders to give Jack every few days; and he also wanted to visit Ruth regularly. Or Susanna, if Ruth wasn't there.

However, now that she was coming out of her childish protective shell, Susanna was blossoming. Rather to her surprise, and certainly to Ruth's, she found that her honest kindliness, intelligence and dry humour — and, as she had the wit to realise, her mother's wealth — brought her many friends. Frank discovered with some dismay that his second choice of lady in the house was almost as seldom alone as his first.

Though her new friends were fine, rich and entertaining, Susanna still wanted this one particular youth. He circled round her like a cranefly round a solid little glow-worm. Susanna carefully kept her own counsel about her defence of Jack. Whenever Frank remembered it, he'd be thinking about her; and she saw to it that he didn't forget. Every time he was deserted by Ruth and came looking for Susanna, in clear, open pleasure she welcomed him among her other friends. The talk might be serious or light-hearted, of maps or music, riddles or religion, gardens or geometry, but it often somehow came around to the theatre, or thieves, or watches, and she smiled sweetly at Frank while he fidgeted. Kate had to leave the room occasionally, to laugh in peace.

Frank also fretted that Babington wouldn't, or couldn't, make up his mind what to do. One day he'd be windily optimistic; 'Tom has two friends who may join us, and Edward Windsor, one of the Gentlemen Pensioners, is interested; our numbers are growing!' Possibly, Frank knew, not certainly, not even probably. Next day Tony would speak longingly of peaceful travel around Europe, far from the risks and pressure of state affairs.

He did, at least, forbid John Savage to try any assassination attempt alone. 'A lone man has no chance, John!' he insisted. 'We must be six or seven to make the attempt. Besides, you must share the glory!' Savage assented amiably. He was quite happy to delay, at Babington's expense, as long as he was the first to strike when the time came. Babington complained, 'He is really quite incredible. No nerves at all, Frank! While here am I, totally worn away by apprehension! Oh, what should I do, Frank?'

When Frank suggested getting confirmation, his friend leapt at the idea. It meant further delay . . . 'Of course! I shall speak to Father Ballard on his return. Such good advice you give me, Frank! An old head on young shoulders! I place the most absolute trust in you!' Frank blushed. He knew better now why Walsingham had spoken of a dirty war.

Babington was easily persuaded to go to see Walsingham at the end of June, to ask in person for a passport.

161

Sir Francis, greeting him most courteously, hinted, 'A passport, Sir Antony, might be more readily available if you would offer to furnish intelligence to the queen.'

Babington agreed warmly. 'Indeed, sir! A Catholic living abroad might well be able to render Her Majesty good and loyal service in this way.'

This wasn't what Walsingham meant; but how to press the young man, without revealing any knowledge of the plot? 'May I ask for details of the service you are prepared to offer? The closer to home the intelligence is, the more grateful the queen will be, you understand.' But Babington avoided the hints, not admitting to knowing anything. Walsingham smiled coldly; he had kept his word to young Verney; Sir Antony had had his chance.

Frank could have kicked Tony in frustration when he heard.

Next evening, he walked into Sir Antony's rooms to be greeted with an excited call, 'Frank! Come and meet a messenger straight from Paris! This is Frank Verney, Master Gifford — Gilbert Gifford!'

Frank gulped, smiled and bowed and tried to say all the right things. He didn't have to pretend excitement. Babington was thrilled. Tom Salisbury and Chidiock Tichborne, sitting in the window seat, looked uneasy.

Gifford bowed, showing no sign of recognition. He was as beautiful as ever, his longish hair gleaming gold above his severe dark brown broadcloth and linen ruff. He appeared stiff and accusing. 'Sir Antony, I am sent by Sir Thomas Morgan, secretary to Archbishop Beaton, Queen Mary's chief representative in France, to discover the reason for your delay.'

Babington was insulted. 'Delay, sir? I am gathering my friends, sir, with care and discretion, to avoid discovery.'

Gifford seemed unimpressed. 'Forgive me, sir, but I must speak as I am directed. Your "discretion" appears otherwise abroad. I am charged to demand of you why has Savage not yet slain the usurper? Do you abandon the enterprise, in dishonourable shirking of your responsibilities?'

Babington stiffened at the attack. His anger gave him an unusual incisiveness. 'Sir, we will do all that an honourable man may! But our honour itself gives us pause. We need written, undoubted authority that the proposed dreadful action is indeed lawful in every part. We must also know whether armed assistance is actually in existence. Without good assurance of these points, we will go no further, and if John Savage persists in his determination, I myself will discover the whole to the queen.' Salisbury was nodding approval. Frank felt like cheering.

Gifford sighed and beamed in apparent relief. 'Sir Antony, I see you have considered the matter most expertly, which you would not have done were you not in earnest about the action. You gladden my mind, sir, and I heartily apologise on my masters' behalf for their doubts of you!' Babington bowed, relaxing slightly. 'I can myself give you some of the information you require. All the professors of Rheims University hold that Elizabeth's excommunication justifies the planned action against her as lawful in every part.' Rheims was a centre of Catholic teaching, Frank knew; what else would they say there? Even if it was true. He had to keep reminding himself that this honest, sincere young man was in fact Walsingham's agent.

'In this letter, sir, you will see that Mendoza, the Spanish Ambassador, has personally assured Morgan that the invasion will take place in September.'

How could that be, Frank wondered. It couldn't be true; a forgery? Or — it suddenly struck him — was Morgan himself one of Walsingham's agents? A spy, in charge of Queen Mary's finances, and in position to recommend Babbington, and Gifford . . . The spymaster was a true genius!

Gifford was clapping Babbington on the shoulder. 'And, sir,' he beamed, 'I may assure you that those who risk most in the enterprise shall be the most abundantly rewarded.'

Salisbury sniffed. Tichborne, not a rich man, rubbed his hands and smiled happily. 'That covers all, does it not, Tony?'

Babington, impressed by Gifford's air of assurance and always easily charmed by personable young men, was about to agree when Frank caught a glance from Gifford. He must remember his duty. 'What about the confirmation in writing?' he interposed, to Tom Salisbury's emphatic nod. 'We m-must have it. How long will it take, to write to F-France?'

Gifford chuckled. 'Why go so far?' As they stared at him, Babington's expression bewildered, he beckoned them into a secret. 'Why not ask the very source of our authority? Queen Mary herself!'

'What?' Salisbury exclaimed. 'God's teeth, we can't reach her, man!'

'I have some letters for her,' Babington said. Jack had had them out for copying weeks before. 'But I know no way to send them.'

'Aha!' Gifford was triumphant. 'But I do! The brewer at Chartley, sirs, is our man. He can pass letters through, hidden in a sealed tube inside his casks of ale! I carry them from him, to and from the Spanish and French Ambassadors.' Via Phelippes, Frank thought. And Walsingham.

'The tube is waterproof?' Babington was enthralled. Silly question, Frank thought, it had better be!

Tichborne grinned widely — always a sign he was going to make a joke. 'Say aleproof, rather!'

'And foolproof!' Salisbury offered. Wrong, Frank thought.

Gifford chuckled with the rest, and then returned to gravity. 'Compose a letter, sir, encode it, and I shall deliver it to Queen Mary. You have a copy of the cipher, Morgan tells me?' Phelippes had one as well, Frank knew. 'Then write, sir, to inform and cheer her and yourself both. Demand what authority you need, tell Her Majesty all your plans, seek her advice and instructions. Within three days, I shall send a servant for it!' And within another five minutes he had vanished, a man of mystery.

His attack on Babington's determination, rather than any attempt to insinuate himself into the plot — that had been totally convincing. Frank had to admire Gifford's acting. But there had been a gloating gleam in his eyes, when his dupes were not observing him, that turned Frank's stomach. He himself wasn't like that. Was he?

For the next few days, Frank couldn't find time to visit Ruth and Susanna at all. Babington was busy composing his letter, and since the ciphering was a tedious, exact business, Frank was called upon to do it, and correct the spelling. He must, of course, use the chance to work for Walsingham. '*An invasion is planned* —' It's too v-vague, Tony. We must say who'll be involved, and where.'

'But we won't know exactly till Father Ballard returns, Frank.' Babington, leaning over Frank's shoulder at the table and admiring his masterpiece, was peeved by any criticism. 'Just put that down for now.' He read on through the letter, enjoying the ring of the words. '"*An invasion is planned . . . and I, Sir Antony Babington, wish to do Your Majesty some service in that connection for restoration of your liberty . . . We pray that any rewards promised to the chief actors shall be given to their posterities if they miscarry in the execution.*" That's well thought of, isn't it, Frank? We must prepare for the worst.' Brave and tragic. '"*We beg your Majesty's authority for all.*" That's your own idea.' Frank nodded. That was the main point; to get Mary's written approval, so that she'd be fully implicated and could be executed. '"*Myself with 10 gentlemen and a 100 of our followers will undertake the delivery of your royal person from the hands of your enemies.*"'

'Can we be sure of so many?' Frank asked.

Babington tutted. 'Tom Salisbury can raise twice that himself, from his own servants. And our friends will rally round when the time comes! Don't be such a kill-joy, Frank!' He puffed out his breath in annoyance and went on in a hurry. '"*For the dispatch of the usurper, I anticipate I may find half a dozen or so gentlemen —*"'

'God's Body, cut it down, Tony!' Frank protested. 'Say "*I and six gentlemen*". Or it won't be ready for Christmas, let alone three days.'

'How efficient you are, Frank!' Babington sounded slightly huffed, but immediately apologised. 'You quite put me to shame. Very well. "*There be 6 noble gentlemen —*" will that do? — "*all my private friends, who for the zeal they bear to the Catholic cause and Your Majesty's service will undertake somewhat for the performance of the tragical execution.*'

Frank sighed. It was like trying to stop a waterfall. He'd be up all night, at this rate.

'"*Upon the 16th of this month, July, I will be at Lichfield, expecting Your Majesty's answer and letters, in readiness to execute what by them shall be commanded.*" Will a week be enough to leave for her to reply, do you think? "*Your Majesty's most faithful subject and sworn servant —*" and I'll sign it.' He beamed with satisfaction. 'There! What do you think, Frank? Is it graceful and eloquent, yet forceful, as befits a man of action?' He was more anxious about his prose style than his head.

Frank nodded, stretching his fingers. 'Yes, excellent. I'll cipher it f-for you right away.' And give Phelippes a copy. Poor, foolish Tony!

On the sixth of July, in his respectable Fulham clothes, Jack came to Babington's door. He waited, drinking a mug of ale in the kitchen, while Babington struggled to decipher the sealed letter he brought, from Mary herself, addressed to 'my very good friend . . .' She asked for the letters he held for her. He parcelled them up with his own. As Jack left, whistling cheerily, Babington leaned back against the door frame, panting in mingled fright and glory. 'My very good friend'!

Round the corner, Jack handed the packet over to Frank. 'There y'are, sir! Babbleton's letters, all alive-o! An' 'e give me a shillin', too. Care fer a glass o' lime juice? Yer lookin' a bit peaky — this 'eat's gettin' us all down.'

Frank was indeed feeling peaky. He was sickened by this whole affair. Babbleton, indeed! Poor, doomed Tony! He knew that what he was doing was right; Walsingham had explained it all. But then, Tony thought that he was doing right, too ... 'That sounds f-f-fine.' He tried to cheer up. 'M-most graciously kind of you to invite me, sir!' He bowed.

Jack returned the bow. 'My pleasure, yer honour!'

They bowed elaborately, back and fore, each in turn trying to outdo the other's flourishes. By the fourth one, Frank found himself laughing. And he didn't want to be alone just now ... 'Come home with me, and we'll sit at ease in the garden. I'll p-pay.'

Jack snorted. 'Huh! Not bleedin' likely, sir! I asked you.' He raced off and brought back a jugful of the sharp, refreshing cordial while Frank found glasses.

Comfortably lolling on the grass in the shade of his landlady's prized walnut tree, they were singing the old song, 'A woman, a spaniel, a walnut tree, The more you beat them the better they be!' when Gifford arrived to collect the letters. He took a glass of juice, but drank quickly. 'I must get on,' he smiled to Frank, with a side glance at Jack. 'Our master grows impatient, and presses for speed. I —'

There was a bustling at the garden door. The landlady called through, flustered, 'Sir, there's a young lady —'

A lilting voice carolled, 'Master Frank, pray tell this good woman that I am quite respectable, and may be allowed to enter even her worthy portals!' Ruth, laughing like a chime of bells, fresh and dainty in pale blue silk as he had first seen her, held out her hands to him as she crossed the lawn. 'Dear Frank, it seems so long since you have called on us! I wondered if you were ill, and came to reassure myself!'

Her maid sat on a bench by the door, glad to rest her feet. There had been no visitors for her mistress this morning, and rather than join the laughing group inventing acrostics with Susanna in the orchard — she, the most sought-after lady in London, to be reduced to joining someone else's party? Making up silly riddles? Besides, she was no good at them — Ruth had walked out herself. This was the fourth house they'd visited; none of the other young gentlemen had been at home.

Frank was thrilled that she had noticed his absence. She let him kiss her hand; carefully ignored Jack — that imp again! What on earth did Frank want with him? — and gestured to the third person. 'Pray name me your friend, Frank! Ah, is that lime juice? A glass, of your generosity! I'm parched!' She turned to favour the stranger with her smile.

Whose glass could he wipe most easily? 'Oh, er, Master Gifford. Gilbert, M-Mistress Ruth Bolsiter.' Absently, Frank made the introduction.

'An honour, Mistress Bolsiter.' Gifford bowed.

Ruth stood in silent stillness, her lips slightly parted, gazing.

After a moment, Gifford coughed. 'I must go, Master Verney. Mistress.' He picked up his satchel and turned away.

Ruth raised a hand and made a sound of protest. 'Oh no! No, sir! I pray you, don't go — er — don't let me drive you away.'

He shook his head. 'No, no, mistress. I was on the point of leaving.'

'Where are you going?' Her voice wasn't quite under control. She was breathing fast, flushed and trembling. This man was so — so — so beautiful . . . Her heart was racing . . . She'd never felt like this before . . .

'Reading, mistress.' Warily, he named not his real destination, but a place in the same direction. He knew that look. God's Bowels, another one in love with him! He was hard put to it not to laugh. Such fools, women were, for a handsome face! It was useful, often enough.

She bit her lip. 'You take boat to Maidenhead? Then you may give me your escort, sir,' she announced, smiling brilliantly. 'For I am going to — to Whitehall.' She couldn't think of any reason for going further, on the spur of the moment. She could scarcely think at all . . . He was gorgeous . . .

Stupid cow! Gifford sneered internally. But her gown was fine silk, and her earrings were gold and sapphire. Definitely worth accommodating. He bowed, with a charming smile. 'Honoured, mistress.'

Frank gasped at her sudden desertion of him. 'But — your cordial —' He held up the glass helplessly.

Who..? Oh, just Frank. Ruth tossed him an automatic, distracted smile. 'I — er — a most important appointment — I must go instantly. Pray you, Master — Master Gifford, give me your arm. The cobbles — I fear I need assistance.' She raised her wide skirts a trifle, to display a dainty slipper, a slim ankle. 'High heels are so impractical, sir! But one must follow the fashion!' Thank God she'd put on her best perfume! Without another glance at Frank, she swept Gifford out.

Jack snorted cynically, not noticing Frank's anguish. 'Appointment in White'all! In me eye she 'as! See 'er maid's face? First she'd 'eard of it. An' showin' off 'er legs.' Slowly, Frank sank back down to the bench. 'Females! All lovey-dovey, an' then when anuvver feller takes their fancy, bang, bump, drops ye in the gutter! Man'untin' trollop! Oy, wot's wrong? Oh. Ye likes 'er, don't ye?' He tutted in annoyance at Frank and himself, and patted Frank's arm in chirpy commiseration. 'Cheer up, sir! She ain't the only one!'

But she was, for Frank. He sat still and white. While

his love loved no-one else, there was hope for him among all the rest. But now — now she was in love with another man. What should he do? What could he do?

Three days later, Susanna sat at the breakfast table staring at her mother. 'Ruth? In love? I don't believe it!' But for a day or two, Ruth had been dreamy, crying in corners, irritable and careless of her suitors. It might be true — and if so . . . 'How do you know?'

Kate laughed, shaking her head in rueful sympathy. 'I know the signs, my dear. I never looked to see it in Ruth, though. But I'm fair worried. I don't know him at all. I fear he's unsuitable. An' from the face o' her, Ruth thinks so too.' She snorted in resigned sympathy. 'Well! My selfish, greedy, ambitious Ruth! Heels over head in love, an' him no an earl! Nor a knight, even! I never thought to see the day.'

'You've no idea who he is? Or how they met, or anything?' Susanna was so used to her mother knowing everything that Kate's shrug was astonishing.

'His name's Gilbert Gifford, an' she met him at Frank's lodgings, an' went wi' him half up the river for no reason but to be with him.' Kate sniffed in annoyance. 'Chasin' a man's never a good idea.'

'What do we do?'

'Well. I'll no have her disgrace herself, an' you an' me both wi' her. I've told her maid she must never let Ruth out o' her sight outside, an' tell me who she meets. Or call me at once, if she tries to get out alone. I've no mind to set up her back by forbiddin' her to leave the house, but we must take care o' her, see she does nothin' foolish. We may be wrong about the man — he may be no that bad. But we can't chance it.' She sighed, and chuckled. 'Bairns! First they make your arms ache, an' then they make your head ache, an' then they make your heart ache.'

'Mother . . .' The hope in Susanna's voice was tentative. 'Do you think Frank knows? That she's in love with this man? What will he do?'

Kate shrugged. 'God He knows, lass. It might work out well for you. Just — kick the ball as it comes your way. Be ready to comfort him, cheer him. If he'll let you. You might get him on the rebound. But you're her sister, an' he might take against us all. We'll just have to wait and see.'

Susanna, whose heart had suddenly started beating wild and high, was as suddenly filled with dismay. If Frank avoided her, because of Ruth — or hated her — 'Mother, what can we do to help?'

Kate twisted her rings in thought. 'I tell you what, my dear. I'll send him a note to come an' see me presently. I'll say I'm worried about Ruth's health. Even if he wants to keep away, that should bring him. Or he may think it's just an illness she has . . . Wait you an' we'll see.'

Susanna nodded obediently. But she knew — if Frank didn't come, she'd go to him. She couldn't leave him to — to go away from her. Whatever she had to do to get him, she'd do it. Anything at all.

Sal

Frank returned home that week-end so sullen and ill-humoured that after supper his mother called him to task for depressing her again. 'Oh, I'm sorry! Mea culpa, mea m-maxima culpa!' he apologised, trying to hide his misery with a joke.

'Frank!' She blinked at him, in sudden, frowning attention. 'Where did you learn that? It's from the Mass. The truth, if you please, Frank!'

Well, why not? 'Sir F-Francis has commanded me to learn what I can of the Catholic F-Faith, mother. To help me in my work for him.'

'Work? For Walsingham?' Her gaze briefly lost its sharp focus. Frank felt cold. While she was sick, he had often sent the maid away, and told all his news to his mother's unresponsive ear. Could she remember it? What had Phelippes said — never, never discuss Sir Francis's affairs? Oh, Lord!

Lark sat up, neatly erect in her high-backed chair, her hands clasped tight, a curious tension in all her figure. 'Frank, exactly what are you doing for Sir Francis?'

He shrugged, trying to put her off. 'J-just gathering information.'

'About Catholics?'

'Yes, mostly.' She looked deeply troubled. He leaned forward to take her hands. 'I m-must, mother! There's a plot to kill the queen!'

She lifted her hands, and his with them, and gazed into his eyes. 'Frank, my dear — which queen?'

He sighed. 'I know what you mean. Elizabeth or M-Mary. But it has to be done, mother. We must get rid of M-Mary. She's p-planning to escape.'

His mother half smiled. 'Do you blame her? The poor woman has been in prison for over twenty years.'

'But she'll bring back the P-Pope and the Inquisition and burnings again! Sir F-Francis has explained it all to me.'

Lark sighed too, and leaned back. 'In that case, Frank, he has lied.'

'What?' The flat statement shocked him.

Her voice was sadder than he had ever heard it. 'Listen, my dear. When I was younger than you, Frank, I heard all the words you hear now about Catholics; blasphemers, anti-Christ, devil-worshippers. All of that. But then, I heard them from the Cardinal of Lorraine, about Protestants. He was fanatical, as is Sir Francis. Each is so certain of his own rightness, he wants to force the whole world to worship as he does, and loathes anyone who dares differ from him in the slightest. And so, my dear, your Puritan Sir Francis wishes to destroy the Catholic Queen of Scots. Not for what she will do, or has done, but for what he is.'

'No! There is a p-plot against Queen Elizabeth's life, truly —'

His mother grasped his hands again. 'Frank, listen to me. You know that my mother was murdered by Catholics. So you must know that I feel no love for that religion.'

'But M-Mary helped you save the man you loved —'

'I repaid that, long ago. I owe her nothing for that. But, my dearest, there's something you don't know. I've never told a soul, till now. Walsingham must never learn it, for it ties me too close for safety to the Queen of Scots. Swear it, Frank! On your honour!'

She waited till he promised before she went on, picking her words slowly. 'I am known to be a good Protestant. People are aware that I was a Papist when I was young, but since I converted and had to flee for my life, that is forgiven me. Especially since when I was fifteen I was involved —'

He nodded. 'In the Huguenot rebellion against King Francois. And you were caught, and Uncle J-John j-just m-managed to save you f-from being tortured to death. Yes, I know. It used to be my f-favourite story, when I was little.'

She swallowed, distressed even by the memory of those days. 'Yes. But what not a soul knows is that before he could get me away, Queen Mary, King Francois' wife, saw me. She knew that I was one of the heretics, as she saw it, who had rebelled against her husband. She knew, Frank. She should have called her guards, had me arrested and executed like the others, and all my family with me. Indeed, her maid was going to call, but the queen stopped her. For no reason but kindness, goodness, generosity, hatred of torture and bloodshed, she let me go free. I owe her my life.' She sat back and sighed. 'And now, my son is trying to kill her.'

Frank sat for a long time, silent, staring into his clenched hands. His duty to Sir Francis, to Queen Elizabeth, demanded that he must do all he could to bring Queen Mary to the block. But she had saved his mother's life. And he owed even more to his mother than most young men; he had caused the deaths of her three youngest sons, his little brothers, of the plague . . . And Mary didn't even know about Babington's plot . . . At last he raised his head. 'What am I to do? Oh, m-mother, what should I do?'

'I don't know, my dear.' She wiped away a tear. 'I can tell you that though Mary insisted on her right to her own religion, she never tried to force anyone to become Catholic while she was in Scotland. I think, after the horrors she saw in France, she'd never do so herself. If she's involved in a plot now, it's because she's desperate. She wants to go home, Frank! Poor woman! She hasn't seen her son James for twenty years, not since he was a baby. He's just signed a treaty of friendship with Queen Elizabeth, and not a word of his mother's freedom. She must feel — desperate. And Walsingham laying snares for her ... Oh, Frank! If you can help her, in any way, I beg you to try! I beg you!'

She didn't know what she was asking. If Walsingham even suspected Frank had helped Mary, it would certainly mean imprisonment; maybe death. Mentally, Frank shrugged. At the moment, after Ruth's desertion of him, he didn't care. This would make some use of the rest of his life ... He nodded. 'Aye, mother. I swear to you, on my hope of Heaven, I'll try.'

Two days later, he met Jack under Nonsuch House to pay him for carrying the letters to and from Babington. He was sick at heart, and Jack frowned at his white face and drooping shoulders. 'Sir, you eatin' proper? The White Boar by the Steelyards feeds ye far better'n the Three Tuns. Yer that skinny ye could 'ire out as a ramrod.' At Frank's blank stare, he shrugged. Well, he'd tried. ''Ow's the plot goin', eh? Seen Ballard back yestidday. Wot's the word from up north?'

He shouldn't speak of it, but what did it matter? 'Nobody's willing to rise for M-Mary. Sixty thousand ready to rise? Not six hundred. B-Ballard's very down. 'Those who should be most f-forward are most cold,' he says, 'and the older, the colder!' It might just p-peter out.' But not if Mary wrote to encourage them. That would be why Walsingham had sent Gifford; to spur them on ... He sighed, and turned south. 'I'm bid call on Lady B-Bolsiter.' He wasn't looking forward to it.

'Wot, big black Kate?' Jack looked up at the tall lad, worried. He didn't want to go that way, risk meeting that girl, but with Bony looking as if he'd collapse on the cobbles at any moment he'd better give him a shoulder to lean on, just in case. 'See ye over, then.'

He guided Frank, walking rather blindly, among the carts and packhorses that crammed the narrow roadway between the shops on the bridge, and out into the cooler, fresher sunlight again at the Southwark end. 'You needn't w-worry about me,' Frank was reassuring Jack as they threaded their way through the crowded marketplace in Saint Mary Overy churchyard. He pointed to the house. 'I'll be all right. There you are — where are you?'

Jack had vanished.

Frank gaped round him, shuffling in an absurd little dance with a tall woman trying to get past him to a fishmonger's stall. He apologised absently as he got out of her way at last. Oh, well, the lad would turn up again. He crossed the road towards Ruth's house. He could always hope . . . He might be wrong. She might have changed her mind. If only she was less beautiful . . . No, that was blasphemy! Oh, God, Ruth . . .

Sal watched him go. Wasn't that the lad from the Three Cranes? She was almost sure . . . Where was he going? If it was to Kate Bolsiter's . . . It was. Let straight in, too; well known there. Aye, he was the one who had taken Jack and the others away in the boat. What luck she'd come late to market this morning! Who was he? She walked briskly after him, and knocked boldly.

Staring after her from under the fish stall, Jack bit his nails. Thank God he'd seen her first! He should have come down to ground level before. From above he couldn't see her height. And with her hair dyed and her waist padded, even he had scarce known her. No wonder he'd had no word of her. Gor, she was at the Bolsiters' door!

176

A girl was driving half a dozen goats past, belling and bleating. He jumped forward among them. One of the goats leapt up right among the codling, and the girl and the fishmonger both cursed him. He cursed back, his voice high and clear above the racket of the market.

Sal was arguing with Kate's porter. 'Young gennelman as just come in, see, 'e never paid me man fer mendin' 'is saddle fer 'im. Sir John 'Ardacre. Certain sure it were 'im! Well, who is 'e, then?'

The porter was looking past her, grinning, and a well-known voice caught her ear. She whipped round. There he was! Jacky himself! She could grab him — say he was a runaway apprentice! But no. With his friend in this house, and servants at call . . . Best leave it for the moment — and not let Jack see her now, either. Before the doorkeeper had finished chuckling at the lad's flow of oaths, she had raised her shawl round her face again and faded away into the crowd.

Jack, ready to run for his life at any sudden move by Sal, wandered off casually. He expected her to follow him, kept her in the corner of his eye, led her onto London Bridge and vanished again. Oddly, considering how well she'd known him, she never thought to look up. She crossed the bridge, peering into all the shops and along the road, but at last gave up and turned back. She'd find him when she wanted him. She'd ask Kate Bolsiter's servants. Billy would be main pleased.

On his perch on the Stonegate below the traitors' heads on pikes, Jack waited for her return. In his turn, he followed her on the roofs above her, till he lost her as she crossed Barns Street to the Gulley Hole behind St Thomas's Hospital; a dangerous, foul rookery of narrow lanes, knee-deep in rubbish between close-set three and four-storey houses let out in rooms. She could be in any one; she could live there, or be visiting; she could be watching for him out of a window, with a gang of roughs ready to grab him. Better stay clear! He'd find her again, now that he knew what to look for.

Instead, he went back to the Bolsiters' house. He must warn Bony about Sal, and beg him to warn the house folks not to tell anyone about Joe and Jess. And it had to be done now; Sal could come back at any time.

His orange suit, he knew, wasn't fit for the front door; The porter'd kick him right over the road into the Clink. But a side door led to the kitchen, carefully separate in case of fire. He knocked urgently. An elderly man opened, and blocked him with an ungentle arm as he stepped forward. ''Ere, wot d'you want, stinky? Beggars waits outside!' Insulted, Jack started to argue, and was summarily grabbed by the scruff of his neck and the seat of his breeches and heaved out. 'An' don't come back!' As he picked himself up, cursing, the door slammed.

Drat that Bony! If it hadn't been for him and his mother and her soap and clean clothes and all, Jack knew he'd never have been so high-and-mighty, and he'd at least have got a message in. He looked round. What now?

Try the rear. Eight-foot walls, no problem to Jack's clinging fingers and toes, sheltered a long orchard of young apple and pear trees. You couldn't hide behind them, as Jack found when a gardener came out of a shed and chased him. The back door of the kitchen opened and more servants ran out. Gor! Up a tree, the branches bending under his light weight, back onto the wall, they could still reach him with their rakes, run along it to the house jumping the striking staves, scrabble up the brickwork of a corner to swing by a shutter onto a windowsill on the first floor.

He perched there while servants on the paving below him waved and threatened. A skinny old man called up to him in a reedy voice, 'You, boy! Come down at once. You hear me? Come down! You'll not be hurt.'

Jack had heard that before, and stayed where he was, but he leaned out and called back politely. 'Sorry, sir, but

I gotter speak ter —' Gor, what was Bony's name? — 'ter Master Verney. I don't mean no 'arm, honest. But it's important, see? You get the bleeder — er, the young gennelman — fer me, an' I'll be off.'

He was quite right.

In the gallery behind him, Frank had been telling Kate and Susanna about Gilbert Gifford. Not that he was a spy, but that he was quite respectably born, with an uncle a professor at Rheims. He couldn't lie, of course, even to win the lady of his love. Especially to win her. Every word made Kate look happier. Every word hurt more. Susanna sat beside him, holding his hand warmly between her own. He didn't know when she had taken it, but it was a comfort, and he let her keep it.

His curly dark head bent sadly beside Susanna's blonde fall made a pretty picture, Kate thought. He might do very well . . . And it was a relief to know that Ruth wasn't totally a fool. She never trusted really handsome men, though; aye vain and unreliable . . . What in God's name was that din? Kate shoved Balthazar off her lap, stood up and went to see what was happening. Someone on the windowsill? Intrigued, she marched over to the shadow on the glass and rapped briskly.

Jack turned and found himself nose to nose with her black face, hideously distorted by the greenish glass. He jumped in fright. Outwards.

It was only about twelve feet, and he was already turning in the air as he left the sill, ready to land relaxed and roll, but a couple of the men tried to catch him. They succeeded in knocking him off balance. He still managed to land on his feet, but askew. One ankle twisted under him, and he crashed down with a yell.

Kate, shoving up the window sash and leaning far out above him, was furious with herself. 'I've less sense nor a wet hen, to startle the lad so, an' you mislushious gomerils cryin' after him! A thief, ye thought? Ye canna think, ye lurdens! He was askin' for Master Verney. I heard him mysel'! Whit's wrong wi' him? His ankle? An' his arm? Broken? In the name o' the Wee Man! Ye hochlin' hempies! Fetch him up here. Master Slim, a pint o' eau-de-vie, an' call a bone-setter. Gently, ye glaikit sumphs!' She hauled herself angrily back inside, and smoothed her satins and herself back to calm. 'Frank, you've a visitor. An' we've half-killed him for you.'

Jack was carried in by the men who had tried so disastrously to help him. He felt quite sick, his pains aggravated by humiliation at making a fool of himself again in front of these women. Amid her concern, Susanna laughed. 'It's your theatrical young friend again, Frank.' Frank flushed. Both lads thought, 'Bitch!'

Whenever Kate was angry enough to use Scots insults that her servants didn't understand, everything moved fast. A bonesetter arrived within five minutes, and there was an unpleasant little episode while he felt Jack's ankle, reassured them that it wasn't broken, only sprained, but the left arm was, pressed the cracked bone into place, splinted and strapped . . . Jack held Frank's hand, swore through clenched teeth and screamed as little as he could. But at last it was over. The bonesetter bowed himself out, well pleased with his fee, and Jack could lie back on the settle where they had laid him, white and shaky, his arm in a sling and his left foot firmly bandaged, and tell them what it was all about.

Unsurprisingly, they got on well together. Jack's nervousness melted under Kate's warmth and Susanna's kindness — and a small glass of brandy. Frank's confusion of emotions at least took his mind off Ruth. He was relieved, and even cheered, as Kate and Susanna asked no awkward questions.

'Never fear, Jack,' Susanna assured the anxious lad. 'We'll help you. The porter knows his duty, not to speak of who's in the house. But we'll warn him to be even more careful.'

Kate nodded. 'An' I'll ask my friends to seek me out

this Ivory Sal. It'll no be easy, mind! There's a hundred thousand folk lives in London an' round about, an' it may be weeks afore I can get news o' her.'

Frank was frowning. 'Why not ask the sheriff to seek her?'

Jack sighed, and exchanged a glance with Kate. Frank might be older in years, but in experience he was a babe in arms. 'This ain't Lunnon, sir. Liberty o' Southwark!'

'Aye, every rogue in the kingdom's safe here, if he pays his dues quiet-like to the sheriff.' Kate's voice was scathing.

'That's true, Frank,' Susanna agreed. 'And then, do you honestly wish the law to pay attention to you? And Jack?'

Her mother nodded. 'Sir Francis might no be best pleased.'

Frank's jaw dropped. 'Sir F-Francis?' He tried to cover his shock. 'Why — what Sir F-Francis?' To hide her smile at his appalled face, Susanna bent her head over the cat jumping up to settle on her lap as usual.

Kate smiled forgivingly, 'Frank, lad, I wasn't born yesterday. An' I have friends. A wee word here and there, an' it's astonishin' what you can find out, an' none notice it. It's as well I'm no in Spanish pay, eh?'

He rubbed his chin in dismay. 'But —'

Susanna laid a hand on his arm. 'We'll not betray you, Frank.'

He eyed their smiles doubtfully. He glanced down at Jack, who shrugged incautiously and winced. 'Can't do nowt about it. Just pray as they 'olds their tongues.' He sniffed. 'Be the first women ever could.'

Kate threatened him with a jesting fist. 'You think I've never had a secret to keep afore? Safe as the Tower, lad!' She smoothed her ruby satins complacently.

Frank sighed. 'Half London seems to know.'

'Not at all! Only me. Or am I half London?'

Susanna couldn't resist it. 'Only in size, mother!'

Kate made a face at her. 'Besom! I'll teach you to mock your mother!'

Jack yelped at the twinge in his arm, as he couldn't help joining the laughter. 'Don't look like ye needs ter, missus!'

That caused another laugh, till Kate sat back more soberly. 'Never fear, Frank. We'll no tell. But I carry a certain weight round here — and we'll have no comments from you, my laddie!' Jack, his eye on her massive bulk, couldn't help snorting with stifled laughter again. She bent a glare of mock anger at him over her chins. 'Impudence! It's my friends among the wild lads here that are our best chance o' findin' your Ivory Sal.'

Jack grimaced. 'Not mine, missus! An' you tell 'em ter be right careful. Seen Sal bend a 'alf-inch iron bar wiv 'er bare 'ands.'

'That's true, Lady Kate. I've seen Billy and Tom f-fight, and if their mother's like them —'

'Sight worser, she is!'

'Yes, well. It could be dangerous for you if J-Jack stays here. I'll carry him home with me.'

Jack shrugged. He'd see Jess for a while, anyway.

Kate, however, had other ideas. 'What! A friend o' mine sent away for fear o' some harridan?' Jack's jaw dropped. Him? Lady Kate's friend?

'Never in life!' Susanna was as insulted as her mother.

Frank felt a fool. 'I beg your p-pardon. I m-merely thought to spare you trouble.' They sniffed. 'Then what have you in m-mind?'

Kate smiled, forgiving him. 'Jack'll no set foot to the ground for a good while.' Jack sighed. It was just what he'd been thinking. Kate chuckled at the look on his face. 'He'll stay here wi' us until he can walk wi' fair ease. Two or three weeks, maybe. Then you can take him home.'

Gor! 'I'll not see Jess an' Joe — Oh, well.' But the fat woman was jolly enough; it might not be so bad.

Susanna leaned forward to suggest, 'Do visit him

182

whenever you please, Frank.' That gave him a reason to call. Another idea. 'You can bring the little girl to visit Jack. Or maybe your mother might . . .'

Kate agreed heartily. 'Well thought on, lass! I've been meanin' to ask her to visit, Frank, since you said she was recovered. Let her choose any day, an' spend a while in the shops on the Bridge if she pleases, an' then rest here an hour or several, or the night if she's over tired. She'll be more than welcome.' Susanna almost purred like the cat on her lap. Her mother always seemed to know what she was thinking these days . . . Kate raised an eyebrow. 'Unless you think we're no respectable enough for her?'

'Oh, no! I never dreamed —' Frank was expostulating, when he saw the gleam in their eyes, and puffed in exasperation. 'Oh, you're p-pulling my leg again! Lady Kate, I'll — I'll get my own b-back on you! Soon!'

Susanna laughed. 'You'll need to rise early, then, Frank,' she warned him. 'There's few as fly as my mother.'

Kate blew her a kiss, as Frank asked, puzzled, 'F-fly?'

'Clever,' she explained. 'Sharp-witted, hard to catch.'

'Hard to catch? It depends how high she's been f-flying.'

The door swung open on their applause and laughter. Ruth stalked into the parlour. She looked round suspiciously. 'Frank!' Her tone was less than welcoming. 'What are you all laughing at behind my back? Me, I'll warrant you!' She didn't know what to do. Gilbert wasn't interested in her . . . In her! The belle of London! With all her charm and beauty lavishly displayed on the way to Whitehall, he'd shown no sign of more than manners. And she loved him so much; why didn't he want her? They had no right to laugh, when she was so wretched. She almost sobbed in frustration and distress.

Kate raised a hand to quiet her. 'Ruth, Frank says Master Gifford —'

She gasped in outrage. They had been discussing her! And him! 'And what's so comical, may I ask? There's naught wrong with him!' She didn't care that he wasn't an earl! 'God's belly, I'll swear Frank's telling you a pack of lies about him, from sheer jealousy!'

Frank's jaw dropped. Susanna kept a demure face, cheering internally. Go right ahead, Ruth! Open your mouth and jump right in! But Kate, her eyes snapping in anger, was smiling acidly. 'No, lass. A fine young man, respectable, gentle born. An estate in Yorkshire, he tells me.' Ruth's jaw dropped. 'We'll invite you an' him over for supper some day, Frank, when your laddie's feelin' better.'

'Laddie — I mean lad? What lad?' Ruth was totally confused. 'What has this to do with Gil — Master Gifford? Do you mean that filthy beggar ragamuffin? Why on God's earth are you still involved with him?'

Frank hesitated, embarrassed by her spite. Jack, hidden behind the high back of the settle, winked up at Susanna, who answered for her friend. 'Kindness, Ruth. Goodness of heart. Generosity. You've heard of them?'

Ruth snorted. 'For one of your own rank, certainly. But to a pauper?'

'Oy, missus, be fair! I may pong a bit, but I doesn't pop!' Jack protested loudly. As Ruth jumped and squeaked, he looked thoughtful. 'Not unless I've ate too much beans, anyway!'

Susanna started to gurgle with laughter. Jack grinned. After a moment, Frank had to laugh too. He suddenly felt as if a weight had dropped from his neck.

Shrieking, Ruth exploded in rage. 'You disgusting, stinking —'

Her mother's hand smacked across her face. 'Mistress! Mind your tongue!' Kate's face was grim. 'The lad's a guest in my house.'

Stopped in mid-screech, Ruth stared. Her lip trembled, and she burst into tears. 'God damn you all!' she screamed, swung round and ran out and along the corridor to her room, her cork heels clacking like a drum-roll.

At Frank's horrified face, a broad grin of satisfaction spread through Susanna's mind. She bit the inside of her cheeks to stop it escaping. Don't spoil it . . . Poor Ruth! How humiliating for her!

Kate, carefully ignoring her elder daughter's behaviour, rang for her steward. 'Master Slim, you'll instruct all the servants, if you please, that Master Verney has unfriends who may seek word of him or the lad here. No information about them is to be given to any inquirer at all, in or outside this house, an' you'll tell me of any questions. Anyone askin' for them at the door is to be brought up to see me at once, an' the menservants warned, just in case they're rough.' She smiled reassuringly. 'I doubt any real trouble will occur. But it's as well to be prepared.'

He seemed to expand, drawing himself up to his full skinny five feet three inches. 'Trouble? I'd like to see it, my lady! We'll be fit for the villains! I'll have pistols laid ready, as well as the porter's cudgel, and a couple of men in the hall. Be easy, my lady, there's no rapscallion will harm you nor Master Verney in this house, no, nor yet a soul will say a word about him, I'll take my bounden oath on it!' He bustled out in a pleasurable flurry of excitement.

Susanna laughed in astonishment. 'Well! "Ha, ha! he sayeth amid the trumpets!" Who'd have thought it?'

Her mother was touched. 'If wishes were horses, he'd be out on a white charger, eh? But we're safe enough now.'

Jack was carried upstairs and settled into a maid's bedroom not far from Susanna's own, whitewashed starkly clean, with a red blanket and a feather quilt, and a bright window looking out north over the woods to the Thames. He was depressed. 'More soap, I s'pose,' he complained to Frank. 'An' more new clobber. I got that much, wiv wot's up in the Plumbers' 'All as well, as I can't get at. I'll be startin' me own flea market.' He sighed deeply. 'Oh well. No 'elp fer it. 'S on'y fer a week or two.'

Elizabeth

Frank was relieved, upset, glad, depressed, at losing Ruth.
No, at losing his love for Ruth. He quite understood,
usually, that she wasn't the ideal goddess of his dreams.
But he missed the dreaming . . .

Anyway, he was still involved with the Enterprise. How
could he make sure Elizabeth was not murdered by John
Savage, and at the same time save the Scottish Queen and
his foolish friends?

Since the letter from Queen Mary had come — 'my
dear friend'! What an honour! — Tony was going round
in a perfect halo of heroism, even ordering portraits to
be painted of all the plotters. 'It's only right, Frank, that
those who risk all for their faith and their queen should
be recorded for posterity!' Idiot!

Frank couldn't just warn Tony straight out; Walsingham would be certain to find out. The best he could
do for the moment was hint that they were betrayed;
there were whispers round the Treasury! Better stop! To
Frank's astonishment, instead of either giving up or going
ahead quietly, Babington requested another meeting with
Walsingham.

He returned biting his knuckles, to pounce on Frank and Ballard who were awaiting him anxiously in his lodgings. 'Oh, Frank! You were right! Oh, Father! I thought to discover what he knew, and he knows! About our plans! About the Enterprise! Not the details, no, but that there is something! And that I am involved! He knows! But if I confide in him, Frank, he offers absolute secrecy, total confidence. I said naught, of course! I could not, without betraying you, and all of us. But he knows!'

Ballard poured scorn on his fears. 'Whatever he may suspect, he knows nothing, or he'd have arrested us! No, no, this is a common trick to entice the unwary to confess. Be calm, my son! Go to Litchfield next week, as you planned, for the Queen of Scots' letter. Then all will be settled.'

Babington agreed. Frank shrugged. But he wondered; why on earth had Walsingham risked warning Tony, by revealing his suspicions?

Babington was away for several days, leaving Frank time to relax and visit Jack and Susanna. Not Ruth; not now.

Jack was in high fettle. He and Kate, opposites in size, were mentally two of a kind, and Susanna informed Frank that his young friend was the most popular person in the house. 'We haven't laughed as much for months! He's been bathed, Ruth insisted, and you should have heard the maids shrieking as they scrubbed him! Peg won't tell me what he said, she says it wasn't fit for a well-brought-up young lady's ears.' She made a face of disappointment, to make him laugh. 'I heard him when he discovered Ruth had burned that hideous orange suit, though. My vocabulary expanded enormously! I keep sending him up to his room to rest his foot, but I always find him in the kitchen or the buttery. He'll be getting fat!'

She ushered Frank into the parlour. Ruth was seated by the window, gazing out down the road. She scarcely took the time to return Frank's bow — no more than polite,

187

as Susanna noted with satisfaction — before demanding, 'Have you seen him? Gilbert — Master Gifford?'

'Yes, mistress. This m-morning. He said he called on you yesterday.'

Kate nodded. 'Aye. For ten minutes, just. A courtesy call. At least we found out what he does and where he lives. He's a messenger for the Treasury, bearin' writs an' letters all over. An' he lodges with a clerk called Phelippes.' Frank nearly choked.

'Mother invited him to supper, but he'd not stay.' Ruth was trying to hide her anguish, but she'd had less practice than Susanna. Frank felt sorry for her. He knew how she felt. 'Did he speak of — of us?' She meant, 'of me'. 'When might we see him again, do you know, Frank?'

Reluctantly, he had to tell her. 'He said naught of you, I f-fear, Ruth. He's going away. In a f-few days. Abroad. To F-France.'

'France? He'll be killed! I'll never see him again!' Her lovely face crumpled. She sobbed once, in anger and distress, and ran out.

Kate and Jack were at the table. She sighed and shook her head over her daughter, while Jack started struggling to his feet from the settle. Frank waved him back. 'Sit still, J-Jack! Your servant, Lady Kate.' Don't talk about Ruth, not yet; let things cool a little. 'You're looking v-very smart, Jack!' The dark grey suit wouldn't be much to his taste, but at least his hair was clean, if it wasn't smooth, and probably never would be.

'Quite perjink,' Kate nodded.

Jack sniffed disdainfully. 'I likes a bit o' colour! 'Eard about me good suit? Huh! Top-notch, it were. Could've went ter see the queen in it.'

Frank had to laugh again. 'Yes, you'll m-miss those f-fleas!'

Jack pretended to glower. 'Just you wait till I can get me clobber from the Plumber's 'All. Then ye'll see summat!'

Susanna exchanged a glance with Kate, who nodded.

'Jack,' she said tentatively, 'I'm afraid I've bad news for you. They're rebuilding the Plumbers' Hall. And when they took off the roof, they found your hoard. I'm sorry. They don't know whose it was, of course, but it's all gone.'

Jack swore vividly enough to make even Kate blink. Then he shrugged. 'Oh, well. Just 'ave ter start again.'

Hastily, Frank changed the subject. 'What's that you've got? Cards? A beautiful p-pack, Lady Kate. What are you p-playing?'

'Whisk. He's a quick learner, this lad!' Kate praised him.

''Course! Gotter be quick in the Vintry!' Jack boasted. ''Ere, Lady Katie, can you play Snap? Come on, it's more fun nor this!'

It was certainly noisier. They played for sugared almonds. The excitement mounted, in happy argument, protest and insults, to climax when 'Snap!' Susanna screeched, slamming her hand down on the table to claim the last cards. 'I've won! I've won all the almonds! Mine, mine, all mine!' She rolled her eyes at them. 'I've beaten you all!'

'You've burst all your hooks, too,' Kate pointed out, chuckling.

Frank was almost sobbing with laughter. 'Right down your bodice. I can see your shift! Shameless hussy!'

She twisted, giggling, to examine the puff of soft linen in the gap under her arm. 'Oh, God amend all! I'll have to change. Now, Jack, you keep your thieving fingers off my almonds while I'm away!' She danced gaily off.

Jack winked at Kate. 'Fingers, she said!' He used his thumbs to fish a couple of pink sweets out of the dish before he lay back on the bright cushions to rest, his arm and ankle aching but his mouth happily occupied.

Frank murmured to Kate, 'Ruth's still — er —'

'Besotted? Aye.' She wasn't unsympathetic, to her daughter or to him, but as brisk as always. 'Half the time she's useless, an' the other half unbearable. About the same as usual, eh? I thought little o' Gifford, I'll tell you true. A right waste o' fresh air.' She sniffed. 'See my wee mirror by the door there? He was aye keekin' in it, like a lassie. I never did trust beautiful men.' She shrugged, with a deep chuckle. 'An' ugly ones are little better!' Ruth had again tried to make her mother increase her dowry, but that wasn't something you told outsiders. 'Do you play Whisk, Frank? Then come an' make a four with us when Susanna returns.' She turned back to the table. 'Well, you rogue, can you mind on the order o' trumps?'

Jack crowed in triumph. ''Course! Cor, peak, demon an' dreadful.'

'Coeur, pique, diamant an' trefle. French. But you're close enough, lad. Come away in, Susanna. My, you've been quick. That green suits you.'

'Yes, indeed,' Frank agreed. Susanna blushed, delighted by the appreciation in his eyes and tone.

Kate smiled. 'Will you cut for partners, Frank?'

It was a good afternoon, for Frank. And Susanna. And for Ruth, who found a sympathetic kitchen lass who'd let her slip unseen out of the scullery door for a shilling.

Babington returned to London on the sixteenth with a letter from Mary's secretary, promising a letter in her own hand in a few more days. He was frustrated at the fresh delay, but relieved too. Knowing Walsingham's impatience, Frank felt an itch in his mind. Something must happen soon!

On the morning of the twentieth of July, it did.

A messenger summoned Frank urgently to Phelippes's office. Had Mary written? Had Savage — dreadful thought — gone ahead alone? He raced up the stairs and burst into the room to find the little man in his best green doublet, laying documents in a flat leather case. 'Come along, Master Verney! Fine feathers on an early worm, as usual, I'm happy to see. Make haste while the Devil drives!' He hurried Frank down to the Whitehall stairs, where a four-oared skiff was lying. 'Get in, get in! Shove off, boatman!' He sucked his teeth. 'Mustn't keep Her Majesty waiting!'

Frank, not yet seated, nearly fell overboard as the boat shot out from the steps. 'Her M-Majesty? You mean we're going to see —'

'Indeed, sir. Queen Elizabeth herself summons us to Greenwich Palace!'

Though it was a falling tide, they didn't wait to change boats at London Bridge. Phelippes, clinging to his hat as they shot the dangerous eddies like rapids, was more expansive than usual. 'Nervous, young sir? Sir Francis is as bad. Unsettled, Master Verney! Unsteady, Master Verney! He sees the apple of his heart almost within his snare, and quails lest it miscarry. Mary might not write. The letter might go astray. His belly is gnawed by horrible imaginings! He thought to double assurance by persuading Babington to turn Queen's Evidence.' He smiled like a weasel. 'He'd lose a knight to take a queen. For without sufficient proof of Mary's complicity, Her Majesty will never act. Huh! She is reluctant even with proof, she so mislikes the idea. But all goes swimmingly, and we will show them Mary's head at a window, as they did to the Admiral of France! Fear not!'

Frank was far from fear. Amid his excitement at going to see the queen — why couldn't they have warned him, he'd have put on his good blue suit, not this brown one! — his heart was racing for another reason entirely. If the letter went missing, Walsingham himself thought there would be no evidence, and Mary would be safe. And he could get it from Babington! He coughed. 'You say all is well, Master Ph-Phelippes. Has Mary written?'

Phelippes tapped the case meaningfully. 'Here, Master Verney! I told Sir Francis, when that note came from her secretary to Babington, that we should have her very heart in the next letter; and here it is! After all these years of discretion, at last she has taken the fatal step too far!'

Frank looked at it longingly. But he'd never get away with stealing it now ... Besides, he was going to see the queen!

At Greenwich Palace steps an impatient usher beckoned. 'Her Majesty awaits!' They were whisked through corridors and anterooms without a single delay. 'Her Majesty awaits!' Doors sprang open before them. Servants and guards in red and black, rainbow courtiers, stood aside. 'Her Majesty awaits!' Frank, dazzled and dazed, had only a vague impression of marble and magnificence before he was stopped suddenly at a last door.

Walsingham himself was waiting for them, in full court dress; doublet and trunks of heavy pewter-grey silk trimmed with jet bugle beads, and a vermilion lining to his short, stiff grey cloak. Inspecting Frank and Phelippes, he nodded. 'Very well. You look workmanlike, not like courtiers — but then you are not.' His thin smile held no friendliness, no humour. He smoothed his short beard over his ruff. 'Master Verney, you will remain silent, save to reply directly to a question. Not a single volunteer word.' Frank nodded dumbly. He would no more have argued with his master at that moment than with a cannon.

At Walsingham's gesture to the guards, the door was flung open. They all three bowed.

A smallish room, panelled in walnut. Queen Elizabeth was standing by the window, two pretty ladies-in-waiting behind her. On her right a bejewelled dandy, rather past his best, in plump fawn silks and jowls, nodded greeting to Walsingham; Robert Dudley, Earl of Leicester, who had come near to marrying the queen ten years before. Now her Master of Horse, responsible for her safety, he strove for first place in her counsel with the other man present, old Robert Cecil, Lord Burghley, honoured by being allowed to sit in the queen's presence, warmly wrapped in violet velvet gown and cap despite the summer heat.

Elizabeth herself was taller than Frank had expected. He knew she was over fifty, but her fine bones and clever painting made her look young. Crystals and silver sequins edged her high-arching collar and lace ruff and glinted on the panels of her stiffly upholstered white taffetas, stretched over a wide farthingale, with a silver under-dress. Every inch, from the pearls on her silver slippers to those looped in her high-piled red hair, was rigid with outrage. 'It is more than enough!' Her white peacock feather fan was tapping, hard enough to break its ivory stem, on the back of a gilded chair. 'These twenty years I have held off from ridding myself of her, for it is not the business of princes to be killing each other. Yet still she wills my death.' She turned a snapping glare on Walsingham. 'Or so I am told. Well? Is this your proof at last?'

Walsingham motioned Phelippes forward. The little man, sniffing ecstatically, knelt to offer his papers to the queen, who looked at him and them as if they were dirty, and gestured imperiously. 'Burghley!'

There were two documents. One, cramped, folded small, in cipher. And another, the translation. Burghley read it out slowly, as if reluctantly.

Mary urged speed and close organisation. They must know exact numbers of horse and foot, assembly points, what foreign forces and arms they would need. They should pretend their preparations were only for defence against the Puritans, who had recently attacked Catholic houses.

Burghley nodded; it was true enough.

Mary asked how the six gentlemen planned to proceed; how they would free her; all should be in readiness, and several messengers sent to her rescuers as soon as the said design should be executed, to be sure to get her away before Paulet her jailer learned of it. The Spanish

Ambassador must be told that even if all went wrong and she was shut up in the Tower, the enterprise was to go ahead, and she would die happy. The Catholics of Scotland must try to seize her son, James; risings should be encouraged in Ireland. The Earls of Arundel, Northumberland and Westmoreland, and Lord Paget would help, she was certain.

Leicester bristled. The queen's raised finger quieted him.

They must be careful of spies.

Elizabeth snorted.

Mary suggested plans for her rescue; attack her lightly-armed guard when she was allowed out to walk on the moors; or fire the stables at night and attack in the confusion; or jam the gate open with a delivery cart —

'Enough!' Elizabeth snapped her fingers like a boy for the letters and sat to read them herself. She tapped the original with a long finger. 'What is this on the outside sheet? A drawing of a gallows?'

Phelippes went bright pink. He cleared his throat. 'My work, Your Majesty, I fear. When I read it, I was so happy I — er — marked it.' He smirked apologetically. She sniffed, sounding very like him, and lowered her gaze to the papers.

While she studied them, Frank was surprised to hear Leicester's drawl, praising Mary. 'Hmph! The woman can organise. She'd match any general.' Burghley glanced at him, humming gently, with a slight smile. Leicester had just made a complete chaos as general of an army against the Spanish in the Netherlands. He spoke quickly to cover his annoyance. 'She wishes to escape. Only natural.'

Burghley agreed. 'Saving this of the invasion, which is scarce under her control, Master Secretary, and of which you have amply warned us, what is in this more than in a dozen other letters she has written before? H'm?'

Walsingham bowed like a fencer saluting his opponent. 'My lord, she speaks of the "enterprise", and the "said

194

design". This is an actual, present plan to murder Her Majesty.'

Leicester swore vividly. 'We must put an end to this Jezebel!'

'It is my constant ambition, my lord.'

'H'm. As we know. H'm. There is naught here to say exactly what is meant.' Though old and unwell, Burghley was Elizabeth's most experienced, trusted adviser, wary, hard to impress, impossible to overawe. Strongly Protestant himself, he still distrusted Walsingham's religious fanaticism.

'I have proof, my lord.' Walsingham gestured to Frank. 'This young man is in my service. He joined the plot at my personal request and at grave risk to himself, to become privy to the secrets of these "six gentlemen".' Frank, flushing at their keen regard, forced himself to bow.

An imperious finger beckoned him forward to kneel before Elizabeth's chair. Hard black eyes studied him suspiciously. 'Your name, boy?'

Walsingham coughed discreetly. 'Madam, may I suggest that it might be wiser to allow him to remain anonymous?'

'You may not.' Her tone was cold. 'I must know with whom I deal. Look at me, boy. Tell me your name. Verney? Very well. You will speak me the truth, Master Verney. I, your queen, require it of you. Are you a gentleman of honour, sir, or bribed, or one of Master Secretary's slaves, speaking words put into your mouth by force or guile? Speak freely. Do not fear him; I shall protect you. But if you lie to me, I shall destroy you utterly. Now, sir; the truth! Is there indeed a plot to kill me?'

Walsingham tensed; he hadn't realised his mistress knew so well how he gained his results. By the Grace of the Lord he hadn't threatened or bribed the boy; any hint of it now would ruin his plans. Had guile been enough?

Frank hesitated. Mary . . . Tony . . . But his queen, his

own queen, demanded truth. And it was true, after all. 'Yes, Your M-Majesty.'

She almost snarled. 'And she — my cousin of Scotland — she knows of it? It is what she refers to here as the "said design"? Oh, God!'

Leicester laid a white hand, heavy with rings, on his sword hilt. 'Fear naught, madam! Your loyal servants will protect you with their lives, though a thousand demonic plots threaten you!'

She glanced at him, irritation lifting her spirits from fear. 'Tchah! They'd better!' With a twist of her lips, she held out a shaking hand to Walsingham, who bowed his dark head to kiss it. 'My faithful servant. All these years, you have urged me to eradicate this constant menace, and I withstood you, but now you have my fullest support! Do whatever you must!'

Burghley cleared his throat. 'Within the law, Your Majesty. H'm. Always within the law, or you encourage others to break it.'

She snorted in irritation. 'Does she observe the law? But yes, I know you're right. I'll give her justice. More than she wants, I'll warrant you! And all of them!' Frank was about to speak, but a scorching glare from Walsingham closed his mouth again. The queen tapped his shoulder. 'Master Varney, you know the plotters? Their names, sir!' She nodded at some, crimsoned with rage as he named the Gentlemen Pensioners. 'God's death! I'll have their heads! Yes, yes, Burghley! Legally! I know!' She rapped her fan on the arm of the chair. 'For complete conviction — God's death, you'd think I was jesting — we need more than your word, young man. Not that I doubt you, but others may. And there may be more that you do not know. Sir Francis, is there room on that paper to add a post-scriptum? To ask for the names of these six gentlemen? It is, after all, what Mary might well demand, and will add to the weight of evidence.'

Phelippes looked doubtful. 'It may be possible, Your Majesty.'

'You can forge her writing?'

'Of course.' He was surprised.

She leaned forward, suddenly piercing sharp. 'Did you forge this?'

He blinked and stammered, like Frank. 'N-no, madam! Certainly not! N-never for your eyes!' She sat back, apparently satisfied by his fright. He coughed nervously. 'I meant merely that there is little space.'

'Do it, sir,' the queen ordered him firmly. 'I must know whom I cannot trust. And as I am most nearly concerned, I have a right to have my mind set fully at rest.'

'Will this not mean more delay, madam?' Leicester demurred. 'We could arrest them all today, with this letter. But awaiting Babington's reply, every day means an unnecessary risk for you.'

She banged a fist down on the arm of her chair. Her fan snapped. 'Will you argue with me, sirrah?'

He bowed obedience. 'It is merely my love that speaks, madam!'

At once she softened. 'Robin, I trust you to keep me safe.'

He bowed again, with a flourish, still disapproving but accepting her decision. 'With my life, madam!'

She noticed her broken fan in annoyance, and tossed it aside. 'Master Varley, what is the latest of the plot?'

Frank cleared his throat. 'B-Babington is uneasy, madam. Since the letter from Queen M-Mary is delayed, Gifford is to go to P-Paris, to get written authority from there, and f-f-find out exactly what Spain will do. They m-meet daily, to discuss f-f-future p-plans.' God damn this stammer!

Walsingham took over the tale. 'Kidnapping Your Majesty, or burning Your Majesty's ships in the Thames, are proposed. Also the deaths of some of the Privy Council. Myself, of course, as I am known to be so strong against Catholics.' Burghley tut-tutted in disapproving sympathy.

'And Lord Burghley, and my lord of Leicester.' Leicester bristled. Burghley shook his head gently. 'One Barnwell was at Court last week at Richmond. He told them that he had seen Your Majesty walking in the garden with only a few unarmed gentlemen about you, open to attack. The news was received with glee.'

Frank opened his mouth again; it hadn't been just like that . . . but Walsingham was watching him. He shut up.

Elizabeth finally dismissed them. 'You will take what steps are necessary, Master Secretary, for my safety. As soon as the evidence has been gathered, we will set in motion the trial of Queen Mary.' Walsingham bowed in satisfaction. She turned to Frank, and held out her hand. 'I thank you, Master Varrey, for your efforts on my behalf. You will not find me ungrateful. And the gratitude of queens is worth having.' He kissed the gem-encrusted fingers reverently, and withdrew with the others.

Walsingham glanced down at him outside the door. 'Do not presume too much on the promise, young man. Princes, like plain folk, dislike having to pay their debts.' Phelippes sniffed agreement. 'Well done, Master Verney. In spite of our sovereign lady changing her mind like a weather-cock, this time I believe we may hope for an end to that bosom serpent at last.'

'What of the letter, sir?' Phelippes asked.

Walsingham pondered. 'H'm. We need it as evidence, but Mary says in it that Babington should burn it. You will, of course, add to it the question that Her Majesty ordered. But then, Phelippes, we will keep it safe.'

Frank, waking from his glory — he'd kissed the queen's hand! — was dismayed. 'Sir, I could easily get the letter from B-Babington.'

'No, we'll not risk it.' They walked out into the gardens, among the fantastical topiary and carved wooden trellises. Walsingham bowed slightly to return smiling greetings from men and women passing them, bright as the peacocks on the lawns in silk and lace, silver and gold, padding, embroidery, slashed sleeves, wide ruffs and farthingales. Where normally Frank would have been in a whirl of delight, now he paid them little heed. He rubbed his chin. He couldn't steal the letter now. Steal . . . Jack . . .

'Make a full copy, with the queen's addition, to give to Babington. Then he may burn it, and welcome! And ask also who besides these "six gentlemen" is privy to the plot, and exactly how they are to proceed. We must make all possible profit from this letter, and his reply.'

Phelippes sucked approval. 'Kill two birds in the one bush, yes, sir!'

Walsingham laughed, happier than Frank had ever seen him since the day in his office in Whitehall when the plot had started to take shape. 'Master Verney, keep good watch on my birds!' Smiling in anticipation of triumph he stood on the river bank to see them off, dark and keen as a Tower raven.

All the way back upriver Phelippes gloatingly planned exactly what to say. 'It may be I shall be able upon further knowledge of the parties, to give you advice, some further advice . . . What think you, Master Verney?'

'What? Oh, excellent, Master Ph-Phelippes.' Frank's thoughts were on Jack. How soon would he be well enough, to set a jackdaw against a raven?

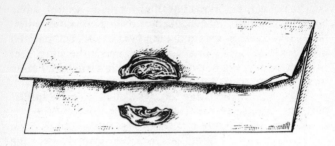

Plans and Plots

Frank called on Jack that evening, arriving amid another row. Hearing the din, he turned at the door to leave, but Susanna, keeping out of it as usual, had caught his voice and ran down the stair to greet him. 'Oh, Frank! I'm so sorry, but you've come at a bad time. They're at it again. Mother and Ruth.' She sighed, looking so weary that he took her hand and drew her to sit on a bench in the cool shadows of the hall.

'Don't f-fret, my dear,' he told her gently. 'You can't help it. Would you p-prefer me to go?'

She gripped his hand in alarm. 'No! Not that!' What had he called her? She must have imagined it. 'You — you came to see Jack, didn't you? I fear he's in the kitchen as usual. Master Slim, call someone to carry Jack up to his room again, and hot and cold water for his foot.'

'Are they arguing about him?' Frank asked as they climbed the stair past the angry voices snapping from Ruth's bedroom.

Susanna laughed, with an effort. 'No, no. Not at all. In here. Listen to the giggles; he's got a maid to carry him up!'

If she didn't want to tell him, he could scarcely ask again. 'Hello, J-Jack! Keeping the house cheerful, eh?'

The lad was sat on the bed, his foot up on a stool, while another maid brought in buckets of hot and cold water. He was pleased to see Frank, but Frank was disappointed by his news. 'Arm's fine, sir, scarce needs the sling, see! Ain't strong, mind, not yet. But me ankle's still bad. Funny that, eh? Gor, wait till ye sees it!'

'Well, you won't stay off it! What d'you expect?' Susanna scolded, carefully unwrapping the bandages.

'Yah! Sittin' still ain't no fun!' He displayed his ankle with gloomy relish. 'See! Bleedin' rainbow! An' swole like a football!' It was a deep mauve bulge with black, brown and yellow blotches, from his toes half up to his calf. He could ease his toes up and down a little, but trying to angle his foot sideways at all was still painful.

Susanna fomented the foot, making him plunge it into the hot and cold buckets alternately, in spite of his exaggerated complaints. 'Gor! Tryin' ter cure me or kill me, Missus Susan?' he moaned.

Rewinding the linen bandages, she made a face at him. 'Big baby! Gaudy, isn't it, Frank? But it's not as swollen as it was yesterday. It is getting better, honestly! Just keep off it, Jack, you hear me? I'll have somebody bring you down to the parlour in a while.'

'Arter the row's finished?' He grinned impishly at her and winked at Frank. 'Never mind shushin' me! Mistress 'Oity-toity's been slippin' out ter see 'er fancy-lad. Got caught comin' in, an' ain't she just 'earin' about it! Been at it fer hours, on an' off.'

Failing to keep him quiet, Susanna shrugged and admitted it unhappily. 'She bribed a scullery-maid to let her in and out by the kitchen door. She'll not say how often, and the girl's run away. But it must have been several times, Frank. Oh, dear!' She sighed deeply. 'I always thought I'd be glad to see Ruth fall in love with a man who didn't love her, get back some of what she's given to other people. But

201

it's making her so miserable, Frank, and causing so much trouble — I'm sorry she ever met that man!'

'I'm n-not.'

There was a second's pause. Jack looked at him in puzzlement. Then Frank blushed scarlet. Susanna's cheeks, after a moment, matched his. Jack's surprise vanished as he looked from one to the other. He opened his mouth to yell in delighted mockery, as he'd have done in the Vintry; and then bit his lips and kept considerately quiet, his eyes dancing.

The talk was rather formal for the rest of the visit. 'Has Lady Alice decided when she'd like to visit Jack here, Master Frank?'

'Er — on Thursday next, Mistress Susanna, if that will be convenient?'

'Of course, sir.'

'She p-plans to leave home at about seven o'clock. That will allow her f-four hours to v-visit merchants, and then if it p-pleases you, she can come here at about noon.'

Susanna assented, rather absently. Her mind was on other things. She was sorry Jack was there. No, she was glad he was there. Oh, she didn't know what she felt, except that it was wonderful! 'We'll expect her about noon, then, Frank — er, Master Frank. Will — will you be with her? Oh, good! I mean — er — I shall look forward to it.'

But Lady Alice didn't visit on Thursday. Because the next day, as he had planned with Babington, Gilbert Gifford left for Paris.

And, as had been planned only with him, Ruth and her mother's biggest jewel-box left with him.

After her first earth-shaking fury, when she'd vented her rage by chasing off all her gushingly over-sympathetic visitors — 'lang-nebbit, ill-faured carline hags!' — and had had a day or two of thunderous silence to reflect, Kate surprised everyone. She walked into the parlour where Susanna was sitting trying to concentrate on her

Latin, and dropped a kiss on her daughter's hair. The girl jumped at the touch; she'd been carefully keeping out of her mother's way. But Kate was smiling. Chuckling, even. 'I never thought Ruth had it in her.'

'What?' Eyes wide, Susanna looked up from her Cicero.

Her mother laughed and kissed her again. 'My dear, I hope you'll no copy her, but when I think back, I did worse myself when I was young. She but took what she thought was her fair share, an' went after her man. I'll no say I don't think she's picked the wrong one, but it's her life.'

Susanna sighed in relief. 'You'll not turn her away, then, if — when she comes back?'

'No, my lass. I'll no turn her away.' She sighed and stretched. 'Lord, what a weight I've been carryin' this week! I feel better now. I've even taken back the kitchen lass that helped her, for she begged so sore to get her place back.' She nodded in satisfaction at her own generosity.

She'd not have said that if she had seen the girl the day before, facing Billy, her hands twisting miserably, her teeth chattering, agreeing with every word that this man with the crazy eyes said to her. 'Aye, sir, I'll go back! I'll beg Lady Kate to forgive me! An' I'll pass you the word whenever the lad's able to get about. No, I'll not tell a soul! As God's me witness, sir! Lemme go, sir! Yer 'urtin' me!'

Billy had tightened his painful grip on the girl's shoulder, enjoying her winces. ''Course ye will, lass! An' see 'ere; 'ere's a shillin'. There'll be anuvver one when ye sends me word!' He'd probably give the lass the money, too. He'd been frustrated so long, trying to find Jack, and then trying to get one of Black Kate's servants who would talk; now that he had a spy in the house, he'd wait till the brat could come out and then grab him. And then . . . The scullery girl had eased herself out of the loosened grip and fled as Billy lost himself in terrible, thrilling fantasies.

Walsingham was furious. Not that one of his spies had ruined a young woman's reputation, but that Gifford wouldn't be returning to give evidence. A report sent from Paris some days after the elopement soothed him only slightly, Phelippes told Frank with a snigger. 'One of our best men, young sir! Years, it took, to find him, train him, set him in the right position, and now he's off! But we must just let him stew in his own goose. He'll be back some day. When all the money's gone. Four thousand pounds' worth, you said — and not the most valuable jewel-box, either! Great Jehovah!' His nose was glowing with emotion.

However, he returned fairly swiftly to business. 'Diggory has an ague, and his hand shakes too much, but he's the best egg in our quiver. We must wait a day or two for his full recovery. We shall soon have the letter ready, Master Verney. Keep them content.'

So Frank joined in the long, anxious discussions. All their friends agreed something must be done, but none would commit himself to actual action except Savage. And Frank's veiled warnings seemed to be having an effect at last on Tony; he became even jumpier than normal, and affected them all. When at last the letter from Queen Mary — well, the forgery — arrived on the twenty-ninth of July, even the ending, 'Your most assured friend for ever,' could scarcely raise their spirits. All these demands for details which they didn't have! What could they do?

Next day a note from Walsingham was delivered, tempting Babington with permission to deal with the principal plotters in the state, to discover their intentions. The discussions turned frantic. Babington was still in turmoil. 'He must know something! Oh, I am torn, torn, Frank! As a Catholic, should I support the present state, or try to subvert it, or avoid the strife, go abroad and live a life of contemplation?' The idea kept returning in greater attractiveness as tension mounted.

'You're not v-very contemplative, Tony! And what about your w-wife and little daughter?' Walsingham wouldn't let Tony leave now, anyway; he'd be arrested if he fled. But Frank couldn't risk his own life by just warning him! 'I think you should tell W-Walsingham. I really do. Killing the queen, and invasion — they're j-just not right, Tony!'

'I half agree with you, Frank.' Babington was looking tired, drawn, older. 'But I feel I must go on ... if I must ... My honour is at stake.'

'More than your honour, Tony! Your head!' Oh, come on! Be sensible for once! Turn Queen's Evidence and save your life. And I'll save Mary's ...

'Yes, dear Frank, but ...' Waffling, wandering, in spite of all Frank could say Tony fluttered finally into dramatic decision; he must go ahead! But, as a stroke of great caution, in case spies were following Ballard and Savage to and from Tichborne's house, he'd move! Into 'The Garden'; the room right beside Frank's. No spy would know he was there!

Typical, Frank thought.

They decided that to put Walsingham off, Babington must reveal something. He'd tell Walsingham he had discovered that yes, there was a plot, but it was nowhere near completion. 'Which is true, Frank. We must always face the facts!' He could name Gifford, who was safe abroad. And he'd also name the main conspirator; Ballard, who would have to escape to France.

Without hesitation, the burly priest agreed. 'I started the conspiracy, my sons. It is only right that I should take the risk of being sacrificed, and if it saves the Enterprise, I'll count my life well lost!' Even as he wrote his report to Walsingham, Frank found himself for the first time respecting the Jesuit.

Babington wrote to ask Walsingham for another meeting, but was put off for some days, on the excuse of illness and press of business.

205

Frank felt torn and squashed at the same time. The tension and suspense of nursing, and betraying, Babington, and reassuring his mother, and waiting for Jack to be well again to deal with Mary's letter, keeping his own counsel, not letting anyone at all ever know what he was thinking . . . And nothing happening for days at a time . . . He felt as if he was juggling grenades. Was this how spies always felt?

But he had at least one relief. Or was she an extra strain? Susanna.

Neither of them wanted to be reminded of Ruth, and the wild passion she had inspired. They were shy, hinting at their feelings, advancing warily and hastily retreating, blushing a lot. Kate smiled on them, and left them alone with Jack as chaperone to work their way to a decision.

Jack's foot, as Susanna had predicted, improved. The swelling shrank, the bruise fading to yellow. He started to hobble gingerly on his heel, with a stick at first, but soon was managing without it, and as he grew more and more restless it became harder to hold him down and make him go easy on his ankle.

At last, at the start of August, Jack and Frank walked down the sweet chamomile path to an arbour right at the foot of Kate's orchard. Jack's foot would bear his weight well, if he was careful not to turn on it. He sat down on the seat under the arching roses, and grinned up at Frank. 'Right, sir! I'm just about fit again. Ye've been like a goose on 'ot tar fer days. Come on, then! Let's 'ave it! Wot're ye wantin', eh?'

He was astonished when he heard. Steal, not for Walsingham, but from him? The great man himself? From his very own office? Gor! But the crazy risk and impertinence of it drew him, and when he looked at Frank's face he realised that yes, it was important. He owed Bony so much; he'd do it!

He kept his comments practical. 'Where's Walsin'am's office? 'Ow 'igh up? First floor, eh? Can't climb, not yet.

206

'Ave ter go up the stair. Is the box locked? Padlock or built-in? 'Ow big's the key'ole? Three on 'em? Gor! Take a while, that. At least I doesn't 'ave ter put it back after. 'S just the one trip.' He sighed in delight. 'Queen's letters! Me! Gor! Now. You knows White'all. 'Ow does I get in?'

Silently as she had approached on the soft path, Susanna stepped round the rosebush. 'If you've half the sense you were born with, Jack, you don't!' She thumped the tray she was carrying down onto the table by the bench and glared at them, her voice high in angry fright. 'I've never heard anything so daft in my life! You're both fit for Bedlam Hospital!'

Jack's reaction was immediate. 'Gor! Females! Useless bleedin' pests!'

So was Frank's. 'Nothing of the kind! Don't be cheeky, J-Jack!'

She was so aware of him! His white tension, his defence of her, the old, weary look on his face as he refused to change his mind. 'I'm sorry, but I m-must! And it's not my secret, Susanna. I must get hold of M-Mary's letter. On my honour, I m-must. P-please don't argue with me, Susanna!'

'I'm not arguing, I'm telling you! No!' But it was no use, she couldn't shift him. He was so determined, and so drawn-looking; she'd do anything to help him. Though she still protested, argued, objected, she was soon deep in the planning.

It was she who had the best idea for getting Jack into the office. 'Let him go in openly, Frank. Get him letters for another department, as an excuse to get past the guards. Then he can hide till everyone leaves in the evening, including you. He'll have all night to find the letter and hide again. And you'll make sure you're in plain sight all day, and the next morning, too, while he leaves openly when the place is busy again. Then you'll not be suspected.' That was most important for her.

Reluctantly, Jack eyed her with new respect. 'Aye, that'd do it.'

There were still details to arrange. When? 'Soon. Your mother's coming to visit us in three days, Frank, on the seventh of August. The best time would be the night before that, don't you think so?'

'I'll m-meet her on the B-Bridge after I leave work at noon, to escort her here, and I'll ask her to take J-Jack back home to F-F-Fulham with her, before the letter's even f-found missing. We might have as m-much as a f-f- two weeks before the hue and cry.'

'And if Jack leaves no sign —' Jack snorted in disgust, and Susanna smiled a quick apology — 'the letter might have been taken at any time.'

'An' I tell yer wot! I'll pertend as me foot's worser again, worser nor it is, an' nobody won't never think as 'ow it coulder been me, even if they thinks so!' The others exchanged smiles.

At last they could think of nothing else. They fell silent. It was actually going to happen; it wasn't a game . . . Remembering what she had come out for, Susanna poured the cider she had brought. The silver flask tinkled against the cups as her hand shook.

Frank raised his cup, to cheer himself as much as her. 'A t-toast! Walsingham's quest is for Queen Mary's death. We'll drink to success in ours, to save her!'

They looked at each other. Frank, newly eighteen, tall and thin in his blue broadcloth; Susanna, sixteen, short and sturdy in almond green damask; and Jack, small and gnome-like in plain grey doublet and hose. They were an oddly-assorted set of adventurers to set against the spy-master of England.

They rose to clink their cups. 'Success in our quest!'

Suddenly Susanna dropped her cup and clasped her hands over her mouth, sobbing in sheer fright, without tears. Frank shyly put an arm round her shoulders to comfort her. It felt awkward . . . Then it felt just right . . .

'Cheer up, missus Susan!' Jack was confident, even if they weren't. 'It'll work. You'll see! It'll work!' They paid him no attention. Grinning, he poured himself another cup of cider.

Next day, on the fourth of August, just as he was about to leave for France, Ballard was arrested.

When he heard, Babington raced home in a panic. 'Frank! Frank! We're lost! What's to be done? Oh, God, who's that on the stair?' It was Savage, strolling in. Tony seized his arm, tugging at him in distress. 'Ballard's arrested, John! What's to do? There are only two courses open to us! Flight, or sudden and desperate action! Oh, God, John! What can we do?'

The tall young man looked down at him, smiling placidly. 'Calm yourself, sir! No remedy but what I've wanted to do these two months past. Kill the usurper at once. That's all.'

'That's all! That's all, he says!' Babington gritted his teeth, trying to look decisive. 'Very well, John. Tomorrow. We'll go tomorrow.'

'Can't.' Savage looked down at his worn old doublet, and tugged at a loose thread. 'Haven't any clothes fit for the Court.' He shrugged like a sad clown. Frank couldn't help it; he started to laugh.

Babington was near hysterics. 'Frank! Stop that! In God's name — John — here — my ring — all the money I have. Buy clothes! Hasten, man!' Savage wandered out, loose-limbed and casual, while Babington flustered after him, turning at last to Frank with his hands flapping helplessly. 'What can one do with such a man, dear Frank?'

For hours they talked in the garden, till Babington slowly cooled down. They sent word of what had happened to their friends; and neither got much sleep that night.

Next day, they went out for dinner as usual at noon to the Three Tuns. None of their usual friends appeared, not even Tichbourne or Salisbury. Babington was near hysteria. 'What is John Savage doing, Frank? Why has he not come back? Where is everybody? Arrested? Dear God have mercy!'

Just as they finished their meal, a man brought a letter for Frank. Turning a little aside at the table with a word of apology to Babington, he broke the seal. His heart seemed to freeze. 'Master Verney, on receipt of this warrant, you will arrest Sir Antony Babington in the name of Her Majesty and convey him presently to the Tower of London. Walsingham.' Oh, God! It had come to it! Had he sent soldiers? Yes. Leaning against the door-post was the competent bulk of Serjeant Palmer himself, grinning.

Could he do anything? No. Not with Palmer there. All he could do was obey his orders. Poor Tony! Poor, doomed Tony!

No! He'd not do nothing! He turned his back on Palmer. 'Tony, sit still and listen carefully, and don't argue. Quiet!' As Tony's eyes widened, he tapped the paper. 'This is a warrant for your arrest. But I'll give you what chance I can. Get up quietly and go out as if you were going to the jakes. Then run for your life. It's all I can do now, Tony. Go!'

His friend gazed at him blindly. 'Arrest? You mean — you're a spy? You? I trusted you, Frank!'

Frank's heart ached with tension, guilt, pity. 'Go, man! Now!'

'But — where? My stable will be watched.'

'Ballard's man has a horse. Run! I'll wait as long as I can before giving the alarm. Go on, Tony!'

'Frank, you're Walsingham's man? All this time? Oh, God, what a fool I've been!' Tony pushed his chair back clumsily and rose, his lips trembling slightly. 'I'll pay the shot. I'll pay for all, will I not? And I thought you my friend!' He smiled slightly. 'But you have been. You urged me to confess, to save my life. And I paid no heed. I thank

you for it. But I fear my stars are against you. And me.'
He was recovering fast.

Frank bit his lips in anguish. 'Oh, stop posturing, Tony! Run!'

Tony nodded, almost gaily. He glanced at his sword and cloak, still hanging on the back of his chair, and left them as proof that he wasn't really leaving. He paid the bill, and with a wave and smile to Frank moved off through the door to the back yard.

Frank sat still. For once, Tony had acted fast. Walsingham would blame him. He turned over the warrant. There was his life-line on the back; 'Warrant; Sir Antony Babington'. In Phelippes' clear, angular writing. He could claim Tony must have seen it, known what it was. It was a way of escape from Walsingham's wrath . . . But not from his own conscience.

It was almost five minutes before Serjeant Palmer became suspicious, and the hunt was up.

Jackdaw

On the sixth of August, Susanna screamed that there were strange cats in the house! There were; three big, battle-scarred veterans which she had smuggled in herself, each in a bag with a cod-head to keep him quiet, and tossed out in the parlour where Balthazar was sleeping. The whole household flurried up to separate the wailing animals, while Jack slipped out of the side door by the deserted kitchen, into the bustle of the morning market. Nursing a scratched hand, Susanna had given him a cold pork pie and a couple of the first of the apples. 'No-one will know you're gone, Jack,' she promised him. 'I'll say you're not feeling well and want to rest before Lady Alice comes tomorrow.' She kissed him for luck. He blushed as red as Frank would have done, she thought. Oh, God, she hoped he'd succeed! If she'd been a Papist, she'd have lit a candle to a saint. A hundred candles!

Heading for the river steps, Jack paid no heed to a beggar girl squatting in a corner of Saint Mary Overy's wall. Behind him, Susanna shut the door and ran up to the parlour again, not noticing a peeping scullery lass. She had been allowed back on probation, but strictly forbidden to set foot outside the kitchen without orders, even when everyone else was yelling and chasing cats. The girl hesitated; she'd promised loyalty, and Lady Kate was a good mistress . . . but the fearsome thought of Billy was too much for her. She slipped out to speak to the beggar girl, as she'd been told. On her return, the cook caught her and beat her for going out. It was nothing to what she'd been threatened with if she didn't.

The beggar scurried off across Southwark.

In the three months since they had settled in the Gully Hole, Billy had plenty to keep him occupied; he had to guard Sal, and to encourage bad payers, which he enjoyed. And now they were successful, growing richer than they'd ever done in the Vintry. Sal had hoped that Billy's hatred of Jack would have faded. But to her irritation, she had to admit to herself that if anything it had grown worse. Every few nights, Billy would riot in his sleep, shouting, swearing, his hands ripping his blankets; and the name he cursed was always the same. Jack! Jackdaw! Jack!

The only thing that would stop it was for him to find Jack. She didn't care if he tore the boy to fishbait, as long as it made him happy again. So when she saw Jack in Southgate, and told Billy about it, she expected the news to cheer him. Instead, he grew sullen and twitchy; his eyes never rested still for more than a second.

At last, the beggar girl they'd left as a messenger brought word from their spy in Kate Bolsiter's mansion; Jack had left the house. Left? By the gate, Billy cursed and punched at the iron-studded wood. Damn that girl! She was supposed to tell them as soon as he could walk! What was going on? He'd murder her! They still didn't know where Jack was!

To confuse any possible inquiry, Jack shared a boat with a party of lawyers, one of whom boasted so arrogantly about his fat fees that Jack couldn't resist lifting his purse. They were only going as far as the Four Brothers, a beer house a quarter of a mile from Whitehall, and he judged it best to walk from there, hurrying to get in before the changing of the guard. By the time he reached the big gates his ankle was very painful again, but he just made it; the marching feet stamped behind him as he crossed the courtyard. Good; nobody would know whether he'd come back out.

In his new grey clothes, he looked smart and dull enough, and the letters he had in the pouch slung over his shoulder were genuine; Frank had lifted them from the Treasury bundles the day before. He hardly needed them, though. There was a lot of bustle, messengers riding and running urgently, and the guard scarcely glanced at him before waving him on. Jack marched in, walking straight and looking confident. He mustn't draw attention by limping, asking the way, or appearing uncertain. Frank's directions were good; along this corridor, and up these stairs, two flights, and there was Frank passing at the top, paying no attention to him, but going into a side office and leaving the door ajar ... Nobody watching; Jack followed him in.

Frank was breathless and pale. 'No trouble? You'd not be noticed in the f-fuss. I j-just hope the letter's still there. The off-office is almost directly below this one. F-facing the stairs. Sir F-F-Francis might have taken it home with him last night, the letter, after it all went wrong. The arrests, I mean. He was in such a f-f-fury ... I saw you out of the window, coming in, and s-said I had to check something with Ph-Phelippes ... Come on. Can you squeeze in under the b-bottom shelf in the cupboard here? I cleared it out yesterday. Oh, give m-me those letters. Here, these are to go out tomorrow. Here's the key. There's a gap f-for you to see when it's dark. W-will you be all right?'

'Oh, geroff, sir!' Jack hissed at him. Make a gravestone nervous, he would, with all his fussing. 'Go on 'ome. See yer tomorrer.'

Frank swallowed, nodded, and hissed 'Good luck!' The

door closed over. In the dark Jack reached up to lock it from the inside, and curled up on the floor, grinning. Gor! Bony wasn't cut out for a thief, for sure!

He was cramped, stiff and aching by the time the light faded outside, and the sounds of feet and voices finally died away, but he'd often been worse. He'd eaten his pie and his apples. His first need was for a jakes ...

The lock on Walsingham's door was easy, to an expert. He locked it again behind him, in case of prowling sentries, and hunted for the box. It wasn't where Bony had said; it was on a side table, not a shelf. However, the triple locks were unmistakable. It was too dark to see well, but his sensitive fingers didn't need light. He spat on them, and settled down to probe gently. There wasn't a sound outside.

Although the locks were tricky, within an hour he had the letter out and the box relocked. It was the right letter; he couldn't read it in the faint starlight, but he could just make out the gallows mark Bony had spoken of. He tucked it carefully into his doublet.

He was finished quicker than he'd expected. Would he try to get away now? No, he told himself firmly. He had a good excuse for being there tomorrow; don't spoil it by being too cocky! He returned to his own office, stretched out on the floor and slept like a corpse, waking just in time to tidy himself away in the cupboard as the office-boys arrived to fill the inkwells.

Getting out went as smoothly as getting in. He listened till there was no-one in the office, cautiously unlocked the door and rolled out. A minute's stretching, and he could walk quietly out and down the stairs. The guards stopped him this time, but his letters were genuine and he was passed out to hurry briskly down to the river steps, whistling. Boat home, and all's well. Easy!

Susanna was watching for him from her window, to slip down and open the door for him. He grinned at her anxious face. 'Trouble? 'Course not!' She was going to drag him upstairs to tell her all about it, but one of the maids passed and nodded to him, smiling. He'd been seen; better make it all ordinary. He shrugged, winked at Susanna, and headed down to the kitchen for a bite and a gossip. No, he'd been a bit off yesterday, hadn't felt like eating, nor talking, but he was better today. He felt fine!

The same beggar girl, crouching in the shelter of Saint Mary Overy's wall, watched him in, nodding; aye, that was him. She was just about to rise when a company of people walked up the street. A tall lad was escorting two ladies, with several attendants behind them, one an old maid carrying a small child, and one a big lurden lurching with a deep basket, all well-dressed and happy. The beggar girl whined, hand outstretched, and the tall lad tossed her a penny as they were welcomed into the Bolsiter house. She scurried off. Better news for big Billy this time.

Tremendous news! In his pleasure, Billy gave her a whole shilling and slammed the gate in the faces of three people waiting to see Sal, snarling, 'Gerrout! No more terday! Go on, clear off!' His grin was enough, as one of the women commented, to put you off your ale for a month. He didn't even wait, as he usually did, to be sure that they had all moved away before he charged into the house, tugging Tom's sleeve. 'Come on! 'E's back!'

Sal was startled when both her sons marched into her room. Billy was triumphant. ''S Jacky! 'E's back in Black Kate's again!'

She gasped. 'And where d'ye think ye're off ter? Ye're like a bleedin' invadin' army! Tom, put down them pistols! Ye're not goin' right inter that 'ouse after 'im, an' that's flat!'

Tom obediently stopped checking the priming of his enormous pistols, but Billy grinned wider. 'Aye, mam. That's just wot I'm doin'.'

Tom's eyes opened wide in shock. Nobody talked to Sal like that!

Sal was as taken aback as Tom. She opened her mouth to curse Billy, but he raised his head and stared balefully, straight into her face. His eyes were wide and wild. ''E's there, mam. An' not just 'im. 'Er wot brung the news says there's visitors in the 'ouse. Jess, an' Joe. God knows why, but they're there too. We can get 'em all, all three on 'em. If we goes now. An' that's wot I'm doin'. Whether you likes it or not.'

For the first time, Sal realised to her shock that he was beyond her control. Not entirely; she could still stop him, by stunning him if all else failed. But if she did, she'd lose him, for good. And that she couldn't do . . . 'Wot about the servants? There's a score on 'em, wiv pistols an' cudgels, the kitchen slut telled ye. An' they'll use 'em.'

Billy chuckled happily. 'No, they won't. Not when we've got a pistol at Black Kate's 'ead, they won't! They'll do wotever we says, won't they?'

Probably true. 'An' after? She'll 'ave 'alf the country 'untin' us! An' a reward out!'

It was a good point, as he could see even in his madness. ''Ow much we got? In ve chest?'

'None o' your bleedin' business!'

He gripped her wrist. 'Aye, it is! Don't me an' Tom work fer it? 'Ow much?' Tom, horrified, raised a fist to knock Billy's hand from their mother's arm, but Billy snarled at him. 'Keep off, knuckle-'ead! Can we leave, mam, gerraway after? Wiv enough ter live on in Bristol as yer aye yappin' about? Well, mam? 'Ave we got enough?'

Sal considered. It wasn't a bad idea. These last few days, there had been men asking about her and her sons. That bothered her. If it was suspected the lads were alive, they'd be found some day, disguised or not. 'Aye. Right. We'll go.' As he stretched high and wide, his fists clenching, his snarl of triumph deep and happy at last, she slapped the table before her. 'But we'll do it proper! You an' Tom go out an' get in all ye can. Don't say as we're leavin', mind! Say we got a new customer as wants a big loan instant, an' we'll take one in five as a payment fer the next six weeks. They'll fight ter give ye the coin. There ain't no 'urry, son!' she soothed Billy's impatience. 'Ye knows Black Kate's reputation. She'll feed 'em an' entertain 'em fer hours.'

Two hours later Sal settled her big ivory beads round her neck and the heavy bangles on her wrists. She smoothed the gleaming white circles with satisfaction. 'I can wear 'em again now we're off. God's tripes, I've missed 'em! But now I'm meself again!'

Her sons were packing gold and silver coins into five heavy little chests, small enough to carry in a wheelbarrow. 'Right. Tuck 'em back o' the door. We'll come back fer 'em.' Tom was grinning, Billy trembling with excitement. She slapped Billy's shoulder. 'Right, lad. We're wiv yer. Let's be off an' see about our little jackdaw, eh!'

What do you wear to greet your future mother-in-law? Susanna had driven Peg frantic for days, trying on dresses. Her final choice was damask, the soft green that Frank liked, with darker green and white trellis-work, and a white silk underdress couched with green. Her hair was shining; nothing to worry about there. Her lace ruff was fine, but small. Silver earrings. She mustn't be overdressed. Oh, she was so nervous!

When Jack returned safe, she fled up to her room to relax and wash her face, but glanced out of her window. There they were, walking up from the river already! Frank was in blue, as usual; on his arm a small, elegant lady in grey-fawn who must be his mother; another lady, in purple, and a group of servants. She flew out onto the landing and down the stair, calling, 'They're here! And the children, too! Mother, they're here!' Master Slim was arranging his parade of maids and men in the hall. Kate surged out of the parlour, and the door was flung open in welcome.

Susanna saw the visitors' eyes widen. For the first time, she looked at her mother with a stranger's eyes. She cringed inside. Kate's beaded cherry-red taffeta was sumptuous, her farthingale like a cartwheel, her winged lace collar embroidered with crystals like a halo behind her dark brown face. Loud? Overdressed? The queen dressed more plainly. No wonder they were shocked!

In fact, it was mostly Kate's rubies that fascinated the ladies.

Lark knew she couldn't match Kate's wealth, and had sense enough not to try. She dressed neatly and wore no jewels except small gold drops in her ears. She sat trying not to gape.

Seated politely behind her mother-in-law, Jane seethed. Her gown was a fine quilted plum brocade, her ruff and farthingale impressively wide, though not gaudy nor ostentatious, she had approved herself smugly. Her earrings were set with good amethysts. But now, as she gazed at Kate, her lips were pinched. What a vulgar display of extravagance! Necklace, rings, brooches, earrings like red-currant tarts! Her Puritan soul was outraged.

Used to the gems, Frank paid them no heed. He tried in vain to catch Jack's eye as the lad limped in, beaming. 'Gor! Jess an' Joe! Wot ye doin' 'ere, then? By, ain't ye smart, eh? Oh, sorry! Fergettin' me manners!' He bowed with a flourish. 'Servant, Lady Alice!' Jess bobbed solemnly in return. Still bent, Jack glanced mischievously aside. ''Ow's that, Lady Katie? Do ye credit, eh?' Noticing Frank's nervous stiffness, he winked reassuringly.

Lark was flushed, her eyes bright. Jack must have succeeded, or he'd not be so chirpy. Queen Mary's letter was safe! She had scarcely breath to speak, her heart was so high in happiness. 'Fine as Lord Leicester!' she praised Jack. Jess was squeaking in fluster and delight as her big brother swung her up into his arms for a quick kiss. 'I thought the children would enjoy the trip. We brought a basket of Jane's new preserves for Lady Bolsiter, of goosegogs and currants that Joe helped grow and gather, so I thought he should carry and present them, and we can all go home together.' And the children were extra proof that no plot was in their minds ... Pleased to recognise his name, but shy among strangers, Joe grinned and shuffled.

While the preserves were examined and praised, Susanna whispered to Frank, 'All's well. He's got it!' At her confirmation, he suddenly hugged her. She squeaked, very like Jess. Their mothers turned to stare. He flushed vividly. Kate chuckled. So did Lark. Jane frowned.

Susanna blushed too. What a way to behave! In public, at least ... But then, they'd just saved a queen! Did she expect him not to rejoice?

'Jack,' Kate said, 'take Joe an' Jess down to the kitchen for a bite. Ladies, would you care to refresh yoursel's? Susanna, why not go out into the garden wi' Frank?' Alone? Jane stiffened, but Kate smiled sweetly. 'I'll keep an eye on you from the window here, till the ladies rejoin me to sip a cup o' iced wine in the coolth, if that will please you, Lady Alice?'

Frank hesitated; the way he was feeling — he might — had he a chance? Susanna didn't; the way he was feeling, he might — had she a chance? As they ran down the stairs and out into the orchard their laughter faded. Their eyes met; they looked swiftly away, and blushed again.

Lark and Jane relished the scented, warm water, the ivory combs and soft cloths spread for them in the guest room, but the offer of chilled wine brought them quickly back to the parlour, where Kate produced printed sheet music of the new madrigals. 'Frank sings with us often. Odd, that his stammer vanishes when he sings. He has a fine voice, Lady Alice.'

Nothing could have pleased Alice more. 'I taught him myself. A score of years ago, and more, alas! I sang for Queen Catherine of France, and also for Queen Mary Stewart.'

'Indeed?' Kate was all surprise and delight. Frank had only mentioned it twenty times. 'Is that no a coincidence! I sang for Mary often in Edinburgh. Her own singin'' was never more nor fair, but she was a dab hand on the virginals. Do you play, Lady Alice?'

Alice's fingers twitched, eager for the music. 'I'm sadly out of practice, Lady Katherine. But pray call me Lark. A silly nickname my father gave me for my singing in my childhood.'

'Well merited, I'm sure.' Kate beamed. 'An' my friends call me Kate. Maybe I could try accompanying us?' She lifted a lute from a side table.

Lark looked round hopefully. 'Jane plays beautifully.'

Jane simpered. Kate beamed again. 'Shall we attempt an air or two?'

After an hour Jess and Joe were growing bored and restless among the servants crowding the kitchen. Jack led them out into the garden. Music was still pouring from the parlour window. They'd not be dining yet; old Danby would be tearing his hair, Jack thought with a grin. Frank and Susanna were in one of the arbours, sitting holding hands among the roses. He started to take out the letter from his doublet, and then stopped. They were holding hands, staring into each other's eyes, smiling vaguely. Leave them be!

Chuckling, he led the way to the ripest apple tree, and set Joe to shaking it. 'Go on, Joe! That's the way! Look, Jess, we'll 'ave a feast. Stop, Joe. Stop!' But Joe didn't stop at once, and as Jess ran forward to pick up the apples, one fell right on her head.

Susanna and Frank, jerked from their idyll by the scream, came running over. 'Oh, dear, my pet! What a big bump!' She looked at Frank, and shrugged. They'd have to go in and tell their mothers soon, anyway.

He picked Jess up. 'Would you like a sugar almond?' The wails faded.

'Tch! My good pippins!' Shaking her head, Susanna looked at the fallen apples. 'Get a trug, Jack, and gather them up.' Jack nodded; it would keep Joe busy and happy. The two lads trotted off to the garden sheds.

Carefully not holding hands now, Frank and Susanna stopped on the stair. 'They're singing. We shouldn't interrupt,' Frank said. They glanced round. The men on guard in the hall below couldn't see them. They kissed, gently ... till Jess started to whine again. Reluctantly, they went on up.

Peg watched entranced from the landing above. She'd known! Right from the minute Mistress Susan set eyes on him in the theatre! She skipped down to the kitchen to tell her news.

'Hey!' the porter called as she bounced past. 'What's the rush?'

'Wouldn't ye like to know!' she teased. Intrigued, the two guards strolled after her. The porter turned to answer a quiet knock at the door.

Frank and Susanna stood bashful by the parlour door, smiling, blushing both. From her perch in Frank's arms Jess saw a dish of sweets on the sideboard, and wriggled till they set her down.

The ladies were sitting back in more than musical harmony. 'Come away in, my dears, an' we'll try a quartet. Aye, Jess, you can have an almond, but offer them round, my dear. Who's a clever lassie! Susanna has a fair gift for music, but not to match yours, Lark.' Happily, Frank noted the nickname. 'It's a rare treat to me, to sing with such a voice, an' such a fine lutenist!' Lark was glowing at Kate's praise. Even Jane was smiling.

But Susanna and Frank didn't reply. 'What's wrong, my dears?' They blushed brighter. Kate looked more closely, and started to rise. 'Or should I say what's right? Have you come to ask me a question, Frank?'

He drew a deep breath. 'Yes, Lady Kate. I beg the honour of the hand of your daughter, Susanna, in m-m-m-marriage!' Oh, drattit!

Jane squawked. Kate beamed. Lark gasped, jumped up and ran to them, exclaiming, hugging and kissing them all.

Behind them the door burst open.

They turned in surprise, not alarm. Three tall figures towered there: a woman in a plain tan gown and white apron like a merchant's wife, broad bangles and two strings of huge white beads, but her face hard and ruthless; a big man in a bulky leather doublet, carrying two pistols; an ugly man in dark green, glaring round with crazy eyes.

Susanna saw Jess's face by the window as the child sank down, hidden behind the settle there. Her chest suddenly hurt. These must be — 'Ow!'

Like a snake striking, Billy had grabbed her wrist and yanked her into his arms. He swung her to face the rest, who stood stunned by the sudden violence, and grinned at them over her head. 'Where's Jacky? I wants 'im!'

Sal's voice was harsh and commanding, to bully instant obedience. 'We wants Jacky. Jackdaw. An' 'is bruvver an' sister, too. We knows they're 'ere. You get 'em in 'ere right away, an' nobody don't get 'urt. You make us trouble, an' she —' she jerked a thumb at Susanna — 'gets 'er neck wrung like a bleedin' chicken. Where is Jacky Daw?'

Billy

In the garden below, Jack chilled at the familiar harsh voice barking from the open window. Ivory Sal! Inside the house! And Jess was up there. Oh, Gor! 'Joe, stay 'ere! Stan' still! Don't move!' He raced in.

The stair was jammed with servants crowding to the rescue, but Tom was at the parlour door, waving his pistols gently, grinning wide. 'Stand! Or yer dead!' Naturally, they stood. The guards couldn't fire their pistols, not with so many women in the room behind. Jack couldn't get by.

Inside, Susanna was too amazed to react for a moment. This lout had touched her! Hurt her! The filthy, stinking — how dare he! Her good gown! Outraged, furious, terrified, she tried to turn and slap him, but her wrist was jerked up behind her till she yelped, in fury as much as pain.

Frank leapt at Billy. In spite of all Jack's tales he ignored Sal, a mere woman, until her fist thudded into the side of his neck, and his knees were folding under him and his face scraping along the carpet . . . It'd have been rushes at home . . . He lay still, oddly conscious but unable to move.

Billy twisted Susanna's wrist again. 'Fetch 'im out!' he yelled over her agonised gasp. 'Jackdaw! Get 'im in 'ere! Now!'

Jane was hysterical. 'What for? Why d'you want him?'

Sal sneered. ''E's me long-lost son, an' I wants ter leave 'im all me gold! Wot differ does it make? We wants 'im! Where is 'e, ye gutter-rakin' sow?' She snatched the lute from Jane's hands and smashed its delicate bowl on a corner of the table.

'Stop that!' Appalled, Lark stepped forward. Sal simply swung a long arm. Her ivory bangles smashed into Lark's face. Bright blood spurted from Lark's split lips, and she fell back with a cry of distress.

Billy laughed, and jerked Susanna's arm again, harder. She screamed.

Sal suddenly found herself on hands and knees, knocked off her feet by an arm like a leg. Kate swept past her.

Billy menaced Susanna with his knife. 'Keep off, ye black savage, or I'll slit 'er throat!'

Jack was climbing the wall outside, ignoring the stabs of pain in his arm and ankle. Whose guts? Jess's? Grabbing the shutter, he hauled himself onto the windowsill, to see Kate heading for Billy in spite of the threat.

She was unarmed, but not helpless. She simply drew breath and bellowed at full pitch. Astonished, shocked by the rage on her dark face; by her wide crimson mouth; by her disregard of his knife; by the sheer volume of noise her trained singer's voice blasted full in his face, Billy froze for the instant it took her to wrench his knife hand safely aside from Susanna's neck and hit him.

Susanna, jerking her wrist from his loosened grasp, cried, 'Look out!' Kate whipped round. Sal was leaping at her like a tigress.

Lark pulled herself up to a stool by Jane, dabbing at her mouth in fright and fury. Susanna ran to tug Frank out from under the fighting women. Using her arm and a corner of the sideboard he hauled himself wavering to his feet. Everyone watched Kate and Sal.

Jack, who had seen many fights in the inn, soon realised that this one wasn't as uneven as it seemed. Sal was taller and longer in the arm, tougher, five years younger, a century more vicious. Kate was softer, older, and enormously heavier, hampered by her gown and petticoats of heavy silk, but her whalebone and braid, seaming and padding also armoured her against Sal's punches and kicks. Trained as a dancer from her youth, she was still agile, fit and quick-moving despite her weight. She also had another, hidden advantage; she was more experienced in the rough side of life than anyone there knew.

Kate screeched as her ruby earrings were ripped out. One eyelid, already blooming like a plum, split at a second blow. Her nose was bleeding from a clawing thumbnail; but to Sal's dismay, the fat rich bitch wasn't an easy victim; she kept on fighting.

Ivory Sal's necklace broke, and the big beads rattled onto the carpet. Her cap came off, and her hair made a good handhold for Kate, whose own black curls were almost too short for Sal to grab. Not quite; Sal hauled her in close and bit her cheek. Kate reared back, pulling free, and then butted. Blood gushed from Sal's mouth and nose, and her eyes were wild. She kicked. As her foot bounced off Kate's whaleboned petticoats, the black woman grabbed it, jerking it on up till Sal fell backwards.

Tom, just behind Kate, hit her with one of his pistols. She crumpled on top of her gasping opponent, crushing her, both equally helpless for the moment. Tom bent to haul his mother free.

But as Sal fell, she had knocked over a settle. Balthazar, the white cat, hiding under it, leapt spitting to the sideboard beside Susanna. And Billy stepped forward with a cry of joy as a small figure was revealed, cowering in the corner. 'Jess! There she is! That's one of 'em, anyways!' Then his eyes lit up. Jack's face, mouth broad with terror, was peering in the open window. 'An' 'im, too! Jacky! I got both on 'em!'

In triumph he charged across the room. He skidded on the broken string of his mother's ivory beads. It slowed him for an instant.

In that moment Susanna shrieked, 'Billy!' He glanced round. Screeching, slung by the tail, the cat hit him full in the face. Its foreclaws clung over his eyes, while it bit, ripped his mouth with its hind feet, screamed as loud as Billy himself.

It was five seconds before he could drag it off and hurl it aside.

For an extremely angry cat, five seconds is a long time.

Cursing, half-blinded, sobbing wildly, Billy swept streaming blood from his face and headed for the window again. He stopped. Susanna was standing there. There was no sign of Jess or Jacky.

'Where is they?' His voice was a howl of rage.

Susanna faced him, her head high, her stomach aching with terror. 'Safe.' It hadn't been hard. Four fast steps, while all eyes were on Billy. Hiss to Jack, 'Get down!' Pick up the child, stuff her through the window, drop her into Joe's strong arms below. They were away.

She'd apologise to Balthazar later.

Billy shoved her aside so hard that she fell to her knees. He leaned out, wiping more blood from his eyes. He could scarcely see. But there they were, all three of them, among a score of angry gardeners and cooks, all out of reach, God damn them! Cursing in a steady stream of filth, he leapt across the room, snatched one of Tom's pistols, shoved his mother aside as she reached to stop him, stumbled back to the window and fired out at Jack. He peered through the smoke. Jacky was still standing, untouched. But Joe was staggering back. He'd got one of them!

Sal grabbed his arm. 'Bleedin' fool! We're leavin'! Now!' He still stared and cursed. She slapped him. 'Listen ter me, ye mollymaggot! That shot'll bring the sheriff! We been 'ere too long! We're leavin'!' Slowly her voice penetrated his raving. His eyes focussed on her. He nodded.

She looked at Kate; unconscious, and far too heavy. God, she felt ill! She stooped to grip Susanna's wrist and tug her to her feet. Frank started to move forward, but stopped as Sal pushed Susanna struggling into Billy's arms. ' 'Ere. You 'old 'er. An' don't let 'er go! She's our safe-conduct!' She glared at the onlookers. 'You try ter stop us, an' she's blinded!'

There was a gasp, and as she moved determinedly forward, Slim shoved the crowd of servants back. Cautiously the four hurried down the stair, Sal first, then Billy with Susanna held cruelly tight, his arm crooked round her neck hugging her close and half-smothering her, his knife at her eyes, and Tom bringing up the rear with his unfired pistol. Out of the front door, and slam it behind them. 'Run!' Sal snapped.

Billy changed his grip to Susanna's wrist, hauling her with them as they charged down the road. Shouting arose behind them as the more fleet-footed servant lads gained on them. Sal was still shaky from Kate's blows and from the dreadful crushing fall, and Tom was helping her along. Everyone was turning to stare, but they were past before anyone could do anything. Susanna was terrified. Wherever they were going, it must be more dangerous for her than the open street — must do something — couldn't get her feet far enough forward to pull back — could stop running, though — didn't want to fall on her face — oh, dear, what a mess her good gown would be in . . . She kicked her feet out together in front of her and sat down.

It didn't work out exactly as she'd planned. Her petticoats certainly cushioned the first thud, but Billy just cursed and hauled her bumping over the cobbles. She wouldn't get up; he yelled to Tom. Tom simply picked her up bodily, slung her over his shoulder and ran with her, while Billy helped his mother. She'd only delayed them by a moment, and it was much more painful jouncing on her stomach on Tom's shoulder than running.

There was a bang behind them. Tom lurched, but he didn't stop. Someone had shot at them! With her there! Good Lord! But they were going slower.

There was more and more shouting. Tom grunted, ''Ead fer ve river,' but Sal gasped, 'Gotter get our gold!' There was a minute of ducking in and out of narrow lanes. A gate swung close by her hair, bolts slammed, dogs were barking, they were inside a building and she was dropped heavily to the ground in a narrow, dirty hallway. Tom was leaning against the wall, a hand pressed to his side, blood trickling through his fingers.

''Ell!' Billy was peering back out of the door. 'Poxy whoresons is at the gate a'ready.'

'It'll 'old 'em fer a while. Tom, you 'urt bad? No, right, then. Reload that pistol an' get out ter the gate. I'll come out an' tend ye in a minute,' Sal panted. 'Shout, tell 'em if they tries ter get in, we'll kill the girl.' Susanna was still too winded by the jouncing ride to react.

As Tom heaved himself off the wall and lurched out, Sal turned viciously to her other son. 'Billy, yer a fool! You an' yer fancies! An' I'm a bigger fool fer 'eedin' ye! No, belt up an' listen! At least ye 'ung onter the slut.' She turned a cold eye on Susanna. 'She's our chance. Our 'ostage. We'll sell 'er to 'em fer a boat.' Panting, she paused for a few seconds while she thought. 'Take 'er up ter my room, an' 'old 'er in the winder where they can see 'er, an' stan' beside 'er, an' put yer knife at 'er throat. I'll go out an' tell 'em.'

Billy hauled Susanna up the stairs and over to the window, where he tied up her wrists behind her to one of the hooks for the shutter bar. She felt the sharp prick of steel at her neck. She could see the crowd outside the gate, and Frank's blue doublet. Sal was at the gate, shouting and pointing up. Other hands pointed. The crowd's din died away.

Beside her, Billy was whispering evilly, 'I'll kill ye, ye bitch! Wotever 'appens, I'll see ye dead!'

She couldn't help it. She started to sob.

Kate was recovering slowly, Lark and the maids clustered round her. The big woman was bruised, bleeding, aching all over, exhausted with exertion and shock, and Lark wouldn't let her be lifted till she was better. She smiled faintly up at Lark, as they both dabbed cold compresses on bruises. 'My certes, this is no the pleasant afternoon's visit we had planned, eh? I'm fine, I don't think there's anythin' broken. Is Susanna right enough?'

There was an unpleasant pause.

Kate's gaze, and tone, sharpened. 'Susanna? Where is she?'

Lark told her. Kate nearly erupted off the floor, but as soon as she was on her feet she swayed, more hurt than she had believed. 'Frank has taken the men after her, my dear!' Lark soothed her. 'He'll see to it!'

'Him! He's but eighteen!' Kate cried in distress. 'I must — I must go —' She was trying to stagger towards the door through a swarm of maids.

'Oh, for God's sake sit down, woman!' Lark snapped up at her. Startled, Kate collapsed onto the cushions of a settle. Lark took her hands gently, encouraging her. 'We're neither of us in a fit state to run about fighting villains, my dear. Leave it to Frank. He's very capable!'

By the door, Jack shook his head. Bony? Very capable? Against Sal and Billy, and no surprise possible? In a pig's arse, he was capable!

Somebody had to do something.

Sal, and Billy, and Tom . . . Gor! Oh, well. He had a debt to pay. To everybody, near enough!

Jess, shuddering with fright, was clinging to Hepsibah like a limpet to a rock. She didn't need him just now.

He turned from the parlour door, and limped down the stairs. His foot hurt, with all the exercise of last night, and today's climbing and dropping from the window. In the hall Joe, his left arm bandaged where the pistol ball had ploughed through the muscle, was grunting uneasily, upset, reacting to the anger all around. Jack sighed. Couldn't leave the big lad here, among strangers, in this state. Besides, he'd be useful. 'Come on, Joe,' he said. 'We'll go an' see wot's ter be did. Gimme a pig-a-back. Kneel down, Joe, an' lift me up.'

It was easy to find out where Susanna had been taken. They just followed the noise. Jack grimaced. 'Gulley 'Ole. Knowed it.'

Outside Sal's gate, Master Slim and Frank were arguing. 'We must wait for the sheriff, sir!' Slim insisted. 'The lads ran for him at once.'

'He'll get Susanna killed!' Frank's head was splitting. Men crowded round, waving axes, cudgels, knives, even a few pistols. He shouted for quiet. In a minute the only noise was dogs barking in the yard.

Sal's face appeared at a peephole in the gate. 'A boat!' she yelled. 'Give us a boat. Or we'll kill the lass! I swears, when we sails off, we'll let 'er go free. But if ye tries ter get us, she's a dead 'un! See!'

They gazed up. Susanna was at a window, and Billy's knife glinting.

Everyone looked at Frank. He was the gentleman; he was in charge. He swallowed. 'Don't attack,' he called, forcing himself to competence. 'But keep good watch. Some of you go round the streets on the f-far side. They may have a way out there.' It was all he could think of, for the moment.

There was a stir at the rear of the crowd. Men, armed soldiers, were pushing through, with an officer in red and gold at their head. Frank swayed. The sheriff? He must be held back . . . 'Sir, there's a girl — Susanna B-Bolsiter — held p-prisoner in that house. They want a boat, to escape, in exchange f-for her life. I can't th-think how to get her out.'

'Your name, sir?'

'F-Francis V-Verney, sir. You can see Mistress B-Bolsiter —'

The officer nodded to his men, and to his incredulous dismay Frank felt himself seized by the soldiers. 'Francis Verney, I arrest you on a charge of high treason. The warrant is signed by Master Secretary Walsingham. Where is the lad known as Jack Daw?'

Frank, gasping, found himself looking right at Jack as he realised what was happening. He was under arrest. The letter's absence had been discovered. But Susanna . . . Oh, God!

He didn't struggle, or argue. He swallowed, and deliberately looked the officer straight in the eye. 'J-Jackdaw? I've no idea, sir. But p-please — I b-beg you! M-Mistress B-Bolsiter's life's in danger!'

Not without some sympathy, the officer nodded towards a richly-dressed companion. 'The Sheriff of Southwark will take charge here. I have no doubt he'll rescue the lass. Come along, sir.'

As he was pushed away, Frank turned towards the sheriff. 'I'll hold you responsible. I trust you w-with her,' he shouted urgently.

Only Jack, perched on Joe's broad back behind the sheriff, realised that Frank's eyes had fixed for one desperate second on his face. It was him he meant. Jack.

He watched as Bony was shoved off towards the river. He looked up at the window where Susanna was held. Oh, well. No help for it. He'd known he'd have to deal with it.

First, spy out the scene. His ankle was aching. No time for that. He left Joe in a quiet corner and climbed up from wall to roof, till he could look down on the rear of Sal's fortress while the sheriff, ostentatiously official and efficient in public, was shouting at the front. The house stood right in the centre of a bare yard, with two mastiffs roaming irritably round it. Beef ribs wouldn't help here.

No way to climb or jump over. But at one place a corner was only about thirty feet from the next roof. Too long for a ladder. But a rope . . .

He slithered back down, mounted Joe, and drove him running for a chandler's. Ten fathoms of good plaited hemp rope, he needed, with a three-pronged grapnel on one end. Against the grain to pay for them, but he was in a desperate hurry. Lucky he had lifted that clerk's purse! Never leave till tomorrow what you can steal today — stop wasting time!

Back to the wall. This time, he'd need help. It'd have to be Joe. At least you could rely on him to do what he was told and not argue.

'Come on, Joe, up 'ere. That's it. Put yer foot on this broke brick. No, the other 'un. An' 'old on 'ere. Now up. An' again. Never mind if yer arm 'urts, this is important. Good man!' He urged the big lad up the wall, to clamber clumsily along the roof till they reached the narrowest gap. He nudged Joe, who was grinning in enjoyment of the unusual view of the yard below. 'Look, Joe! See that roof! Throw this 'ook 'ere ter catch in it.' It was no good asking Joe if he could do it; you just told him what to do, and he'd do his best. Sal and Tom were down at the gate, and Billy at the front window with Missus Susan. He'd get across unnoticed. He hoped . . .

'Stand up.' And pray nobody down by the gate, or at the windows round the yard, saw them and started pointing and waving. They stood up by a tall chimney-stack. 'Right, Joe? 'Ere y'are. I'll 'ang on ter this end.' Just in case he threw the lot. 'Take the 'ook, Joe. Now throw it ter catch on over there. Throw it right over.' And hurry, but get it right first time . . .

Joe took the grapnel. Humming, he swung it to and fro three or four times along the wall below him, whirled it up round his head, and let go in a great heave. The grapnel flew out, high above the other roof. At the full length of the rope, jerking at Jack as he held the loose end, it flew over the ridge, and the sharp prongs caught in the thatch.

Jack tugged at the rope. The grapnel was solid, no doubt about it. He'd trust himself to it. But Joe had thrown it much further than he'd planned, and the chandler had cheated him in the rope's length. There wasn't enough left to tie it round the chimney. Gor!

Only one thing for it. He turned to his brother. 'Joe, can I trust ye? Gor, wot a daft question! Joe, you stand 'ere, see. 'Old the rope in that 'and, see, an' the chimbley in this 'and. An' don't let go!' There wasn't even enough rope to tie it to Joe's wrist. He knotted the end for a better grip. 'Stand there, Joe. 'Old on tight! 'Old the rope, Joe!' Joe was strong enough to hold a carthorse, Elijah Parry had said. He hoped so! Even with his arm hurt, he should easily bear Jack's weight on the rope. And he'd stand there till he was told to move. Jack hoped . . .

Oh, well. Tightrope across? It would be quicker, but his ankle was too sore to be reliable. He gripped the rope, swung his knees up to cross over it, and started to swing across under it, hand over hand forty feet above the yard. He felt Joe sway, and recover easily. In twenty seconds he was across, sliding off onto the thatch. His arm hurt a bit, but not too badly. He didn't dare wave to Joe, in case Joe dropped the rope to wave back. ''Ang on, Joe!' he hissed, slid down the roof and swung round an open shutter to a dormer window. Right!

Fire!

Inside, all was quiet. A fine carved bed and chests, stools and a tall cupboard. Jack tiptoed over to the door; inched it past the squeak. Nobody about. He ghosted down the stair. That must be the door to the front room; yes, he could hear Billy cursing monotonously. Right. How to get him out?

The problem was solved for him. From below Sal shouted, 'Billy! Come 'ere! Tom's worser'n 'e said!' Jack had barely enough time to crouch low against the wall behind the door before Billy raced out and down the stair. As soon as he was past the turn, Jack nipped into the room, his knife out already as he glided across the floor, and Susanna was cut down almost before she knew he was there. In less than ten seconds she was hushed and hurried out and up to the bedroom.

Jack pegged the bar firmly down, and frantically started dragging the bed over. 'Gotter jam the door. It's strong, but so's Billy,' he grunted. ''E breaks in while we're out on the rope, an' 'e'll just shake us off like raindrops. Or cut it.'

By the window, Susanna was easing her arms and rubbing her hands. 'We've to climb across that rope?'

Jack grinned to encourage her. ''S easy. Jest 'ang by yer knees an' 'ands, an' sorter crawl upside down. Can't fall, less'n yer daft.' Susanna eyed the height, the cobbles, the roaming dogs, the thin line and Joe its only support on the other side. Her hands were turning purple with returning blood, and starting to burn with pain. She still couldn't move her fingers, let alone hold anything. She shivered.

Dowstairs, Tom was unconscious on the passage floor beside the chests of money. 'They've agreed, Billy,' Sal was saying. 'A boat at the Bridge steps fer us in ten minutes. But wot d'we do wi' Tom?'

Billy looked down at the giant slumped at his feet. 'Will 'e waken?'

'Dunno. Even if 'e do, 'e'll need 'elp ter walk. One on us ter wheel the barrer; one ter 'old pistols an' the girl. Neither on us got a spare 'and ter 'elp 'im.'

Billy shrugged. 'Ain't no choice, mam. Gotter leave 'im. We'll tell 'em 'e's goin' ter guard the lass whiles we sees as the boat's ready. An' we'll just not come back. Tell 'im the same, if 'e wakes. 'E'll keep 'em off our backs fer an hour. An' if 'e don't wake, they'll not know it.'

Sal nodded. It was her own thought. A pity, but needs must, to get Billy and herself away safe with the gold. 'Right. I'll tell 'em.'

But as she opened the door, she heard the crowd. Jack had been seen to cross the rope. They had kept quiet then, waiting; but when he cut Susanna free from the window frame, some fool had started cheering. Axes began thudding against the yard gate. 'Wot's that? They can't! Not when we got a 'ostage!' Frightened for the first time, Sal slammed the heavy door shut.

Pistol in hand, Billy was already racing for the stairs. From above came a howl of anger. 'She's gone!' The cheering outside redoubled as his bloodsmeared, scarred face appeared raging at the window. He whirled away to

236

search. Sal's own bedroom door was shut and jammed. 'She's in 'ere!'

Inside, Jack stuffed the rolled-up mattress in behind the door, to finish a line of furniture jammed from the door to the opposite wall under the window. 'Dunnit!' He grinned breathlessly. ''E'll not shift that!'

He was just in time. Billy crashed against the door, bellowing in fury. 'I'll kill ye! Jackdaw! I'll rip yer guts out!' His shoulder made no impression; he kicked, and a rotten plank cracked. He kicked again. Susanna yelped as his boot-heel came right through. His hand appeared, tugging aside splinters, scrabbling at the mattress.

'Come on! 'Urry up! Can ye grip yet?' Jack was urgent.

'I can't! Not yet!' She rubbed desperately at her hands, and never mind the agony.

'Gor!' Fighting his fear, Jack drew his knife again. As Billy's hand shoved past the mattress up towards the peg holding the bar, he slashed at it, cutting deep gashes in the hand, and the mattress as well.

Billy roared. Susanna cheered. 'Well done, Jack! that's put him off!' Only for a moment, though. Screeching with rage, Billy kicked the hole bigger, and then his hand appeared again, dripping blood, but groping, gripping the straw bursting from the cut mattress and tugging it in handfuls out through the hole, clearing a space to reach the bar.

At last, Susanna thought she could grip the rope. Jack left slashing at Billy's hand, and climbed out first, to help her. Tucking up her skirts, she grinned faintly. 'I'll have you know, Jack, that I'm terrified of heights.'

'Well, don't look down, then! Gor! Females!' That spurred her to action even more than the threats screeched through the door. She set her knee on the sill, grasped the sides of the window and pulled herself up.

Peering in past the sagging mattress, Billy saw the movement. He stuck the muzzle of his pistol through the hole and fired.

Susanna, on the windowsill, screamed and tottered. Only Jack's hand held her from falling out. 'My arm!' she whispered. 'He hit my arm.'

'Bleedin' 'ell! Of all the luck!' Jack tugged her out and round, to collapse onto the thatch, crying out in pain. 'Let's see!'

She supported her right elbow and fore-arm with the other hand, blood pouring over her fingers. It was a far worse wound than Joe's. The bone of her upper arm was broken. She struggled not to faint or be sick while Jack cut strips off one of her petticoats, bandaged her arm and strapped it hastily to her side. Then, her lip bitten to bleeding, she looked up at him. 'You must go on, Jack. There's no way I can swing across there now.'

'Stupid cow!' He was frantic with worry. ''Ow can I leave ye? Bony'd ne'er fergive me. Nor Jess neither.' He'd not forgive himself, if it came to that. Thuds and oaths rose from the window opening beside them. Billy would be able to reach the peg any second now . . .

But a worse danger than Billy threatened them.

When Billy fired his pistol, a spark had fallen onto the straw round his feet. The tiny flare caught the corner of his eye. It was still so small, a foot would crush it out instantly. But he paid it no heed; all his mind was set on getting through this door, killing Jackdaw . . . He kicked and tugged at the planks, knelt down and strained in through the hole to free the bar. His scrabbling boots shoved glowing straw, wisps of flame, through the banisters to the rushes on the floors below. There had been no rain for a long, hot month, and the timber was all dry . . .

There was a sudden scream below. 'Billy! The 'ouse is on fire!'

'Fire? Can't be! We just been in there.' Jack looked round him. 'Gor, so it is! Look! Smoke, up by the ridge!' The wisp grew thicker, heavier even as they stared. The air quivered with rising heat.

Susanna yelped with painful, hysterical laughter. 'That's all we need! The house burning under us! At least we'll not need to worry about Billy!'

Jack grunted in disgust and decision. 'Right. Gotter do it.' He stood up grimly. 'Climb on me back.'

'What?' She gaped.

'On me back. Walk across wiv ye. Pig-a-back.'

'Walk across a rope? You're joking!'

'Joking?' He glared. 'No time fer bleedin' jokes! Done it afore now.'

'You couldn't do it! Your ankle! And Joe couldn't hold us both! He's hurt! And you're smaller than me! You can't. Can you?'

Why did she keep on talking? 'Billy'll be out arter us, or we'll burn. Which d'ye fancy? Right, then.' He shrugged impatiently. 'If we gets over, fine. If we falls, there's a chance. If we stays, there ain't. Gor! Come on, gerrup! Don't waste time!'

Oh, no ... But the smoke was thicker, the crackle of the fire hoarser. And Billy ... Shakily, fighting the sickening agony of every movement, she let him help her up. He crouched. She clambered onto his back, her good arm round his neck. Her head whirled; grimly she stayed conscious.

He was strong, and she wasn't very much bigger than he was; he lifted her with a grunt. 'Now don't throttle me, an' keep dead still!' He hoped Joe could hold them both. Thank the Lord he'd practised so much! His arm hurt as he held her. Ignore it. No more need for silence. He yelled to Joe, ''Ang on, Joe! 'Old 'ard, now!' and set foot on the rope. Balance, with the extra weight high up his back; get set; ease up ... It sagged. He slipped down again. Ow! His ankle! ''Old the rope tight, Joe! Tight!'

Joe firmed his grip. His left arm, crooked round the chimney-stack, hurt. 'Pull tight, Joe!' He always did as he was told. No longer humming, but moaning slightly with the pain, he hauled with all his vast strength. The rope stretched taut.

Jack stepped up again; swayed. His bad ankle stabbed with the strain. Forget it! Concentrate! Steady! One step. Another. Out over the yard now. Head up, don't look down. Was the door still holding? Or the rope burning through? Concentrate ... Feet easing down, step and step and step ... Susanna tried not to breathe ... Step and step ... Almost there ...

'Gotcher, Jackdaw! Ahaah!' His blood-stained face grinning in crimson triumph, jeering wide, Billy was at the window. He reached out to tug on the rope, to send them smashing to the cobbles.

Four arquebuses boomed from the yard below. The sheriff's men, once Susanna was free, come to support the lad who was saving her.

Without another sound, Billy fell back from the window.

Totally absorbed, Jack didn't even twitch. Two more smooth steps. The thatch behind them flared with a bellow of flames. The rope parted. Susanna, still clutching him, shrieked as they crashed to the slates beside Joe and slid towards the eaves. Joe lurched as the weight came off, and stood on her skirt. They all stopped moving.

Susanna lay back, sobbing, moaning with pain, recovering slowly. Beside her, Jack trembled with relief from the strain. All round, men scrambling onto the roofs to beat out sparks were cheering them. After a while she looked up at Joe, grinning happily because his arm didn't hurt any more. 'Thank God!' she whispered. 'And thank you, Jack. And you, Joe. And isn't it a beautiful day?'

As the flames spread through the house, Tom wakened. Frantic, Sal helped him out. She'd been going to leave him, but not to the fire. She had one of the chests of coins under her arm, a pistol in her hand to hold off the soldiers, Tom's weight leaning heavy on her shoulders. 'Billy! Get down 'ere! Where are ye, Billy?' she screamed wildly, over and over. 'Billy!'

When the arquebuses fired at the side of the house, she dropped the chest, left Tom swaying and ran round. She saw the faces looking up; the gun barrels smoking. She knew . . . Her boy . . . Screaming, she raced to the front door again. 'Billy! I'm comin', Billy!' Without hesitation she hurled herself inside, into the brilliant furnace of the hallway.

Tom's eyes focussed. 'Mam! Stop!' Two men tried to hold him back, but he pushed them aside and charged to rescue his mother. 'I'm coming, mam!'

The house timbers cracked and collapsed, in a roar of flames.

Above, Jack sighed with satisfaction. Sal and Billy both. Pity about Tom, in a way. But he'd said he'd do it, some day . . .

That evening Jack sat on a stool in Kate's bedroom, his ankle freshly bandaged, while three rather battered ladies sat in conference. Jane had been packed off home with Jess and Joe, but Lark was staying as close as she could to her son. Kate, extensively bandaged and aching all over, propped on her softest pillows, listened carefully while Susanna sat beside the bed and told them the story.

'Well!' Kate leaned back against her cushions. 'I knew somethin' was goin' on, but I'm bound to say I'd no idea I'd raised two fools, no just the one.' She glared at her daughter. 'Have I no told you often enough about the time I got involved wi' a daft lassie an' Mary Stewart's affairs? An' it ended up wi' a man dead, an' Mary betrayed in spite o' us. An' this time there's you near lost an arm, an' might yet —'

'The surgeon said it'd heal, mother.' Susanna eased her sling.

'Don't interrupt me! There's three dead, an' your lad

241

in jail, an' Walsingham huntin' Jack here. Heaven knows how we'll come out o' it.'

Susanna was serious and almost withdrawn. Her good hand stroked the white fur of Balthazar, who had forgiven her. She hoped it was a good omen. 'I know too, mother,' she said.

Lark's mouth was swollen and red, her face grey with exhaustion and worry. 'You know? How, then?'

Susanna smiled at Jack, crouched on a stool by Kate's chair. Nodding, he pulled Mary's letter from the breast of his doublet.

Lark tensed to rise. 'No! You can't give it back!'

'Gotter, Lady Lark. Nuffin' else fer it.'

'Yes.' Susanna was resolute. 'If it's important enough to Walsingham, and it is, I can get anything from him in exchange for it. Frank doesn't matter to him at all, really.' She looked sadly at the little lady sitting so stiff, dwarfed by the high chair and brilliant cushions. 'Which is more important to you, Lady Alice; an old debt of honour, or your son's life?'

After a pause, Kate observed, 'A man would say the debt, no doubt. But women have more sense. I've aye said it.' She sighed. 'Mary was — is — a gallant, kindly, gracious lady. If she'd no been a queen, she'd have lived long an' happy. But she was. An' she was raised in France, high-spirited an' stubborn, but soft at the heart. An' then, who had she to help her? The Scots lords are all out for theirsel's, an' deil take their country. Or their queen. Elizabeth at least has Burghley. An' she had it hard, early on. She was raised an' dashed a dozen times afore she was twenty. She learned the false masks o' policy. She saw the death an' despair marriage brought to her mother an' stepmothers, her sister Mary an' her cousin Jane Grey. Her stepfather charmed her to love him; but then she found he was doin' it for ambition. He ended on the block, an' near brought her there too. No wonder she never trusted a man enough to wed. Besides, she knew that while a queen is unwed, all men woo her. It's one o' her few advantages, an' no to be wasted. But Mary wanted love an' marriage, without the judgement to pick the right man. Maybe there wasn't one. An' Knox, an' her religion — ach, there was just too much against her.'

She sighed again. 'An' if she survives this plot against her, there'll be another, an' another. She'll never get back to Scotland. Nor anywhere else. Nobody wants her. Her son, her country, France, Spain — she'd be an embarrassment to them all. She'll bide in prison till she dies.' She turned to Lark. 'My dear, why no let her do what she's wanted for long enough? Be a martyr for her faith. That's how she'll see it. Let her die happy, in glory, knowin' she'll be remembered, rather than fade away.'

'You're saying that the kindest thing I can do for the woman who saved my life is send her to her death?' Lark's voice was a whisper.

Slowly, Kate nodded. 'It's no death that matters, Lark. The one thing every soul born on this earth is sure o', my dear, is dyin'. It's how, an' why, you do it that's important. Give Mary her moment o' triumph.'

Susanna had always respected her mother. Now, listening as Kate judged a queen, she found her awesome. Kate was telling Lady Alice, as she had once told Susanna, to face reality; then you can decide . . .

She held out her hand to Jack. 'The letter, if you please, Jack.'

Jack didn't hesitate. He'd known for hours what he had to do; he was just uncertain exactly how. If Missus Susan was willing to take over dealing with the authorities, he was happy to let her.

Kate smiled at her daughter. 'I'm thinkin' you've grown up, my dear. Well, Lark? Do we save your son for Susanna here?'

Slowly, Lark nodded. Tears were running silently down her face.

Kate looked at her with sympathy, and turned again to Susanna. 'You know what you're goin' to do wi' it, my dear? He's tricky, Walsingham, an' dangerous if he's crossed. Do you want me to come with you?'

'You're not fit, mother, and we can't wait. Jack and I will manage.'

Jack looked up in alarm. He'd thought she'd do it! Face Walsingham? After robbing him? And him with a bad ankle, so that he couldn't even run away? Gor! But if she needed him . . . And Bony . . .

At the Palace of Greenwich next day, Mistress Bolsiter sent in word that she sought an immediate interview with Master Secretary Walsingham.

'Come to beg for her lover, no doubt, Phelippes,' Walsingham snorted. They were examining the last letter Babington had sent to Mary, to see how they could alter it to be more incriminating. 'No, no. He's ruined months, years, of careful planning. I'll not relent for a teardrop or two!' He had hoped so much for the lad . . . He tutted. He must be getting old.

Phelippes was nodding in commiseration. 'Indeed, Sir Francis. I fear we skinned the bear before it was hatched. But we've caught three of our little plotters, and soon we'll have all. They'll make our humble pie, and mayhap enough to snare their mistress Mary, too.'

The messenger coughed apologetically. 'Your pardon, Master Secretary. The lady directed me to give you this.' He held out a paper. There was a little ink drawing on it, of a gallows.

Within a minute, Susanna was sitting in Walsingham's office, trying with fair success to stay calm under the gaze of two pairs of shrewd eyes.

They waited, to unnerve her.

She settled her sling to rest on her farthingale, and sat quietly.

At last, in some surprise, Walsingham found himself

having to break the silence. 'You have a letter of mine, I believe, Mistress Bolsiter.'

'No, Master Secretary.' He stiffened. 'It was sent neither by you, nor to you. Therefore you cannot claim it as yours. Nor do I have it. However,' as he started to draw breath, 'I do, to a certain degree, control it.'

Walsingham leaned back. Phelippes was sucking his teeth. 'We are, I presume, speaking of the same letter?'

'From Mary of Scotland to Sir Antony Babington.' Susanna nodded.

'And you — control it, Mistress Bolsiter?'

She nodded again. 'In a sense, sir. If I may explain?'

'Pray do.' Not a simple barter, then, letter for man. He suddenly felt a surge of pleasure. This self-possessed young lady was worth attention.

'I thought it unwise to bring the letter with me, sir, in view of the temptations it might arouse.'

'Very prudent, mistress.' He smiled tightly.

'It is in the hands of a friend of mine. I do not know exactly where he is, nor how to get in touch with him. I assure you, that is the truth.'

'I'd not dream of doubting you.' His respect for the intriguing young lady was growing every moment.

'If I do not leave this office and take boat within two hours, sir, free and alone save for my escort, the letter will be destroyed. I cannot prevent it. And I am sure, sir, that neither of us wishes that to happen.'

'Indeed.' To ensure her safety. What a girl!

Susanna had expected opposition; this smooth agreement was unsettling. She drew a deep breath. 'I propose that we exchange letters, sir. Two of little value to you, for the one of great worth which my friend holds.' They looked politely attentive. She suddenly saw that this was the same trick as the silence, and chuckled disconcertingly. 'One letter, sir, will be written here and now. It will say that you arrested Master Verney because he knew of your forgery of letters supposedly sent by Mary, Queen

245

of Scots, to Sir Antony Babington. That is all. It will be sent to my mother, Lady Kate Bolsiter, who will put it in a place of security.'

Walsingham sighed in disappointment. *A mistake, my dear. I can get at anything, anywhere . . .*

Susanna smiled. 'She is today being visited by several friends, and may ask any one of them to keep it safe for her. Sir Robert Cecil. William Davidson. Lord Howard of Effingham. And others of their party.'

Walsingham's lips twitched, and Phelippes snuffled with laughter. All were his rivals at court. A hint of search for the letter from any of them would raise a storm of scandal. He bowed appreciation of her stratagem.

'When the messenger brings me back a note from my mother to say that she has safely received this letter, I shall take boat up to the Tower, with the second letter which you will write for me in the meantime, if you will be so kind. It will be —'

'An order to free Francis Verney forthwith.' It wasn't a question.

She returned his bow. 'Exactly, sir. Since, you will say in the letter, you now have proof that the information which led to his arrest was false. And my friend will presently return the queen's letter to you.'

He pursed his lips. 'And if I refuse your offer?'

'With regret, I shall not quit the palace till the time is past.'

'Leaving Master Verney to his fate?' Had she the steel to face it?

She had. 'And the Queen of Scots to hers, lacking the evidence of the letter. It is for you, sir, to judge which is of more importance to you.'

'H'm. How do I know that you will, in fact, give me the letter, mistress? You went to considerable trouble to get it.'

She'd won! Hiding her delight, she smiled. 'Sir, if we had got it without your knowing who had it, we should have kept it. But as affairs stand . . .' She shrugged one shoulder. 'We must face reality. You are a man of immense power. Frank — Francis Verney and I are going to be married. We wish to live at peace with you, and could scarcely hope to do so if we had wantonly cheated you.'

'But Master Verney did so, Mistress Bolsiter,' Phelippes interjected.

She shook her head. 'A conflict of loyalties, sir. It caused him, I know, great turmoil of mind. But,' she paused thoughtfully, 'I could not positively swear that it would not occur again. Therefore, for his sake, sir, as well as yours, I feel he should quit your service.'

'Hah! I'd scarce wish to take him back! But tell me; why the other letter? About the forgery?'

'To cement our friendship, sir. In the future —' when Mary was dead; she chilled for a moment at the thought — 'it would cause you mere embarrassment. But even that would surely be sufficient to deter any action against people who truly intend harm to neither you nor England.'

He laughed, rising to take her good hand and kiss it. His spirits were lighter than they had been for days. 'Mistress Bolsiter, I wish I had met you thirty years ago. Before I was wed! Phelippes, write me the letters the lady requests. I bow to all your demands, mistress, with awed alacrity!'

An hour and a half later, Kate's note and Frank's warrant of freedom in her purse, Susanna was the centre of astonished attention as Master Secretary Walsingham, Privy Councillor to Her Gracious Majesty Queen Elizabeth, escorted her through the crowd at the Greenwich steps, kissed her hand again, and carefully helped her embark, totally ignoring Sir Roger Frame, her escort. While the boat pulled away, the great man stood bareheaded, hat respectfully in his hand as if she was the queen herself.

Then he clapped his hat back on his head and returned chuckling to his office. 'Well, Phelippes. I wonder how long it will be before her accomplice — Master Jack Daw, I presume — finds a means to return the letter to me. I must admit I hope he does not simply hand it in at the door. I look for something much more flamboyant from these young people!'

He suddenly realised that Phelippes was chortling, quite pink with glee. 'What is it?' Phelippes was pointing upwards, over his head.

Walsingham glanced up, puzzled, annoyed by the impertinence; then took off his tall hat. Stuck in the band, beside its feather, was the letter.

Within an hour, Frank, sitting in a cell in the Tower with his head in his hands, heard the stamp of feet, the rattle of the lock. He scrambled to his feet, trying to be brave. The last time, they'd taken him down to the dungeons to watch as Ballard was tortured. Was it his turn now?

Susanna stood there, her right arm in a sling, grave and somehow older. She held out her left hand to him. 'Frank,' she said quietly. 'I've come to take you home.'

He stood still, his heart pounding. 'Mary's letter?'

'A fair exchange.' His lips tightened, in spite of the relief trying to well up inside him. 'Your mother agreed. Or would you have her lose another of her sons?' At that, his head sank. She stepped forward and took his hand. 'We did our best, my dear.' And at last he came to the draw of her hand, since no more could be done.

Epilogue

On the 20th and 21st of September Sir Antony Babington and Father Ballard, with Tichbourne, Salisbury, Savage, and seven of their friends, were most cruelly executed for treason. They all died bravely.

On the 7th of October Lady Kate Bolsiter, Lady Alice Verney and Mistress Jane Verney solemnly swore that the woman known as Mistress Banks had in their presence stated that Jack Downie was her son, and that she intended to leave him all her wealth. Jack, shining and innocent of face in a new, excruciatingly respectable and boring brown suit, was formally declared heir to all the coin and melted silver and gold found in the house in the Gulley Hole, together with all other moneys held for Mistress Banks by various bankers, and all properties owned by her.

He threw a wild party for his friends in the Vintry, and then settled down with Kate as a kind of unadopted nephew. 'A good laugh, Lady Katie,' he told Frank. 'Gor, that fight! An' sir, the lawyers says it's near eight thousand pounds Sal left! An' the inn, as Craddy'll rent, an' the site in the Gulley 'Ole wot there's a merchant lookin' ter buy. An' I gets it all! Ooh, wicked, they was, the ladies, in court! Couldn't scarce believe me ears, 'earin' 'em tell all them lies about me bein' Sal's son. Missus Jane, even, an' 'er a Puritan! Were her remembered wot Sal'd said, too! But Lady Katie said she'd give me laldy if I argued, an' I dunno wot that is, summat Scotch an' nasty, I s'pose, so I just shut up an' let 'em get on wiv it.'

Frank couldn't help laughing. Jack saw he'd cheered up his young Bony, and grinned. 'Dunno wot I'll do wiv it all. Got a grand suit fer meself, fer you an' Missus Susan's weddin' next week! Red velvet, an' gold braid! An' a present, too, a silver salt-cellar from me an' Joe an' Jess. They're 'appy wiv yer mam, an' I'd not disturb 'em. Can give Jess a good dowry now, get 'er wed later on. An' Joe, maybe, we'll get 'im a good wife. That'll take some o' the money. But arter that, I dunno. Lady Katie's on about lessons. Fencin's fine, an' 'orse-ridin'. But Latin, an' dancin' — not if I can 'elp it!' He picked his nose thoughtfully. 'Summat'll turn up!'

He didn't tell Frank that, the previous day, he had nervously visited a small, bright office in Whitehall, to speak to a small, sniffing man about getting some excitement back in his life. Discretion, Jackdaw!

In February of the next year, 1587, Frank and Susanna rode over from their estate near Verneys, their wedding gift from Kate, to tell Lark the news they had just heard.

Mary, Queen of Scots, had been executed at Fotheringay Castle.

She was forty-five years old, her tall head stooped, wearing a wig, for she was nearly bald with constant illness. She had been Queen of Scotland since she was six days old; Queen of France for a year and a half; ruler of Scotland for less than six years; and in prison for nearly twenty.

As she mounted the platform where the executioner's block stood, she was urged to repent and become Protestant. 'Sir, I am settled in the ancient Catholic Roman religion,' she proudly told her tormentor, 'and mind to spend my blood in defence of it.'

They all wept for her.

They had some more cheerful news for Lark, too. The baby was due in August. They'd call it Mary, if it was a girl. John, if it was a boy; Jack, for short. But not Jackdaw.